From Aberystwyth with Love

MALCOLM PRYCE was born in the UK and has spent much of his life working and travelling abroad. He has been, at various times, a BMW assembly-line worker, a hotel washer-up, a deck hand on a yacht sailing the South Seas, an advertising copywriter and the world's worst aluminium salesman. In 1998 he gave up his day job and booked a passage on a banana boat bound for South America in order to write *Aberystwyth Mon Amour*. He spent the next seven years living in Bangkok, where he wrote three more novels in the series, *Last Tango in Aberystwyth*, *The Unbearable Lightness of Being in Aberystwyth* and *Don't Cry for Me Aberystwyth*. In 2007 he moved back to the UK and now lives in Oxford.

THE LOUIE KNIGHT SERIES:

From Aberystwyth with Love

Malcolm Pryce

BLOOMSBURY
LONDON · BERLIN · NEW YORK

First published in Great Britain 2009
This paperback edition published 2010

Bloomsbury Publishing, London, Berlin and New York

Bloomsbury Publishing Plc, 36 Soho Square, London W1D 3QY

A CIP catalogue record for this book is available from the British Library

ISBN 978 1 4088 0102 4
10 9 8 7 6 5 4 3 2 1

Typeset by Hewer Text UK Ltd, Edinburgh
Printed in Great Britain by Clays Ltd, St Ives plc

Mixed Sources
Product group from well-managed
forests and other controlled sources
www.fsc.org Cert no. SGS-COC-2061
© 1996 Forest Stewardship Council
FSC

www.bloomsbury.com/malcolmpryce

To Tony, Marie, Ryan and Daniel

S IXTEEN CROSSES glimmering beneath the waters of a lake are all that remain of the Chinamen who built the Devil's Bridge narrow gauge railway. Sixteen unhappy wretches who left their native land in the nineteenth century thinking they were going to build the great Union Pacific Railway across the United States and learned too late the bitter lesson that life so often conceals in the small print. From the comfort of your Aberystwyth hotel with all its modern amenities – its electric elevator and sophisticated telephone switchboard – it is easy to believe the official account of their deaths. A simple linguistic mix-up that transubstantiated gelignite for jelly in the dessert. But if you forsake the comforting embrace of civilisation and pass by the shores of the lake late on a winter's day when the curlew haunts the land with its uncannily human cry, you may hear a different story. You may chance upon the humble peasant carrying brushwood home upon his back who will tell you about the trolls living deep in the belly of the mountain, and about the Promethean arrogance of the railway company that scoffed at the superstitions of the locals and carried on blasting despite the warnings. The peasant may tell you stories of his childhood when village girls were offered to the trolls as brides. Perchance he will point you in the direction of a forgotten parish museum where photos gather dust that show the many hairy babies born in those parts. And he may add with a glint of pride in his eye that many of them went on to achieve great renown and bring honour to the village as school games teachers.

From *In Deepest Cardiganshire*, by Colonel Sir Henry Lyons

Chapter 1

FOR A WHILE He just sat there and hovered, taking it one step at a time. He moved upon the face of those waters and made light. That was OK, but He really needed to set it off a bit, so He divided it from the darkness. It gave Him what you might call a framework. That was good, too. Then He tried out a firmament and after that he gathered all the waters in one place to make a thing called land. That was where it started getting tricky. Once you've got land there's always the temptation to make things to put on it. It's like having a toy farmyard with no animals. At first things went OK: seeds and trees and grass; and herb yielding seed after his kind; and no one would begrudge the herb the opportunity to do that. On the fourth day He had a brainwave: lights in the firmament, a big one and a small one. As soon as He saw them He knew that they were good; and there isn't a single soul born since He first switched them on who would disagree with that verdict. They sure are lovely things, those lights, especially the ones down the coast from Aberaeron and Cardigan glimmering across the water at night. Drive through those places during the day and there's nothing there: a scrap of village green, a few dogs and a bus shelter that smells of urine with a tattered rag that details the arrival and departure of buses as rare as comets. But at night, on the Prom at Aberystwyth, they twinkle and sparkle to you from down the coast, over the dark water, in strange agonised beauty. On the fifth day He thought up fishes and whales and birds, and that was enchanting too. When you look at birds, the way they fly, the freedom and ease and grace with which they glide around, it ravishes the soul. That was really where He should have called it a day. The hardest thing in the world is knowing when to quit. He was just like the guy in the casino who can't leave the table: just one more throw of the dice. We all know what happened on the sixth day: He got out of bed on the wrong side. After breakfast it was kine and creeping things that creepeth over the earth; and after lunch He came up with the creepiest thing of all: man. The creature that was always getting into trouble. Six thousand years later one of them walked into my office.

He was wearing a museum curator's uniform buttoned up to the throat: four solid brass buttons in a row up the front of the Prussian blue serge. He had epaulettes, gold braid at the cuffs, and the general air of a Ruritanian dignitary that you sometimes find in the doormen of a certain class of hotel; and in leaders of banana republics, the ones who get their portrait painted in oils the morning after the *coup d'état*. I could tell his museum wasn't one of those modern affairs where kids are encouraged to press buttons that make things light up. It was strictly Sumerian clay tablets imprinted with cuneiform markings like bird footprints; tablets of no interest to anyone, least of all the Sumerians. Rivulets of sweat ran down the man's cheeks and formed dark lines in the serge collar. We were midway through the great August heatwave at the time and it was already unbearable by 9 a.m., which is the time he walked into my office. I didn't know it then, but the uniform belonged to the Museum Of Our Forefathers' Suffering in Hughesovka. The man had also placed a sock on the desk. Hughesovka is a town on the lower Don River in the Ukraine that was founded by John Hughes from South Wales, a steelworker who left the land of his birth in 1869 to build a town that bore his name. At least until the Bolsheviks renamed it Stalino to commemorate another famous man of steel. That's not the sort of thing you can do any more, found a town that bears your name, and you have to admire the achievement. Louie Knight, Private Detective, is written on my business cards and on the frosted glass in the top panel of the door but that's about as far as it goes. Half the people I give the cards to throw them straight in the bin. He was the first man I had ever met from Hughesovka.

For a while we sat peering at each other across the desk; he wasn't smiling but some people can look amiable without having to smile and he was one. I could tell he was a connoisseur of that most under-rated of God's inventions, silence. If you work in a museum a pin-dropping hush is your bread and butter. I like silence too and it's hard not to warm to a man who has the manners to walk in and say nothing. Most people start gushing the moment their backside hits the chair. If I ever meet God I'll tell Him. The best thing you ever came up with, better even than the firmament or the lights in the sky to rule over the darkness, better even than the birds, although I admit the birds are special, the best was the silence. If only there had been more of it. And He'll probably say, 'You know what? That's the one bit I didn't invent. It was already there when I started.'

We waited some more, the only sound the distant gulls, the sleepy traffic drone and two men sweating. Then I said, as the distant clock struck a quarter past, 'It's always nice to meet a quiet type.'

As if grateful for the hint, he told me to call him Uncle Vanya. I told him to call me Louie. I turned the Bakelite fan to a higher setting, stood up and opened the window wider; then sat down again. The heatwave had been going on since June. Each morning we peered through the curtains in the hope of seeing some sort of cloud that might spell the end of it, and each morning all we saw was a malignant glare, a sky bleached out to a sickly pallor. Walking along the Prom was like wading through gelatinised air.

I made no reference to the sock on the desk. Instinct warned me not to go too fast on that one. Clearly whatever the case was, the sock played a pivotal role and some people don't like being rushed when it comes to pivotal things. Without even having to look closely I knew the sock was an item of fundamental importance and in this respect I was more right than I realised: it was my fee.

Calamity Jane, my partner, walked in and introduced herself to Uncle Vanya. She didn't mention the fee on the desk, although she definitely saw it. Calamity was seventeen and, following a brief and ill-fated attempt to set up on her own last Christmas, was now a full-time partner in the business. Three or four years ago I had rescued her from the dark belly of the bingo hall, that subterranean cavern seamed with veins of fool's gold where she had been one of the many teenage troglodytes with pallor similar to the one in the sky at the moment and a sullen resentment towards just about everything in life. I never ceased to wonder at the speed with which that attitude evaporated after I removed her from the milieu. Within a week it had been replaced by a bubbling silver brook of optimism, the sort that runs dry or gets blocked up in later years, but about which no one would ever dream of disabusing the young. They will find out soon enough.

Calamity drew up a chair to the desk, sat down and opened her notebook.

'For many years,' began Uncle Vanya, 'I was a cartographer. I explored a wild and marvel-filled *terra incognita*, criss-crossed by rivers that scorned the puny attempts of man to navigate them. Though many men had passed before me and tried to fathom its secrets, all had failed and that dark centre remained on the map as a white expanse marked merely with the supposition that there might be dragons living there. It was a crazy realm containing extremes of joy and misery; troughs of despair, and peaks of felicity. I traversed its oceans of longing, I crawled on my slimed belly through the dark caves of its terror . . . I charted it all. You will by now have guessed the continent to which I refer is the human heart.'

We both nodded to signify that this thought had indeed occurred to us a while back.

'I was the first to apprise mankind of the exact boundaries of this landscape. I traversed it all in that train wagon named after a Czarist prime minister, a man whose death was foretold in 1911 by Rasputin but who is now remembered by posterity chiefly for giving his name to a railway carriage. That particular contrivance that was to convey those vast armies of the damned, swept up in the terrible purges of the thirties, to the precinct of their damnation along the banks of the

Kolyma River and other sundry hell holes of the Siberian prison system. I am referring of course to the Stolypin car.'

He turned to Calamity and said, 'S, T, O, L, Y, P, I, N.' I had not yet made up my mind whether he was sane or not. I've learned it doesn't pay to jump to conclusions in this respect, but I admired his grasp of detail. You could tell that in his museum the cards that labelled the artefacts were yellowed round the edges to exactly the same degree; that nothing was written on those cards that couldn't be absolutely verified by the latest scholarship; and he typed them all himself, at home in the dim light of a forty-watt bulb amid the fug given off by socks drying next to the fire, while his loving wife placed a gentle hand on his shoulder and set a dish of cabbage soup down before him. If a man could speak typeface this man spoke Pica at ten characters per inch.

'It may be that I make an error in bringing my story to you. It may be that the vessel of your heart is not sturdy enough to accept the dark wine of my woe. The Russian heart is vast and contains multitudes. Is it really possible to pour out its contents into the puny vessel of your Welsh heart? I see you people selling your toffee apples and renting out deckchairs and I ask myself: where are their parricides, their swindlers, their crazed monks and dark malfeasant convicts? Where is the mother whose love is so great that she strangles her own babe in the crib to save it from the cruel death of hunger?'

'Tell us about the sock,' I said.

'I was just about to.'

'I'll make a cup of tea,' said Calamity.

'The sock is from the Hughesovka Museum Of Our Forefathers' Suffering. I used to be the principal curator. As you know, this museum charts the centuries of tyranny and oppression that caused that great Welsh Moses, John Hughes, to throw off the imperialist yoke and lead his people out of servitude to the promised land.'

'Is there really such a place as Hughesovka?'

'You ask such a thing of me?'

'We learned about it in school; they told us it was the only Welsh-speaking community east of the Greenwich meridian – it always struck me as improbable.'

'In our schools we found tales of Aberystwyth equally hard to credit. But please!' He pointed to the sock as if to remind me of his true business here. 'After the long arctic winter of suffering I found a short-lived but intense degree of happiness. I met Lara. I was employed for a while as an assassin for the Hughesovka criminal underworld. I first set eyes upon Lara while staring down the telescopic sniper scope of the rifle with which I was commissioned to shoot her. Ah! If I were as richly endowed in gold as I am in woe I would commission a statue to that great man, Carl Zeiss of Jena, who fashioned a lens of such perspicuity that tragedy was averted. Just as I was about to pull the trigger she turned and smiled directly into my cross hairs. A smile like the break in the clouds after forty days of rain in the time of Noah. In short, I forbore to squeeze the trigger and took instead an arrow in the heart.'

He paused and took a sip of tea.

'Our union was blessed with a little daughter, Ninotchka, and for a time my happiness was complete. But then I was arrested and sentenced to penal servitude in the labour camps north of the Kolyma River. This was in 1950 when little Ninotchka was barely two years old. Being torn away from my family by the cruel men of the State Security Apparat caused me suffering beyond the power of words to describe. But also it gave me strength: every day in exile I thought of my little daughter and the day when I would see her again. And then in 1955 I received a strange letter from my wife. There had been an outbreak of diphtheria in Hughesovka and in order to protect our daughter she had kept her at home and prevented her from playing with the other children. Naturally little Ninotchka was cast down and in order to lift her spirits my wife bought her a little Welsh doll from the Museum Of Our Forefathers' Suffering. Whereupon a very strange thing happened. Ninotchka acquired an imaginary friend: a little Welsh girl. This is of course a familiar and often charming aspect of many childhoods, but Ninotchka's friend was no happy playmate with a funny name and odd ways for whom we were required to lay an extra setting at supper. She was a fiend. Her name was Gethsemane Walters and she claimed to be the spirit of a dead girl who had been murdered in Wales, in a town called Abercuawg. She tormented our poor daughter with shocking and grisly tales of death in a small town in Wales far away. How could she know of such things? My wife pretended for a while it was just a figment of her imagination. Gethsemane is a Biblical name which she could have overheard somewhere, and Walters is a common surname in Hughesovka. This is how she consoled herself. But to tell the truth she didn't really believe it. Imaginary friends are usually called Mr Bumpy or something, not Gethsemane. She called a doctor, she called in priests who baptised and blessed and tried to drive out the evil spirit. She took Ninotchka to a special school for psychic investigation.'

He paused and removed a white handkerchief from inside his tunic and unfolded it with the meticulousness of one who intends refolding it exactly as it was. He dabbed the sweat from his forehead.

'I did not expect Aberystwyth to be quite so warm,' he said.

'It's not normally sunny in August,' said Calamity. She stood up and walked over to the window to open it further. It was already as wide as it could go. Vanya continued with his story.

'Not long after receiving this terrible news, I undertook a daring escape and after many adventures I arrived back in Hughesovka and into the bosom of my family. Ninotchka's first words when we met were to tell me I was not her daddy. And then something happened that caused the imaginary friend to disappear for a while. It was 1957 and a little dog became famous around the world. It was Laika the first dog in space, a supreme achievement for Mother Russia. For a time Ninotchka became entranced with the fate of this little dog and forgot all about her fiendish playmate. And we rejoiced.' He stopped and looked at me wistfully. 'But, as you know, those clever scientists who sent the dog aloft had made no provision for her safe return.

She died after a few hours, from heat exhaustion. Her death fell like a thunderbolt upon the roof of our house and destroyed the happiness that we had built. Even now, more than thirty years later, it is too painful for me to recall in detail what took place. The death of Laika affected Ninotchka terribly. The imaginary friend returned and took over completely. She refused to answer to the name of Ninotchka and insisted she was Gethsemane, and she denounced both her parents as impostors. There was a scene. A terrible scene involving vodka and violence during which, I regret to say, I raised a hand of violence to my wife. I was thrown into prison for murder. And I never saw my daughter again. This was all many years ago. I will not waste your time with the details of where I went or who I saw during those years. It is enough that you understand that there was never a day when I did not think of this terrible story.' He stopped and looked at me, eyes full of agonised appeal, as if my task was clear.

'This is a very strange and tragic story,' I said, not sure of an appropriate response. 'And we are deeply touched by your suffering. But what is it you want us to do?'

He took out a copy of *National Geographic* and opened it to a marked page. It was a picture of a lake in Wales. The spire of a sunken church protruded from the water like a witch's hat floating on the surface. The same picture had been on the front of the *Cambrian News* the week before. It was Abercuawg, a town drowned when they built the new reservoir in 1955 and whose ghost had made a reappearance during the recent heatwave.

Out of respect for Vanya I feigned interest in the article, even though like everyone in town I knew all about Abercuawg. Nine hundred people had been evicted and forced to watch their homes demolished. Everything was razed except the church because none of the wreckers' men would raise a sledgehammer against the House of God. They called it the reservoir filled with human tears; some even said the water in Birmingham had tasted salty. Of all the myriad spectacles life has devised to break a heart, that one belongs in the top five. You don't have to die to lose your life, the folks said. The magazine article recounted the various ways the lost town had made its presence known over the years. Old ha'pennies washed up or fragments of Coronation mugs; tins of boot polish with unfamiliar markings on the lid; and once a slick of eye ointment that made the water shimmer with amber translucence. At times, too, winter storms had churned the water and brought forth the scent of mothballs and corset soap; or left gossamer rags coating the shoreline that the superstitious said were the exfoliations of fairies but which were really integuments of Anaglypta shed by dead living rooms. This year the corpse of the town itself had been washed ashore.

'You see? Abercuawg! This is the very name my daughter's imaginary friend mentioned. Gethsemane claimed to come from this place.' He paused and gave a beseeching look. 'And this is your task. You must find Gethsemane. You must find out what happened to her. You must find her bones so that she may be given a Christian burial. It is my belief that only then will my daughter be released from the thrall of this terrible wandering spirit, and perhaps my beautiful Ninotchka will come back to me and my lost happiness will be restored.'

'What's the sock for?' asked Calamity as she poured out more tea.

'That is your fee.'

There was a slight heightening of tension in the room. As a private detective in Aberystwyth one has to negotiate many formidable hazards but few greater than the question of the fee.

'Is it a valuable sock?' asked Calamity.

Uncle Vanya nodded. 'No sock in the history of the world has been further, gone faster or seen more. Or indeed been engaged on a more noble enterprise. It was worn by Yuri Gagarin during his first space flight, the first man to leave our earth's atmosphere and orbit the earth.'

'Where did you get it?' asked Calamity.

'For many years it was in the collection of the Museum Of Our Forefathers' Suffering and was presented to me as a gift in recognition of my long years' service on my retirement.'

'Normally, we charge fifty pounds a day plus expenses,' I said.

'Then you must be delighted to receive a payment so much over the odds. This is a very valuable collector's item. People would pay very handsomely for such a garment.'

'Not round here they wouldn't.'

'On the contrary, according to my research, there is a firm in this town called Mooncalf & Sons that handles this sort of merchandise.'

'They handle stolen goods.'

Uncle Vanya gave a wan smile. I picked up the sock. It was made of something like asbestos and there were two initials, YG, embroidered inside the hem. In all other respects it didn't seem to differ greatly from an oven-glove with toes.

'Technically, this counts as a missing person job. Despite what they say in the books, private operatives are not the best way to deal with this sort of thing. You really need the help of the police, it takes time and resources—'

'You think if I went to the police they would help me? I know exactly why I am coming to you.'

I made a conciliatory gesture with my hands. I always gave the same spiel; they never listened but I told them anyway. 'I just wanted to let you know. It would be wrong to take the sock without letting you know, that's all.'

'We'll need a description of the imaginary friend,' added Calamity, anxiously trying to skirt over the awkwardness that arises from such disagreements. I was about to laugh when Uncle Vanya took out a photo and laid it down on the desk.

It was a black-and-white shot showing a group of children and adults in what appeared to be the room of a hospital. There was a gap in the row of children and, surprisingly, in the gap there was a dog in mid-air. Uncle Vanya pointed to the empty space and said, 'This is the imaginary friend holding the dog. It was taken at the school for remote viewing and paranormal research. As you may know, such schools were operated by the military who made a systematic study of various psychic phenomena during the fifties. Unfortunately, the photographer was inept, the shot is badly composed. You can't see Gethsemane – she is standing behind the principal, here. This might be her foot. See? And this man is Premier Nikita Khrushchev who was gracious enough to honour our town with a visit.'

I gave Uncle Vanya a receipt for the sock.

Chapter 2

THE SKY was as blue as a cockatoo's eye. If they have blue eyes, I wasn't sure. The sickly pallor of dawn had evaporated. The sand was still damp from the receding tide, still reeking of brine. Individual crystals of mica glittered and sparkled with pink flashes, and every little stone and pebble cast a shadow, like the rocks on the surface of the moon. The larger stones sunk into the sand were a yellow bone colour, worn smooth with indentations that collected clear water, like molars in the gum of the shore.

Fencing the sock was the second priority of the day. First was a visit to Sospan's ice-cream kiosk. We went there at the start of each new case. Just as ships are baptised with champagne, so each case is launched with vanilla, and occasionally a Flake, although my instinct warned that the value of the sock would not run to such luxuries on this occasion. Sospan was the secular confessor of the town who absolved freely from his blue-and-white wooden box situated on the Prom midway between the bandstand and Constitution Hill. On the roof stood a fibreglass cone adorned with the motto *Et in Arcadia ego*, 'I too am in Arcady.' The exact meaning of the phrase was the source of dispute among scholars and also among the townsfolk of Aberystwyth. Some claimed it referred to classical Arcadia, the idyllic pastoral homeland of nymphs and swains, and birthplace of Zeus. According to this interpretation the words were spoken by Death and served as a bitter-sweet counterpoint to our heedless revels. Others insisted it was an oblique reference to a long-lost period in Sospan's life when he worked on a cruise liner called the *Arcadia*.

He was reading a letter and looked up at the noise of our approach. He folded the letter and put it back in the envelope but instead of putting it away he laid it carefully down on the counter. He had the air of someone who wanted to talk about its contents, but would prefer to be asked rather than bring the subject up himself.

I nodded towards the letter. 'Good news?'

'Very good actually, Mr Knight, since you ask. Usual is it?'

Without waiting for the answer he turned to the ice cream dispenser, held a cornet under the Mr Whippy nozzle and laid a gentle hand on the tiller.

'Is it a girlfriend?'

'You know very well my vocation forbids such pleasures. Since you enquire, I can tell you my letter is from a publishing firm in London who have expressed interest in my treatise on the role of ice cream as analgesic of the soul.'

'You've written a book?'

'My life's work; not finished, of course.'

'What's it called?' asked Calamity.

'*The Primal Ice Cream*.'

'What's it about?' I asked.

'It is difficult to sum up in a few words, but it concerns the nature of vanilla as the spiritual keyhole to paradise.'

There was a slight pause in which we strove to formulate the obvious reply, but there wasn't one.

'Got any good flavours coming up?' said Calamity.

Sospan brightened. 'Autumn season starts in September, it's going to be a humdinger. I think you'll be impressed. Lot of cutting-edge stuff, flavours that haven't been seen before in ice cream.'

'I expect it's still all under wraps for now,' I said.

Sospan considered. 'Well, seeing it's you, Mr Knight, and Calamity, I might just give you a little peek.' He pulled a notebook from the breast pocket of his white ice man's coat and flipped it open. 'You'll like these.' He put on a pair of reading glasses and read from his notes. 'Rose water.'

'Mmm,' said Calamity, 'that sounds good.'

'Although I'm not sure whether to call it that or something more evocative such as Scheherazade.'

'I think Rose water is better, if you call it that other name no one round here will know what it is,' said Calamity.

'Does it matter? They can always taste it, can't they?'

'But they'll say, hey, tastes a bit like roses.'

Sospan looked a trifle flustered. One of the continuing struggles of his life was the disconnect that seemed to exist between his role, as he saw it, and the way the townspeople viewed it. To Sospan, to classify his vocation as dispensing ice cream was like saying the priest who administered the sacrament handed out biscuits.

'Tell us another one,' I said.

'Ginkgo Biloba.'

This time he read the puzzled expressions on our faces and continued quickly, 'That's a sacred tree, much prized in Chinese and Japanese cuisine. It was the only tree in Hiroshima to survive the atom bomb.'

'I'm not sure about that one,' said Calamity.

Sospan consulted his notes again. 'Then we've got Sea Cucumber, Ambergris, Spanish Fly, and Potato.'

Calamity looked glum. 'Potato sounds a bit boring.'

Sospan acquired that look of infinite patience that the artist who paddles in the wilder experimental shores learns to assume. 'I tell you what,' he said, 'try this: it's the centrepiece of the autumn collection. I have high hopes for it; it intertwines a variety of approachable themes that even the day-trippers can enjoy while at the same time it contains within it notes of complexity that will satisfy the educated palette.' He pulled out a tub from the fridge that was marked only with a code as if the exact identity must remain a secret for a while. He scooped out two small testing samples and laid them on mini wafers like canapés. We popped the morsels into our mouths and savoured. It was very fishy and sharp, even seaweedy.

'I haven't decided on a name yet,' he explained, 'but I was thinking of Mermaid's Boudoir.'

'It's very fishy,' said Calamity. 'What's in it?'

'Fish milt,' said Sospan with evident pride at his ingenuity.

I choked.

'Fish what?' said Calamity.

'Milt.'

'What's that?'

The ice-cream man turned pink. 'Well . . . not sure if I should . . . you know . . .'

'It's OK, Sospan, she's seventeen now, she's grown-up.'

'I saw a corpse last year,' added Calamity as further illustration of her maturity.

Sospan rubbed his neck with the palm of one hand. 'It's, you know, well . . .'

I tried to help him out. 'When daddy fish and mummy fish want to start a little shoal . . .'

'Yes?' said Calamity.

'Daddy fish sprays something on to mummy fish's eggs,' said Sospan.

'Oh that,' said Calamity, as if it was a substance one encountered every day.

'They eat a lot of it in Russia. You needn't pull a face, it's quite a delicacy.'

'Your new flavours are certainly . . . brave,' I said.

'Brave?'

'Avant-garde.'

'I know what you are trying to say, the people round here will hate them. Of course they will, do you think I don't know that? Do you think a man could remain sane making ice cream for the people of Aberystwyth all his life? What do they care about art? All they want is chocolate, strawberry and vanilla. Not just in their cornet but in everything. Louie, I'm not doing this for them, it's for me. For my self-respect, to assuage the yearning . . .'

'But if no one eats it, won't it upset you?'

'The only people who I need to care about are the reviewers for *The Iceman Cometh*. I don't need to make a lot, just a few scoops, that's all.'

'Any others on your list.'

'Just one, Tempura.'

'Mmm!' We both chorused bogus enthusiasm to soothe his wounded pride.

'How do they collect the fish milt?' asked Calamity.

Sospan blushed.

Fortunately, before he could reveal this particular trade secret we were distracted by the sharp cry of a gull swooping low over the kiosk. It was followed by a short intense bray of joy, and the smell of donkey wafted across signalling the arrival of my father, Eeyore, leading the donkeys on the morning's first traverse. In contrast to the rest of the townspeople that hot August morning he was wearing a suit, with bits of straw stuck to it. He greeted us with a sprightly cheer that belied his age and slung the halters loosely on to the emergency-exit door bar at the back of the kiosk. Sospan put down a washing-up bowl of water for the donkeys and they lapped happily. There were seven that morning: Escobar, Spinnaker, Uncle Ho, Squirrel, Invincitatus, Anwen and Piper. There were no riders. Eeyore had long ago relinquished all pretence that the job of the donkey man had anything to do with giving rides to children. Partly because he did not like the modern variety of children very much, and partly because the job had a deeper significance. Or so he thought. Years ago, Eeyore had been a cop. When he retired, a community grateful for all the crooks he had removed from their midst presented him not with a gold watch but a different sort of time-keeper: a pendulum made of donkeys. And every day he led the caravan of mute and obliging beasts along the perimeter of the town with a rhythm that was as reassuring and predictable as the bright star that traces across the screen of an oscilloscope on a heart monitor.

Each pulse across the dark green dial proved that Aberystwyth was still hale and the fathomless oceans that lay before the cradle and beyond the grave were being held in check by the thin brown line of beasts measuring out their metronomic dung-beat.

He ran a gentle hand of greeting down Calamity's cheeks and said, 'What's up?'

'We're looking for a ghost called Gethsemane from Abercuawg,' she answered indiscreetly.

Eeyore's face darkened. 'You shouldn't joke about such things.' Sospan tut-tutted in rebuke.

Calamity looked from face to face in search of an explanation. 'We shouldn't?'

'Gethsemane Walters,' said Eeyore. 'That was a terrible case.'

'You mean,' said Calamity, 'you've heard of her?'

'Happened in 1955. I remember it well because I was courting Louie's mum at the time, before we moved to Llandudno. The little girl was eight or nine years old, I think. Disappeared when they were building the dam.'

Calamity stared at him, eyes wide and shining. 'So what happened to her? Did someone do her in?'

Eeyore pulled a face as if such bluntness was inappropriate. He sighed. 'They convicted a boy for it, young chap called Goldilocks. I was never convinced about it to tell the truth, he was no angel, used to hang out with the mob who worked at the slaughterhouse, but it never felt right to me. He was due to hang that autumn but he escaped. Hasn't been seen since. They never found Gethsemane's body.'

'The girl's mother was Ffanci Llangollen the singer,' said Sospan. 'She was pretty big in the forties. That was her stage name of course.'

'That's right,' said Eeyore. 'She used to run the village school. After Gethsemane went missing she left town, and set off to look for her. Far as I know, she is still looking – comes back from time to time. But the really strange thing about the case, as I remember, came the following year. On Ffanci Llangollen's birthday a spiritualist sent her a tape recording she had made at a séance, apparently it was the voice of Gethsemane. Of course, that's a bit hard to believe but Ffanci swore it was her and the father killed himself on account of it. Said now he knew for sure she was in heaven there was nothing worth living for.'

'Where's the tape now?' I asked.

'Stolen,' said Eeyore. 'They reckon it was the work of snuff philatelists.'

We bought two vanilla cornets and walked along the beach in the direction of the Pier. There was no breeze and the surface of the sea was the colour and lustre of mother-of-pearl; it was so hot the air zinged. The heat was tangible, audible . . . it quivered and made the air tingle as if it had been struck by a giant tuning fork.

'Boy!' said Calamity. 'If we were in a movie we would be walking across the desert and they would be playing that violin sound they always play, the one that goes Eeeeeeeeeeee!'

'That's right, and then one of us would look directly at the sun and they'd play an organ chord to show that we were going to die out there and be left as bleached bones with rattlesnakes living in the breast cage.'

'Rattlesnakes die in the direct sun, they have to keep in the shade. That's why you have to check your boots before you put them on.'

'I know that, it's the movie makers who get it wrong.'

'It's best to move about at night. If you want to shelter in a cave during the day you throw a rock in to see if there are any rattlers in there.'

I stopped for a second; it was surprisingly difficult walking across the carpet of pebbles. Calamity paused and looked up at me. Her face was washed with honey by the early morning sun. I smiled.

She had been thirteen when we first met, with spiky hair and jeans and a scruffy parka coat, chocolate-rimmed mouth set into a permanent downturn of sullenness. You don't need to be much of an amateur psychologist to know that the sullen resentment and aggression is mostly just a defence to hide the confusion which swirls beneath the waters of the teenage heart. It seldom goes deep. Within hours of becoming my junior partner a smile had begun to tug at the corners of her mouth which she struggled to suppress with no more success than a man on a park bench trying to read his newspaper in a gale. Like most kids she takes life at face value. This can be a disadvantage in a crime fighter but this is counter-balanced by the certainty which it gives her. Her heart is not gnawed by doubt. She has the bright unsullied soul of a puppy, and the same propensity to make innocent mistakes. But there is also an air of street wisdom about her, a suggestion of savvy that contrasts with the dizzy confusion bubbling inside her young heart. In many ways she is the daughter I never had. Only once during our years fighting crime together has the fire that dances in her eyes been dimmed. It was when she returned after her ill-fated attempt to set up on her own. We were looking into the murder of a department store Santa at the time, and unusually for us it turned out to be a case with international ramifications. Calamity ended up liaising with the famous Pinkerton Detective Agency in Los Angeles. They made a fuss of her and suggested the possibility of a preferred associative relationship, whatever that is. So Calamity made a go of it on her own. She thought the business from the Pinkertons would see her through. I was sceptical: how much business does a West Coast American operation do in Aberyst-wyth? But, at the same time, I was worried that my objections sprang from the selfish desire to hold on to her. I didn't want to see her go but I felt at the time I had no right to stand in her way; if you love someone, they say, let them go. It took me a while to understand that this motto, though widely quoted, is not true. If you love someone, you'd be nuts to let them go. The whole venture only lasted a couple of weeks, just long enough for the tumbleweed of fate to pile up outside her door. I don't think she even had a client. It was painful to watch, but I could see it taught her an important lesson about life, the one that says: in this world, people like the Pinkertons never call twice.

'Where are we going?' she asked.
   'To see Mooncalf.'
   'Right. We could ask if he does tickets.'
   'What sort of tickets?'
   'Travel ones. To Hughesovka.'
   'Who wants to go to Hughesovka?'
   'We do . . . might. To take a witness statement from the imaginary friend and stuff like that.'
   'What will we use for money?'
   'We'll use part of what we get for the sock.'
   'Oh of course, I forgot. We'll use the change left after buying the marble palace.'
   Calamity's brow clouded. 'You don't think it's going to be worth much?'
   'My feeling is, this sock is going to bounce.'
The thought that the Yuri Gagarin sock might not be a source of great wealth silenced Calamity for a while, at least as far as the Pier.
   We stopped in its shadow, and looked up. It was little more than a shed on stilts in which two tribes co-existed: the adolescent girls from whose numbers I had extracted Calamity, and the grannies. Invisible to each other, they occupy the same space without ever meeting like wanderers in those Escher engravings where staircases interlock along the planes of incompatible dimensions.
   It was cool in the shadow, like the glade of a forest. Cool and damp and reeking of seaweed and guano. This was the real wonder. Not the tawdry scene up above but the bit underneath: the vast intricate criss-crossing web of ironmongery that held the whole thing suspended at the same level as the Prom. People claim the death of British manufacturing came when the last car factory was sold into foreign hands, but the real death was in 1980 when they stopped making Meccano in Liverpool. When the Pier finally falls down, no

one will have the know-how to fix the ironwork. Until that time, uncountable starlings roost there and emerge at dusk in twittering skeins, endlessly, like a string of black handkerchiefs drawn from a magician's pocket.

We climbed the steps that curved up the buttress of the sea wall, on to the Prom and back into the light.

'How come Gethsemane's spirit ended up in Hughesovka?' Calamity asked.

'Maybe if you are a spirit you don't have much control over who you end up possessing.'

'Yes, it could be like hiring a car, you just have to take what they give you.'

'That's if it is her spirit.'

'What else could it be?'

'I don't know.'

'We need to get hold of that séance tape,' said Calamity, and then added, 'What do you think the chances are of us solving the case?'

'I'd say no chance whatsoever.'

'We can't really fence the sock unless we make at least a token effort, can we?'

'No, it wouldn't be right. Although I have a terrible suspicion that the man-minutes we just used up in our brief conversation have already exceeded the value of the sock.'

'Yuri Gagarin socks must be worth more than that.'

We walked through town to Chalybeate Street where Mooncalf & Sons had, according to the silver copperplate shop sign, been dealing in antiques since 1834. I wasn't sure there had even been a street here back then. The Mooncalfs were originally brothers and two of West Wales's most respected fencers of stolen goods. The shop in Chalybeate Street handled antiques and 'special requests'. The other branch had operated out of a caravan in Clarach and dealt with stolen religious icons. This branch had stopped trading a while back when mobster Frankie Mephisto had incinerated the caravan with one Mooncalf brother still in it.

Mooncalf was a small man, and the counter behind which he stood reached up to his chest. He was amiable with a wizened, sharply pointed look common to men in fairy tales who are prematurely aged by evil witches, but which can also arise from spending too many hours late at night scheming. In former times he would have made a living operating a string of child pickpockets, or chimney sweeps whom he would have discouraged from dawdling on the job by lighting a fire in the grate while they were halfway up the chimney.

He threw his arms out in delighted greeting. 'Mr Knight and Calamity! What a lovely surprise. Welcome to Mooncalf & Sons.'

'Since 1834, eh?' I answered.

'The brand has been around since then, Mr Knight. Mooncalf & Sons is the soul, the actual premises are merely the physical body that houses it.'

'How's business?'

'Slow, but the long-term prospects seem assured.'

'I suppose there is always a market for stolen goods.'

Mooncalf winced. 'Stolen goods! Who deals in stolen goods? If that is what you have in mind you would appear to have come to the wrong shop. Mooncalf & Sons is a respectable business with a spotless reputation.'

'Not according to the police.'

'Mr Knight, you walk into my shop and make these . . . these insinuations. You remind me, if I may be permitted an indelicate turn of phrase, of a man who engages the services of a prostitute for the night and spends the whole time berating her for the shameful way she makes her living.'

'Do you do tickets?' said Calamity.

He paused and reassumed the look of Buddhist serenity with which he had originally greeted us. 'What sort of tickets?'

'Travel ones. We need to go to Hughesovka.'

'No, we don't,' I said.

'We might do.'

'It's really not likely.'

'Hughesovka!' exclaimed Mooncalf as if it were the name of a favourite son. 'What a noble goal! And what a wise choice in coming here to make your travel arrangements.'

'Is it expensive?' asked Calamity.

'Ordinarily the cost of a ticket – like that of a virtuous woman – is priced above rubies, since it is impossible to get there by conventional means. Hughesovka is, as you know, a closed city along with Gorki and numerous others.'

'What's a closed city?' said Calamity.

'One that is closed to Western tourists. As such you will find no travel agent in town will be able to help you, but since Mooncalf & Sons is no ordinary travel agent, you are in luck. When would you like to go?'

'We're just enquiring at the moment,' said Calamity. 'How much does it cost?'

'That depends on a number of factors. Whether you are reasonably flexible about dates and routes, and whether you would like to delegate to me the delicate business of travel visas and aliases. This is highly recommended.'

'What are the aliases?' asked Calamity.

'Normally you need two, I always recommend a belt-and-braces approach since we are talking about quite a high cost of failure here, including potential loss of liberty for a considerable length of time and possibly torture using psychotropic drugs. Thus I would urge you to go for two aliases. The first is to get in and the second is a form of insurance should the first alias cause you to run into difficulties – say your alias describes you as a spinning-wheel mechanic and by some terrible fluke of fate you are called on while you are there to repair a wheel, and your ignorance is thus laid bare—'

'Or you go as an obstetrician and a lady goes into labour at the back of the number 15 tram,' I said.

'An all too frequent occurrence,' said Mooncalf. 'Never go as an obstetrician. Fortunately, Mooncalf & Sons protects its clients against such cruel exigencies of fate by virtue of our unique, patent-pending, double-ID indemnity procedure. Once the first alias becomes corrupted, you can still invoke, as a form of reserve parachute, the second and return safe and sound, albeit a touch chastened by experience, to the comforting embrace of the Aberystwyth bosom. I'll arrange for you both to have a day on the road with Meici Jones.'

'Who's that?' I asked.

'He's the spinning-wheel salesman. A great and trusted associate of the firm Mooncalf & Sons. It will be a great help with your alias: spinning-wheel salesman is a superb disguise.'

'Wow!' said Calamity. 'How much will all this cost?'

'I'll need to make a few enquiries, so give me a few days to put a proposal together. You might need to join the Communist Party.'

'We also need you to put us in touch with some snuff philatelists,' I said.

Mooncalf laughed unconvincingly. 'There's no such thing.'

'Yes, we know, but just pretend there is. We have a rich client interested in buying the séance tape sent to Ffanci Llangollen in 1956.'

Mooncalf removed his glasses and polished them with the tail of his shirt. 'I'll see what I can do, very difficult, very difficult.'

I put the sock down on the counter. 'And we'd like to talk to you about this.'

Mooncalf put on a neutral expression, the sort a man assumes in order not to give too much away at the start of a negotiation. Or maybe he just thought it was a sock.

'It's a sock,' said Calamity. 'It was worn by Yuri Gagarin.'

Mooncalf made a small 'ah' sound indicating the arousal of his professional interest. He pulled a jeweller's loupe from under the counter and screwed it into his eye socket. He held the sock up and examined it.

'We were hoping it was worth something,' said Calamity.

I spluttered, 'Worth something! Of course it's worth something, it's one of the most famous socks in the world. It's worth . . . lots.'

'Yeah, that's one valuable sock,' said Calamity.

It was clear to all that in the manner of driving a hard bargain we were both newborn babes; in the souk they would be fighting over the chance to sell us a used camel. Mooncalf sucked air between his teeth to suggest the prospects were not good. 'It seems to be genuine, no doubt about that, the weave of the asbestos is definitely Soviet and the style of sock was popular in the artistic and scientific communities of Moscow during the late fifties. The problem is, the market for Yuri Gagarin socks is very slow at the moment.'

He lowered the sock from his eye and a photo fell out. It was the picture Uncle Vanya had left with us. Mooncalf picked it up. 'What's holding the dog up?'

'An imaginary friend,' said Calamity.

Mooncalf nodded as if to indicate this was a reasonable hypothesis, although one among many. 'Might be wires,' he added. He held the photo up to his loupe. 'Difficult to say without the negatives. It looks like one of those schools for remote viewing and associated paranormal investigation, which lends credence to your levitation claim. But it could be an ectoplasmic projection.' He laid the photo down on the counter. 'Not really my line.'

'We came about the sock,' I said. 'We'd like to fence it.'

Mooncalf contorted his features into a look of fake shock. 'Fence? We don't deal in stolen goods here, Mr Knight, and I would thank you to remember it.'

'What do you call it then?'

'Facilitation. We help the police. We help them by bypassing them.'

'OK, if we decided we wanted to be of assistance to the police in the way you describe, how does it work?'

'I would be able to let you have a modest, non-refundable deposit on the sock while I made enquiries about the best way to return it.' He pulled open a drawer and removed a thick paper-bound catalogue; it looked like the sort stamp collectors use as a reference. It had Cyrillic script on the front and assorted Cold War memorabilia, such as medals, hammer and sickle lapel pins, stamps, currency. He flicked through the pages and, finding the one he was looking for, scanned it with an unhappy mien, intended to lower our expectations of his first offer. Then he stopped and his eyebrows shot up, he peered closer at the page in the time-honoured manner of someone doubting the evidence of his senses. He stood transfixed for a second before slamming the book back in the drawer, and turning the key. 'As I thought, the market is very slow. I'll give you five hundred in cash.'

And he did.

Chapter 3

I ARRIVED at the office later and found Calamity leafing through a pile of press cuttings that she had retrieved from the *Cambrian News* clipping archive. There was a cardboard box full of items relating to the case of the missing girl, dutifully collated over the years and filed away without much expectation that anyone would ever want them. She greeted my arrival with the pleasure of one who has a story to share and has been waiting for the audience to turn up. I leafed through the cuttings as she ran through the background to the case.

'Gethsemane spent the morning in town with her auntie, Mrs Mochdre, buying a present for her mother's birthday the following week. They went to the Pier amusement arcade as a treat, then returned to Abercuawg around lunchtime. Gethsemane went out to play with the neighbour's dog, Bingo. The dog came back on its own later that afternoon. They used him as a sort of bloodhound, sent him off to search for her with the whole village following. They lost his trail and the dog was never seen again.' She pulled a photo out of the box and slid it across the table. 'This is Bingo, sired by the famous Clip—'

She broke off and gave me a look of guilty complicity. Clip had featured in one of our previous cases. He could now be found stuffed with sawdust sitting in a glass case in the museum on Terrace Road, one ear permanently cocked for the whistle of the Great Shepherd in the Sky. In his heyday he had been a star of the newsreels from the war in Patagonia in 1961, the Welsh Lassie. In moments like this, when a ghost from our past resurfaced, we struggled to recall whether the case had turned out well or not. There was one key criterion for deciding: did the client die? But we never actually met the client in the Clip case; she was, or claimed to be, the Queen of Denmark and our business was conducted over the phone. But since her head is still on the postage stamps we take it as a positive sign. And none of the postal orders she sent bounced. Calamity, remembering this vital fact, continued.

'Goldilocks was a local hoodlum attached to the Slaughterhouse Mob – a bunch of tearaways who worked at the slaughterhouse and hung out at the Pier ballroom. They were into the usual small-time stuff: robbery, extortion, violence. The evening after Gethsemane disappeared someone saw Goldilocks burying something in his garden, it turned out to be one of her shoes. He couldn't account for it and wouldn't say where he had been on the day in question. He was convicted of her murder and escaped from Aberystwyth gaol the following November.' She slid another photo across the desk. 'This is him.'

He had an angelic face with tight blond curls. He didn't smile and didn't look like he understood the purpose of the expression. His eyes were dead, like those of a mackerel in the fishmonger's. They were the eyes of a man whose heart is cold as a fireless grate, one who never takes pleasure or mirth from his passage through this world and is irritated and bewildered by those who do. You can tell a lot about the soul from a photograph. Or at least you think you can. Maybe I was just projecting into the image what I already knew. If I had been told this was a photo of a boy who had rescued a baby from a burning building I might have been touched by his gentle aspect and said he looked a little angel.

'The only member of the Slaughterhouse Mob still alive is the chief typographer down at the rock foundry. We can go and see him.' Calamity took out another cutting. 'This is the only photo the newspaper could find of Gethsemane.'

It was a school nativity play: shepherds in dressing gowns and tea towels on their heads; a Roman centurion; a crib; Mary and Joseph; angels.

'Gethsemane is the robin redbreast.'

She had bird's feet made out of rope, a dark cloak and a cardboard beak. In her eyes there was a certain wistful awareness: staring out across the years from the grey fog of a tattered old photo, it betokened the early understanding of what life held in store for a misfit doomed to wear a cardboard beak when others among her peers were centurions or angels.

'The guy playing Joseph is Rwpert Valentino, the star of the TV soap *North Road*. We can check him out, he hangs out every night after the show at the railway station buffet.'

'How did you find that out?'

'It's in the scandal pages in the *Cambrian News*. He's got a girl who works there.'

'OK, that's good stuff. Anything else?'

Calamity slapped the back of her hand against one of the news reports for emphasis. 'This lady, Mrs Mochdre, interests me. Gethsemane's aunt, the one who took her to the Pier that morning. Last one to see her alive, that's always a red flag.'

'Not always.'

Calamity scowled at me and carried on. 'She's married to the Witchfinder, keeps pigs, used to be pretty big in the ABLL.'

'What's that?'

'The Anti-Bearded-Lady League.'

I blinked. It seemed like an appropriate reaction.

'A lot of the champs on the Pro-Bearded-Lady circuit from the forties and fifties used to come from the area around Abercuawg,' Calamity explained. 'Mrs Mochdre used to campaign against it on grounds of idolatry or something. I thought we could talk to a few.'

'A few what?'

'Bearded ladies, get them to dish the dirt – there can't be much love lost between them and Mrs Mochdre.'

I looked at her through narrowed eyes. Calamity inspires a curious mix of emotions in me: pride and a desperate desire to protect her from the bad things in this world; I want to stop her from even knowing about them, even though she probably already does. Maybe this is how fathers feel all the time. Is this how Eeyore feels when he sees me?

There are certain subjects we never discuss. Her father is one. He does not live in Aberystwyth; according to her mother he lives at the racetrack, but no fixed racetrack, in England, or sometimes the Republic of Ireland. The other subject is boyfriends. I do not think Calamity has a boyfriend, and her behaviour and dress do not betray any interest in that direction. I know how painful it would be for her if I mentioned it, with that clumsy well-meaning insensitivity of adults who have forgotten the grief of their own youth.

She wears jeans and T-shirts and arranges her hair in an untidy spiky pile that is somehow arranged in its lack of arrangement. She is not a tomboy but she has a slight fear of girly things. On occasion I have seen her wearing eyeshadow but so little the lack of confidence shone through.

Calamity tilted her head to one side to express mild puzzlement at the reverie that had caused me to be silent.

'Talking to former bearded ladies seems like a . . . a . . . a very left-of-field way to begin a case,' I said.

'Exactly,' said Calamity. She paused and said with a casual air that was slightly forced, 'I thought we could use it as an example of superseding the paradigm.'

'That sounds like a good idea.'

'I think so too.'

'What does it mean?'

Calamity pulled a piece of paper from her back pocket, and unfolded it. 'I saw it in this month's *Gumshoe* magazine. It's called "The Existentialist Detective and Non-Linear Cognition". It's all about superseding the paradigm.'

'We've managed well enough without superseding it so far but I'm always open to new ideas.'

Calamity began to read. 'Traditional detective methods which rely on deductive reasoning are premised on the belief that life makes sense. This is a mistake. Normally, life only makes sense in novels and movies where events are shaped by the hand of a creative artist. In the real world events are born of contingency and are frequently shaped by the hands of people who are often clinically insane. Thus, because no rational process can be discerned behind the events of life, deductive reasoning is not best suited for unravelling its mysteries. In the past one means of countering this problem was the frequent use of the policeman's hunch which proceeds by non-linear and counter-intuitive methods and aims to break the straitjacket of conventional thinking. Deployed successfully the hunch often re-arranges the pieces of the jigsaw in such a way that old paradigms are superseded. Though a reliable method of unravelling stubborn mysteries, the hunch suffers from the drawback that it occurs but rarely and, crucially, is not subject to conscious control. The advanced detective seeks to summon up the paradigm-busting thinking that hallmarks the hunch by deliberately entertaining hypotheses that are absurd.' She put the article down and looked across.

Before I could think of something to say, the phone rang. Calamity answered. She wrote something down, thanked the caller and hung up. 'That was Mooncalf. He's arranged for us to spend tomorrow morning with Meici Jones the spinning-wheel salesman. This is his address.'

'Did we ask him to arrange that?'

'I don't think we told him not to.'

That night the sky over the beach at Ynyslas had the translucence of a cathedral window on a moonlit night. I opened the door of my caravan to air the inside and went to sit on the brow of the dune behind. For the first time in days, the night was cool. The heat had gone with the setting of the sun, and a soft breeze wafted in off the sea and raised goosebumps on grateful flesh. The beach was dark, the tide far out, you sensed it rather than saw it. On the horizon there was a thin band of lighter blue, the same shade as the neon letters on the 'Eats' signs that flash above so many diners down this coast. I lay back on the sand, felt the rasp under my hair, the sharp ends of the marram grass spiking my cheek. I kicked my shoes and socks off and buried my toes in sand that was still hot. In the morning the same sand would feel as cold as bathroom linoleum on a winter's morn. There was no sound, not even the customary susurration of the sea, it was leaden, unmoving; the sand grains stopped tumbling and hissing like snares on drums; not even a dog dared to bark.

The noise of a van pulling up disturbed the silence. A door slid open, followed by the crunch of a man jumping down on to gravel. I sat up and looked over. He was outside my caravan, knocking on the door. He was wearing a light summer macintosh and a panama hat with the brim pulled down low over his eyes; it didn't look like the postman. In this twilight he could have walked up to the caravan carrying a bloodstained chainsaw and no one would have batted an eye, but the hat brim pulled down was like a big advertising hoarding announcing nefarious intent. I could hear a thousand net curtains rustle, hear the quiet melancholy of eyes staring out in the night at a stranger. I climbed to my feet and wandered down the face of the dune, annoyed at the intrusion. He climbed the caravan steps and peeked inside.

'If you're selling encyclopaedias you're wasting your time, the guy in there already knows everything.'

He turned to face me. 'Looks to me like he needs a brush salesman.' He stepped down off the step. 'Or maybe I'm not here to sell anything, maybe I came to set a cross up outside his caravan and set it alight.'

'That would certainly get his attention. Tell me what you want to tell him and I'll see he gets the message.'

'They told me you were an entertainer, but I'm not in the mood, I've got a bad stomach, so maybe you'd like to get in the van.'

'Where is the van going?'

'To see some of Mr Mooncalf's friends.'

'Stamp collectors, huh? That explains why they sent a tough guy.'

'Don't waste your time trying to pump me. I'm just here to take you. You need to put this on.'

He handed me a blindfold.

'Is it all right if I get in the van first?'

'That would be the smart way to do it, but no one's insisting.'

I climbed in and put on the blindfold. The driver checked to make sure it was placed properly, started up the engine and drove off.

All things have their polar opposites: hot, cold; day, night; love, hate; the Roman Catholic mass is sometimes refracted through a dark lens of wickedness into the black magic rite, the cross inverted and the ritual debased. So it is with stamp collecting. Generations of schoolboys sifting through the little squares of coloured paper have given this pastime a reputation for dullness. The snuff philatelist however is a different beast. He lives in the shadows and meets under the arch of the railway bridge, out of the penumbra of the streetlamp, his collar raised to the level of his eyes, the brim of his hat pulled down low. His trade is one that must hide its face from the light of day. He delights in murder and mayhem, but only at the arm's length of correspondence that passed through the hands of the crook. Letters that are decorated with the fingerprints of the criminally insane, letters postmarked Sing Sing or San Quentin, Holloway or, better still, because insanity adds an extra frisson of terror, Broadmoor. He takes the necromancer's delight in the bizarre, perverse and crepuscular ravings of man, in the freak shows that are played out after hours in the hinterlands of the human heart. The snuff philatelist is not concerned about the lives of the various heads of state, the profiles of Victoria or George, but lives only for the tongue of the serial killer who licked the back of the stamp, or failing that the tongue of his mum or someone who knew him. Except when writing deliberately badly spelled letters to the press to taunt the cops for their lack of success the serial killer seldom writes letters. And this makes his stamps all the more rare. For the collector, the thought that within those molecules of glue on the stamp's back can be found the saliva and DNA of a monster, who once made the front page and caused a whole town to avoid the streets at night, makes his viscera quiver with pleasure.

I listened intently. When we reached the main Borth Road we turned right and continued for about two minutes and then left the road and drove on to a car park of rough stones from the beach. We drove around this a bit, doing some reversing and three-point turns, clearly intended to disorientate me, but when we returned to the main road we turned left so we were going back the way we came. We kept to the main road and omitted the turning to the caravan park, not long after that we went over the railway tracks. A couple of minutes after that, I got lost.

A while later, we drove over a cattle grid and then the world became muffled and my nostrils filled with the smoky, woody smell of old forest and dry pine-needles. We stopped and the driver helped me climb out. We began to walk through the forest, somewhere to my left a stream babbled. We walked for a while and then emerged into a clearing, the smell of pine needles was replaced by cooking smells and woodsmoke. A dog barked and a voice cried out, 'Gelert! Here boy!' The sounds took on a modulated quality that suggested there was a body of water nearby. There was also the crackle of fire burning bone-dry twigs and a wooden pole stirring a heavy metal receptacle that my heightened sensitivity and general knowledge of the vicinity led me to imagine was a cauldron. A girl's voice sang a soft melody on the scented breeze of the summer night.

> Liver of blaspheming Jew,
> Gall of goat, and slips of yew
> Sliver'd in the moon's eclipse,
> Nose of Turk, and Tartar's lips . . .

I was taken into a cottage or barn, a low lintel at the entrance was kindly pointed out. I walked down a corridor of stone flags, under another low doorway, and was ushered on to a wooden chair with a wide back. A man spoke to me.

'This is the last time we will ever talk so listen carefully. Firstly I apologise for the theatrics necessary to bring you here but, as a dealer in our hidden world, you will no doubt understand. All further communication between us will take place via Mr Mooncalf who will deny at all times that the merchandise of which we talk even exists. He will tell you that you are bonkers but you must not be dismayed by this essential security measure. In a minute your blindfold will be removed and you will be left alone for ten minutes to examine the stamps. We have a First Day cover celebrating the formation of the SAVAK, the Iranian secret police, circa 1957; a letter addressed to 39 Hilldrop Crescent, Holloway, London, the house where the notorious Dr Crippen murdered his wife, although the letter post-dates this incident; a letter from a soldier at Maindiff Court Military Hospital in Abergavenny, written at the same time that Rudolf Hess was an inmate there. We also have a ransom note from the kidnappers of a German businessman in Kinshasa in 1978. And the envelope and tape that was sent to Mrs Walters. You have ten minutes, no more. After your ten minutes you will be taken back to the main road at Tre'r-ddôl, after which you may make an offer through the office of Mr Mooncalf if you so wish.'

The blindfold was pulled off, the door slammed, I was alone at a kitchen table with some old letters spread out in front of me. Next to them was a cigar box in which they had been stored. The room was small with a low ceiling in which wooden beams could be seen. A cold empty fireplace yawned in one wall, and next to it was a traditional oak dresser. It was set with plates and cups and some tins of paint and glue stood on it with brushes soaking in turpentine, giving off a strong odour. Next to that was a spinning wheel. At the time it was just a wheel, but a week later and I could have told you it was a Semi-Saxon horizontal, sheathed bobbin, slip-backed flyer with five-speed twin treadle array – basically a souped-up 'Cinderella'; you could cover a lot of yarn on a job like that. The owner of the house was a pro. I turned my attention to the letters.

The envelope was postmarked Aberaeron and contained a small spool of tape and a typewritten letter from a spiritualist who explained that she was familiar with the story from the newspapers and had made the recording at a recent sitting. There was no name and no signature. On impulse, I held the letter up to my nose. Despite the passage of time it still held a scent, that was the remarkable thing about paper, you can leave it lying in the back of the cupboard drawer for years and when you take it out it retains a trace of scent, sometimes enough to ambush the heart with the memory of a long-lost love. I sniffed again and my heart quivered, my head filled with a dizzy sensation of long ago. What it was I didn't know, but I knew that I had smelled it before. The sound of footsteps outside made me realise time was short. It was too risky to steal the tape now, I needed to come back, and to do that I needed to know where I was. There were more footsteps outside, voices, whispered conversation. I looked at the spinning wheel and wondered. Tomorrow morning I had been booked for a day on the road with the spinning-wheel salesman. Maybe if I just . . . more footsteps. I walked across to the spinning wheel, picked up the brush from the glue pot and smeared it on the axle of the flywheel. I sat down again. The man came in and put my blindfold back on. I heard the cigar box snap shut. The man walked over to the dresser on my right, I heard a door being opened, a drawer opened and shut. Then we left. Behind me, the resin slowly thickened and turned to stone, fusing two pieces of wood. All I had to do was ask Meici Jones about reports of jammed wheels on his patch. Piece of cake. It was my first act of spinning-wheel sabotage.

Chapter 4

MEICI JONES stood with his hands on his hips and complained about death taking away his customers. 'It's a dying business, all right. The young ones aren't interested in spinning, and the rest get fewer each year. The number of funerals I attend! You wouldn't believe, sometimes I wonder if it's worth it. It costs me more in dry-cleaning getting me togs ready than I ever get out of the will when it's read.' He shook his head in disgust. 'It's not like the old days. What did you say your name was again?'

'Louie, and this is Calamity, my niece.'

Meici Jones sized us up, and nodded. 'Mooncalf's a good guy.'

'Yes,' I said, 'one of the best.'

'I do a lot of business through him, a lot.' He tapped the side of his nose. 'The sort of business that if you asked about it I'd have to say was none of your business, if you see what I mean.' He was short, in his thirties, with the melancholy eyes of a spaniel. 'I was quite surprised when he said you and your niece wanted to learn. Not many people do these days. You hoping for some action on the bequests and legacies stuff, are you? You're wasting your time if you are.'

'No, it's for the coming apocalypse.'

'What's that then?'

'You know, end of the world, nuclear Armageddon. Civilisation will be destroyed, it will be back to the hoe and plough, armed marauding gangs infesting the radioactive countryside, a man will need to survive by his own wits. Spinning will be an essential.'

'I hadn't thought of that.' He stood back and surveyed the scene. His Cavalier estate was parked outside our office in Stryd-y-Popty, the boot raised. Sample cases and bits of wood and rubber were strewn around the boot. 'Let's see what we have here, then. Good salesman always runs through the checklist.' He pulled a sample case forward and opened up the lid with two snaps of the fasteners. Bits of spinning wheel, cut into sections, lay embedded on green velour in form-fitted depressions. The high-gloss finish flashed in the sun like a welder's torch. 'This is what the guy in *The Day of the Jackal* used to keep his sniper rifle in,' he said. 'The ladies love it when I tell them that. That's what it's all about, you see, the old black magic; know what I mean?' He picked up a quadrant of wheel rim cut from deeply polished mahogany. 'Look at that, quality that is. Last a lifetime it will, not that we want it to, of course, but you can always go back and bugger the thing up every now and again, can't you? You're in luck, as it happens, Mrs Eglwys Fach was on the phone, her wheel's jammed up. Might be able to get her to take a new one.' He banged the side of my head with the piece of spinning wheel. 'Feel that? This is from Marmaduke & Sons. Best there is. Marmaduke Semi-Saxon horizontal, sheathed bobbin, slip-backed flyer with five-speed twin treadle complete with Teflon-coated dérailleur gear change by Shimano of Japan.'

He closed the case and ran his hand across the various items in the boot, talking to himself as he mentally ticked them off. 'Gasket, polish, order book, resin, spare treadle, distaff balance, counterweights . . .' His hand came to rest on two stovepipe hats. 'Not forgetting the most important thing of all . . .' He turned round and said with a wink, 'Couple of stoveys for the ladies!'

We drove up Penglais Hill, windows wound right down, squinting at the bright asphalt that rose ahead of us. Meici had a Tupperware sandwich box balanced on his knee, and took periodic bites from a bacon sandwich that dripped fat on to the steering wheel.

'My mam makes them extra greasy,' said Meici. 'I told her I like them like that but I don't really. I'll cop it if she ever finds out the truth. She says every time I tell a lie an angel marks it down in a book. Does your mum say that?'

'My mum died when I was little.'

'Oh. Who do you live with then?'

'Nobody.'

Meici looked across at me as if to check whether I was being serious. 'Really? Where?'

'I have a caravan out at Ynyslas.'

Meici nodded. 'We live near Bwlchcrwys.' He considered for a second and then said suddenly, 'Guess how many games teachers there are in our family? Go on, guess.'

I looked puzzled.

'Four,' said Meici with evident pride. 'Three uncles and my grandad. What do you think of that?'

'Very good.'

'Yeah, isn't it?'

'Weren't you tempted yourself?'

'No, not for me. We thought for a while my brother Esau might . . . he was born hairy, you see . . .' A thought clouded his brow. 'But I don't want to talk about Esau.' He turned round to Calamity in the back. 'Did you bring any crayons?'

I could sense her eyes narrowing.

'What for?' she said.

'You might find it a bit boring watching me doing the old black magic. Thought maybe you could go outside and draw some nice pictures or something.' He finished the last sandwich and handed me the Tupperware box. 'Hold on to that, Lou, I'll be needing it later.' He licked the snail trails of grease that ran down the back of his hand.

We drove over the brow of Penglais Hill, a flow of cars bumper to bumper headed past us on the right, into town. Some were going to work but their numbers had been swollen by those staying in caravans up and down the coast. Meici expounded on the subtle art of the spinning-wheel salesman. 'The main drawback with wheels is they are traditional, see, so there aren't many firms left that still make them and the ones that do take a lot of pride in their work. The stuff they make lasts a lifetime, but what's the good of that? One month on the road and you would have saturated the market. This drawback is your opportunity, too. Delicate things they are, spinning wheels, that's if you want to keep the yarn at its optimum, so they always need a little tinker under the hood. They could probably do it themselves, the dears, but it voids the warranty doesn't it? That's the trick, you see. Always sell the extended warranty, and all the other bits and bobs, the wheel is just the beginning.' He looked over and asked, 'Know what of?'

'Er . . . I don't know.'

'Beginning of a beautiful relationship.'

'Of course!'

'They get to trust you like a son after a while so then you can start hitting them for stuff they don't need, persuade them to have a service that isn't necessary.'

'How do you do that?'

'Fiddle the log book, put it down for more spins than it's had. Sometimes, if you've been with them for a few years, and they seldom change once they've got a relationship, they start asking you to fetch their pension. You can always skim some off that. "Oh it's not as much as it used to be," they say, and you sympathise: "Oh I know, it's the economy, you see." Stuff like that. Here listen—'

Meici reached across and turned on the cassette player. A tape squeaked into life and a female voiceover chirruped in that bedtime story voice that all adult education audio tapes seem to have:

Welcome to unit 5 of Selling Isn't Telling, the pro-salesman's guide to Ninja selling. In the last unit we discussed the key importance of the 'close' as the foundation of all successful sales pitches. Do you remember how novice salesman Frankie Marshall saw all his hard work go to waste because he was too shy to ask for the order? We learned that it often helps to memorise this lesson in the form of a little mnemonic, didn't we? Did you do one? If you did, repeat your mnemonic now.

Meici said, 'Don't sell like a girly, close that sale and close it early.'
There, that was fun, wasn't it?
Meici turned to me. 'Some of this stuff might be a bit advanced for you, Lou, but try and follow as best you can.'

Today we will be looking at an advanced closing technique based on the trademark exit routine of the famous 1970s TV detective, Lieutenant Columbo. See how salesman Harry Pryce uses this technique to get his prospect to sign the order. But before we go on, did you spot the deliberate mistake I just made? [Pause.] That's right, we never ask the prospect to sign the order, do we? What do we do instead?

Meici answered almost before she had finished speaking. 'Ask him to OK it.' He switched off the tape. 'We probably won't need to do the Columbo today, Lou, I'll stick to the basics so you don't get confused. Just watch how I do it. And if there is anything you don't understand, don't be afraid to ask.'

We passed Tre'r-ddôl and turned right and drove up a pot-holed road into a forestry commission plantation.

'Lives with her son, she does,' said Meici, 'although he's not around much, thank God. He deals in rare stamps and coins and things, so he travels a lot. Good job, too, he's the sort of guy who reads the small print on behalf of his mam. Her granddaughter lives there, too, lovely girl she is, only seventeen and never been kissed. Well, that's what she says, but who knows with kids these days?' He turned to Calamity. 'I'spect you've got a boyfriend, have you?'

'Not until she's twenty-one,' I said quickly, to spare Calamity, or at least stop her saying something that might get us thrown out of the car.

'Lot of guys my age wouldn't stand a chance with a looker like her,' said Meici, 'but I been working on Arianwen for a while now, using the old black magic. Wheels in motion, if you see what I mean.'

He turned and gave me his inscrutable look, the one that said, 'Strangle me.'

'Is there something wrong with her eyesight?' said Calamity.

Meici thought about his answer. 'Not that I'm aware. Although you could say she only has eyes for me.' The road narrowed to a single track without tarmac and the car began to bounce violently; we lurched from side to side. Meici chuckled and continued, oblivious to the bumps. 'Yeah, you could say she was my girl in a way but don't tell anyone in case it gets back to my mam. I sent her a dress last week, really nice one, it was – from the catalogue. I had to wait for the postman at the end of the lane so mam wouldn't find out. It's got polka dots on it, they're supposed to be the best, but when you look at them closely you'll see that they are really tomatoes. That's called an optician's illusion. She'll be wearing it today so you'll be able to see it for yourself.' He pulled over to the side of the road and parked, saying, 'What time is it, Lou?'

'Just after ten.'

'Wrong! It's black magic time. Pass me the sandwich box.' He took out a comb and dipped it in the grease lying at the bottom of the Tupperware container, and then combed his hair, leaning sideways to check it in the rear-view mirror. After that he took out a bottle of perfume from the seat pocket and sprayed it on liberally. 'This stuff's really good, it's got a special ingredient from a place called Provence, that's in France. They know how to charm the ladies over there. *Ooh la la!* and that, I've been reading about it.'

It was the sort of cottage where they kept a cage in the back room with a boy called Hansel in it, sticking gnawed chicken bones through the bars every time the woman went to check. The roof was slate that gleamed with damp, even though the heatwave continued unabated; houses like this have their own micro-climate of grey mist that hangs permanently above the roof. A blackbird in the undergrowth a few feet away stopped hunting for a grub and looked up. He followed us with his cold dark eyes, scrutinising us with the intensity of the inhabitants of Mexican border towns peering at strangers riding into town in the spaghetti westerns.

'Cooey!' shouted Meici. 'Mrs Eglwys Fach! Are you there?'

Mrs Eglwys Fach came out of the front door and did a little pantomime of surprise and joy commingled, ending in her two hands coming together in front of her face, as if the Lord had answered her prayers, even though she should take the lion's share of the credit since it was her, and not the Lord, who made the phone call to Meici. She was bent forward slightly at the waist, wore a black wool cardigan over a drab grey skirt that reached to the ground. Her hair was tucked into a white bonnet and she had the sort of sweet and spite-free face that belonged on the lid of a confectionery box. Some people wear a lifetime's accumulated care and resentment when they get old but Mrs Eglwys Fach was clearly one of those who maintained the belief that for all the bad things life was still a gift for which she gave thanks every day. Meici introduced us and she clasped her hands even tighter at the unexpected treat, since now she would be given the opportunity to make four cups of tea instead of two. She hobbled up to Calamity and peered at her in wonder. 'What a sweet little girl!' she cried. In this remote dingle on the dark side of Talybont you could be forgiven for thinking she was sizing Calamity up for the cauldron, but with Mrs Eglwys Fach you could tell it was the simple goodness of her heart pouring out even if it was guaranteed to infuriate any self-respecting teenager. Calamity bore it with the patient restraint of a policeman's horse being offered sugar lumps while on duty.

Mrs Eglwys Fach led us into the kitchen. It was the same room I had sat in the previous evening looking at the stamps. Meici walked over to the wall and dragged the spinning wheel out.

'I just don't understand it,' said Mrs Eglwys Fach. 'It was working fine on Saturday and then this morning when I tried it, it just sort of seized up. Jammed it was, the beggar!'

Meici gave the wheel a gentle push with his index finger, but it didn't move. He put on an expression of deep concern. 'Ooh, dear, dear!' he said. 'Dear oh dear. Doesn't look good.'

Mrs Eglwys Fach bit her lip.

'You haven't spilled any glue on it or anything, have you?' said Meici.

'Ooh no,' she said. 'I would never do that.'

Meici probed and checked and tapped and accompanied it all with strange unvocalised noises, grunts from the time before man invented speech but which communicated in a language available to us all that Mrs Eglwys Fach's spinning wheel was buggered. He stood up wearily, rubbing the small of his back with one hand, and returned to the table with a look of grave sorrow on his face.

'I'm not sure what's made it stop like that,' he began. 'But it looks to me like you'll need a new wheel.'

'Rhun says it might just be swollen because of the damp.'

'No, I don't think so,' said Meici with barely concealed contempt for the opinions of a layman. 'It's not water in the wheel. In fact, it doesn't look mechanical at all. Could someone have put a spell on you?'

Mrs Eglwys Fach put her hand to her mouth and considered the suggestion. 'Of course it's possible, but I'm usually very careful – I've always made a point of putting a little protective spell on all my wheels.'

'Is there someone who might know the structure of the spell? They're easy enough to crack if someone knows the structure.'

'I don't see how they can know, I make all my own charms. And I don't let anyone watch.'

'What about the birds? Do you trust them? They can spy through the window, you know. There's no point going to all the trouble of making new charms if the birds are snitching on you.'

'The wrens and the thrushes are OK, but I will admit I've had one or two problems with the blackbirds—'

There was a sharp fluttering at the window; we all turned and saw a whirl of feathers and flash of hastily departing bird.

'Caught in the act,' said Meici with the air of one having his professional diagnosis confirmed by events.

'Oh dearie me,' said Mrs Eglwys Fach feeling betrayed. 'They are beggars, those birds. Last week they stole some things from Arianwen's dressing table.'

'You need to teach them a lesson,' said Meici. 'What you have to do is find the nest, and then when the bird is not looking you swap her eggs for turtle eggs.'

'Where would I get turtle eggs from?'

'*Exchange & Mart*,' said Meici.

'Does it stop them stealing?' said Mrs Eglwys Fach.

'Not exactly, but you get a bird who spends a month hatching her eggs and a turtle comes out; you never get any more trouble out of her after that.'

'It sounds a bit mean,' said Mrs Eglwys Fach.

'And stealing things from your dressing table and snitching on you to the witches isn't?' said Meici. 'Point is, some of these new wheels are a lot more resistant to the old ways. These new carbon fibre ones, for example, you'd have a hell of a job putting a spell on one of those.'

'Are they expensive?'

'In the long run, if you factor in the cost of the days lost to bad spells and stuff, they can work out cheaper.' Meici took out a pocket calculator and started punching in random figures. Mrs Eglwys Fach watched, fascinated. Meici murmured to himself with evident satisfaction, the figures were looking good. He stopped and looked up, shoving the calculator over towards her. 'There you go. That's five grand I've saved you.'

She took out her reading specs and bent over the calculator. She leant back and said, 'My, my!' And then a thought clouded her brow. 'But they have fewer spokes those carbon-fibre ones, don't they?'

'Absolutely,' said Meici. 'Stronger material, greater rigidity, fewer spokes—'

'Hmm, but does that mean you don't get that wagon-wheel effect you see in the old westerns where the wheels seem to be spinning backwards? I like that bit.'

Meici scoffed at the naïvety of her question. 'But of course you get it! Don't you see? Fewer spokes, lighter weight, less drag, you can go fast as you like!'

Mrs Eglwys Fach quivered with an excitement that was almost carnal, all common sense had departed and in her eyes there burned the fierce gleam of a woman now picturing herself cutting a dash and inviting all the envious scorn of her neighbours as she sat at the helm of a new carbon-fibre wheel. In such a mood she would have signed away the deeds to the cottage. Meici studiously filled out the order adding in every conceivable extra, including anti-spell coating which I'm sure he had implied was rendered unnecessary by the advanced technology of the design.

Calamity whispered, 'You go outside and create a diversion, I'll get the tape.'

'Why don't you go out and create the diversion?' I hissed back. She gave me an impatient look and Meici looked up to see what the problem was.

Calamity said, 'No, Louie, I think I'll sit here for a while, I'm feeling a little faint from the heat. You go out and take the air.'

I walked outside and heard a voice singing, a young girl's voice. I followed the sound into the thin grey miasma that passed for summer in this dingle and walked round to the back of the cottage. The girl was sitting on the edge of a well washing her hair in a wooden pail. For a while she continued, unaware of being observed. She was bent forward over the bucket, wringing her hair, which the wetness had rendered dark and colourless. Soap suds glistened. She continued singing and I coughed politely. She started and looked up.

'I'm with the spinning-wheel man,' I said politely.

'I know, I saw you arrive. I've seen you before somewhere, too, but I can't remember where.'

'Perhaps in church,' I said.

'Definitely not there.' She picked up a towel and began to dry her hair. Colour emerged from the dark mass, like flowers appearing in the undergrowth of a gloomy wood: russets, mahogany, rosewood, copper. Then she swept the hair up into a white turban of towel.

'If you were looking for the outhouse it's through the kitchen.'

'I just came for a walk. My name's Louie.'

'Arianwen. It was so nice of you to come, grandmother is lost without her wheel.'

'It looks like she's going to need a new one.'

'Can't you fix it?'

'No, we think someone must have put a spell on it, probably in league with the birds.'

She giggled. 'I don't believe in spells.'

'Nor do I.'

'If you ask me, someone spilled some glue on it.'

'But who would do a thing like that?'

'I don't know, an intruder I expect; definitely a very wicked person.' She let her gaze linger on me for a second that might have been a hint of forbidden knowledge or simply the absence of guile. 'You're quite good-looking for a spinning-wheel salesman.'

'No one's ever said that to me before.'

'That's if you really are a spinning-wheel salesman.'

'What else could I be?'

'I think you are a rogue.'

'I could be both.'

'We get quite a few salesmen pass this way and you're not like the usual ones. They're always so corny: "My word, how pretty you are! Here, try this stovepipe hat on. Wow! Just look at that, have you ever thought about starring in the Butlies?"'

'What are they?'

'You know, the "What the butler saw" flicks.'

'I didn't know they were called Butlies.'

'Just shows you're not a real spinning-wheel salesman, then, doesn't it?' She emptied the pail down the drain next to the kitchen wall. 'And besides, you don't smell of air freshener.' She slung the pail down next to the drain, straightened up and smiled. 'I bet he told you I was seventeen and never been kissed, too.'

'Yes, he did.'

'It's because he heard the line in a song once. I'm twenty-one, in case you were wondering, and I've been kissed by three different boys, although I've never gone further than that, well not much.'

'It's never a good idea to rush these things.'

She feigned disappointment. 'Oh you're not much fun, are you? You sound like my grandmother.'

'One thing you learn in life is almost everything your grandmother told you when you were young, and which you thought at the time was just the lunacy of old age, is actually true.'

Meici Jones appeared round the corner of the cottage, holding a stovepipe hat. He gave me the black look of a man who finds another trespassing on his territory. 'What are you doing here?'

'I just came for a walk.'

'You should have asked me first.' He explained to Arianwen: 'This is my assistant Lou.'

'Yes, we've met.'

'I'm sorry if he's bothering you.'

'Oh there's nothing to be sorry for.'

'He's still learning, you see. Lou, get back to the car and write up your report on the call.'

'Oh you're a spoilsport, sending such a handsome man away to write a boring report.'

Meici's face reddened and his eyes misted up. He ploughed on with dogged determination. 'I bought you this.'

'Not another silly hat! Granny never wears them.'

'It's for you.'

'Oh. I see. It's very kind of you.'

'I was a bit surprised you weren't wearing the dress.'

'I wore it so much it had to go in the wash.'

I made a slight chivalrous bow to Arianwen, because I knew it would annoy Meici, and walked back. Calamity came out of the kitchen and gave me a wink that said, 'Tape retrieved, mission accomplished.' We waited next to the car for Meici to return. When he came back he was miserable and said he wouldn't be driving us all the way, but would drop us off at the bus stop. I sat in the back with Calamity. Meici kept his eyes fixedly on the road and didn't speak. As we exited the cottage, we passed a field in which stood a scarecrow wearing a red-and-white polka-dot dress that flapped in the breeze.

Chapter 5

'SPOOKY,' said Calamity. 'Really spooky.'

We walked in single file down a narrow track of loose shale through gorse bushes and found ourselves on the lake's shore. The waters were dark and sombre, and clouds brooded on the surface. Far out, in the centre of the lake, the spire of a church broke the surface. Birds wheeled about the sky, the waters lapped the shore gently. The world was quiet; even the bees had stopped humming. The only other human life came from a group of three artists painting in watercolours.

'Spooky,' said Calamity. 'Really spooky.'

The reservoir lay on the east of the Penpegws massif, north of Devil's Bridge. We had asked Meici to drop us off on the way back to town; we would get the bus back.

'Spooky,' said Calamity.

She was right. Towns that have vanished from the face of the earth, beneath the waves or buried beneath desert sands, are not supposed to reappear. It is disconcerting; a rupture in the fabric of time that undermines the comfortable certainty which helps us get through the succession of days we call a life. Sometimes in periods of drought the outlines of ancient Saxon farms appear in the desiccated ground, visible from the air, like the bone structure of the earth revealed by X-ray photography. It is as if Father Time leaves ajar a door to a room that is normally locked. Such rare glimpses, like the appearance of comets in the heavens, make the skin prickle with primeval feelings for which we struggle to find names but which, no doubt, would be familiar to the Iron Age watcher of the skies.

It had been thirty years since the sun last warmed the slate tiles of that spire; how different had the world been then! A world of rationing and post-war austerity, of bully-beef and powdered egg, in which a pretty tram conductress caught the eye of Eeyore and beguiled his heart. Together they produced me. A world so different, but the troubles were the same, they never change. A little girl went missing and broke her mother's heart. For all the differences that divide us from humanity across the sea or down the centuries, it is through suffering that we maintain a common bond.

We followed the path along the shore for a while, drinking in the strangeness of the view, haunted by the spire. We stopped and stared, lost in thought. Calamity took out an Instamatic camera and took some shots of the shoreline. We were about to turn and return to the car when Calamity spotted something floating in the water at the shore's edge. She trotted down to the water and bent down. I followed, squinting into the fierce reflected glare. I kneeled down beside her. It was a body: a woman, floating face-up in the shallows like Ophelia, wearing what appeared to be a navy-blue pinafore dress over a white blouse, like a school uniform from long ago. We pulled her on to the sand and she opened her eyes. She giggled and looked at us with impish mischief in her eyes and handed us her hat which she had been holding in one hand. It was a straw boater. Calamity took the hat and said thank you. The woman made an excited gurgling sound, like a baby, suddenly jumped up and ran off along the shore. She ran with the speed and agility of a gazelle. We watched, rooted to the spot, immobilised with astonishment. Calamity bent the hat slightly to read the name tag inside the brim and said, 'I think we've solved the case.'

The great thing about being Chief of Police in Aberystwyth is nothing shocks you. Being taken by surprise is for the amateurs. I had known Commander Llunos for fifteen or so years, and had worked with and against him at various times in the past. I'd lied to him a lot, often on occasions when we both knew I was lying, and I had told him some strange stories. On more than one occasion he had thrown me down the police station steps which was his home-spun method of processing criminals without the need for paper-work. I liked him.

He stood in the layby holding the hat and pondering. For once he was not wearing the standard police issue weather-stained, pre-crumpled macintosh. Without it he seemed strangely denuded like a freshly plucked hen; he stood instead perspiring in a short-sleeved shirt, wearing the melancholic expression of a bloodhound that has woken up with a hangover.

'We'll go and see Mrs Mochdre,' he said to no one in particular. 'Ffanci Llangollen's sister, Mrs Mochdre. She lives in Bwlchcrwys. We'll go and see her.'

Llunos drove a tan Montego with crushed velour upholstery, and tartan fabric panels in the door to add a touch of class. It wasn't much good in car chases but he had long ago outgrown the need for such vulgar ostentation. Once you passed a certain point in life as a cop in Aber, if you weren't already dead or invalided out of the force on a tiny pension, you achieved a sort of wisdom and maturity. Cops like Llunos didn't need to chase, by some paradox the crooks came to him, one way or the other.

The cottage was on the right as we entered the village. It was built according to the traditional building regulations, which decreed the walls should be the colour of smoke and the smoke that issued from the chimney should be the colour of the roof which should be the same tone as a field at dusk and this should mirror a rainy sky. Mrs Mochdre stood in wellingtons in a pig pen, emptying swill into a trough and booting the pigs away as they crowded round.

Llunos explained about the hat.

Mrs Mochdre took it, gave it a cursory examination, her face twisted in a frown of disapproval. 'Tomfoolery,' she said and handed it back.

'I guess Ffanci Llangollen is not in town,' said Llunos. Mrs Mochdre didn't deem it worthy of an answer, perhaps it was common knowledge. 'When did you last hear from her?' he added.

'Never. I never hear from her. She just goes her own way, wandering around the country pushing that wretched shopping trolley, still clinging to the hope that her daughter is alive somewhere. I mean, even if she was, what would be the point of finding her now? They would be strangers. Nothing good would come of it.'

A sow started trying to sniff Llunos's shoe; Mrs Mochdre kicked her away.

'So you are not expecting her back any time?' asked Llunos.

'No, but she'll turn up now, won't she? After she reads about the town reappearing in the lake like that. You mark my words, she'll be back.'

'What's she like?' said Calamity.

Mrs Mochdre stared at Calamity for a while and then spoke over her shoulder, to the middle distance. 'My sister had so much going for her. Not like me. She was always the pretty one, you see. All the lads used to come round courting her! I never minded, of course. I was happy for her, we had such great hopes . . . Then she threw it all away. Married the balloon-folder. Not much of a job really, is it? Balloon-folding. They practically fold themselves, don't they?'

'What was Gethsemane like?' asked Calamity.

'The child needed a firmer hand, if you ask me, but it was no good me saying anything, no one listened. She knocked my cruet set over once, and scratched it. Her mother wouldn't pay for it neither. She said it was probably already scratched – as if I didn't know my own cruet set!'

'I hear you used to be in the Anti-Bearded-Lady League,' said Calamity.

'Ignore that,' said Llunos.

It was late afternoon when we got back. The office felt like a greenhouse without the comforting warm earthy smell of peat and tomatoes. Llunos slumped into the client's chair. Calamity pulled open the desk drawer and took out the latest issue of *Gumshoe* and left for the day. I sat down opposite.

'What was that about bearded ladies?' asked Llunos.

'Calamity's superseding the paradigm.'

'How do you do that?'

'I don't know. It's the latest bee in her bonnet.'

'She'll get her ears boxed if she carries on like that. You can't talk to people like that.'

'I'll have a word with her.'

He stood up. 'Let's go for a walk.'

We strode along the Prom towards the Cliff Railway station at the end. As usual the two cars were frozen on the hillside, not moving, like two garden sheds built at the wrong angle. The immobility was an illusion. It was like the brass weights under a cuckoo clock: if you watched long enough you would be aware of a change in position.

The world was the colour of concrete dust, washed out like an over-exposed transparency. The occasional sharp flashes of light from chrome bumpers or hub-caps, from open windows, or the steel frames of pushchairs made the heart wince with unfocussed longing. Holidaymakers ambled up and down wearing expressions of patient suffering.

'I don't mind telling you,' he said without preamble, 'that thing with the hat was a bit strange.'

'Yes.'

'It's not the only strange thing, either. I've been rushed off my feet since that old town reappeared in the lake.'

'How so?'

'All sorts of rum things going on, people behaving oddly. Chap who winds the town hall clock lost the key. Men leaving their families and running off to join the French Foreign Legion. I've got two members of the town council buying guitars – Fenders, too, not cheap ones.'

'Maybe it's just the heat.'

Llunos gave a short sudden shake of the head. 'It's the lake. The reappearance of the town has precipitated a spiritual crisis in the town.'

'Says who?'

'My teacher. He says it's stirring things up, the repressed memories of the townsfolk, it's like our collective unconscious.'

'I didn't know you had a teacher.'

Llunos cast me a sheepish glance. 'Night school, been doing a course in psychology.'

'I'm surprised to hear that of you.'

'Me too.'

I could sense he was torn between distaste for the confessional mode, and the need to share these thoughts with someone.

'You have to move on, though, don't you? Move with the times. The world is changing and you either adapt or get left behind. That's what they say, isn't it?'

Llunos was a lawman in the old-fashioned mould, the sheriff of the frontier town whose methods were rough but reasonably effective. He preferred to beat rather than entreat, he liked the old-fashioned certainties of occasional short-term injustice that through the finely grinding mills of time and God ensured a form of justice not perfect but recognised by all as an acceptable accommodation in an imperfect world.

'These new boys with degrees and stuff, they don't approve of violence as a means to solving crime, they prefer modern scientific methods, they use psychology.'

I said nothing. Today I had been invited along to listen.

'Maybe if I can brush up on the textbook stuff I may make a move down to Cardiff, you know, the Bureau.'

I nodded.

Llunos adopted a deliberately casual tone: 'What were you doing out there anyway?'

'Where?'

'Where!'

'Like I told you, we just went to look.'

'Were you on a case?'

'No.'

He nodded thoughtfully. He didn't believe me. This was the pantomime we often enacted called Protecting the Client; Vanya's privacy had been entrusted into my safe-keeping. Maybe he wouldn't have minded cops asking him his business but most people who walk through my door do and I respect that. Cops, though, they hate it. Llunos knew all this but he still had to ask.

'You just happened to be going for a walk and found the hat.'

'No, we found the girl who was wearing the hat. She ran off. Like I told you.'

'Oh yeah, the girl. I forgot.'

Chapter 6

WHEN I ARRIVED at the office the next day there was an overhead projector set up on the desk. I asked Calamity what it was for and a slight air of coyness slipped into her voice. 'Oh, I've been superseding the paradigm.'

'That's good. How did you do it?'

She walked over to close the curtains, but it did little to lessen the fierce light from the street outside. 'I've been looking into the bearded lady angle, I think I've found something interesting. She flicked a switch on the side of the overhead projector and a wonky square of light illuminated the wall. Dust danced in the well of light above the platen. She placed a transparency down. 'Take a look at this. This is the area round Abercuawg, this line here is the Devil's Bridge narrow-gauge railway line.' She placed another acetate cell over the first. It superimposed a pattern of stars over the map. 'See these stars? Each one represents the birthplace of a champion on the Pro-Bearded-Lady circuit over the past fifty years. See? Classic clustering pattern. And there's more—'

'Could be just a statistical anomaly.'

'Maybe, but look at this.' She put a third acetate over the first two and this time a pattern of skulls was superimposed. The skulls clustered in the same patterns as the stars.

'Same clustering, different occupation. Guess what?'

'You tell me.'

'School games teachers.'

I laughed.

'You can laugh if you want, but the facts can't be laughed away. These clustering patterns are mathematically significant.

Now look at this.' She put another acetate down, this time showing a series of dots. 'Each dot represents a parish museum that has a photo or photos of hairy babies born in the neighbourhood. You see? There's a clear pattern, this area round Abercuawg has a rogue hairiness gene among the populace. Where did it come from? That's where it gets interesting. This line here is the working of a spur line to Devil's Bridge that was suddenly abandoned in 1872 after an accident during blasting. The official history of the railway says they hit a pocket of gas, but the oral histories claim the explosion released a "thing" imprisoned in the belly of the mountain. No one knows exactly what it was, but it was pretty angry and very hairy.'

'So where is all this leading?'

'Folklore also relates stories of village girls being offered to the "thing" over the years as brides, and there is talk of intermarriage between local women and the "thing"; this may explain the hairiness.'

'OK, sleuth, what is the "thing"?'

Calamity paused for effect, allowing her gaze to linger on me melodramatically. Finally, she said, 'Trolls.'

'Trolls?'

'Trolls.'

'There's a troll living in the mountain near Abercuawg?'

'It's a possibility we have to consider.'

'Is it?'

'We have to consider it even if only to eliminate it from the inquiry. The investigator doesn't get to choose what goes into the pot and what doesn't.'

'This one does. If we don't admit it into the inquiry, we don't have to eliminate it.'

Calamity looked flustered. 'Louie, you don't get this sort of thing just by chance. Maybe one or two games teachers, and one or two bearded ladies, one or two hairy babies, that I grant you. But not this many.'

I threw up my hands in mock despair. 'Maybe the pattern of hairiness is interesting but what does it mean? We've already got a suspect, a flesh and blood guy called Goldilocks who was sentenced to hang for the murder. We just need to find out what he did with her. Why bring in the trolls?'

Calamity's brow furrowed as she considered the implications. 'I don't say I believe it, I do say it has to be checked out and eliminated from the inquiry. I was thinking maybe you could help out on that . . .'

'I'm not talking to my old school games teacher.'

'No, I meant with the bearded ladies. I thought you could speak to a few.'

'Calamity, the world has moved on since those days. We don't have bearded ladies any more because it's . . . it's . . . I don't know, it's not right. Competitive bearded ladying went out with all the other freak shows. We don't laugh at people like that, we try to help them, or at least good people do. I'm not going to remind them of the old days, and if I did they would probably slam the phone down on me. What's to stop you from talking to them?'

'I tried but they slammed the phone down on me.'

'See!'

Calamity sighed. 'We just need to find a way to crack the culture of Omertà surrounding the bearded ladies.'

'When can we hear the séance tape?'

'I'm still trying to get hold of an open reel deck, it should be round later today.' She opened the curtains again and it was like leaving a darkened cinema for the bright daylit street.

'I guess there's not much point me asking you to talk to Meici Jones, either,' she said.

'What's he got to do with it?'

'Don't you remember him saying there were four games teachers in his family?'

I said nothing and stared instead at the innocence and candour that played in her eyes. When she came back at Christmas it was with her tail between her legs. She saw it as a failure but in reality it was nothing of the sort. Winter is a bad time to set up a new venture. Because of this I try to bolster her confidence without letting on. But the trouble is, I too suffered in a different way from her temporary absence. In the time she was away I noticed something in my office that I had never seen before. It was surprising how it had escaped my attention all those years but life is like that sometimes: we fail to see things on the end of our noses and it takes a renewal of perspective brought about by a change to make us see. And what I saw was this: the office was empty.

Footsteps echoed up the stairwell, we both looked expectantly at the open door. A small man appeared.

'Mr Knight and Calamity! I'm so glad I caught you, I was afraid you might be out.' It was Mr Mooncalf. 'I have some good news for you.' He opened his briefcase and pulled out a folder. 'A very old and dear customer of the firm Mooncalf & Sons living in Romania has requested I courier a certain item to him. If you were to agree to undertake the task it would so defray the cost of your trip to Hughesovka that you would be able to go for about . . . er . . . nothing.'

'Where in Romania?' I asked.

'I believe the town is called Sighişoara.'

'Wouldn't it take us out of our way?' I said.

'A short detour through a most beautiful landscape, dotted with perfectly preserved medieval villages and abounding in wolves and bears.'

'Sighişoara is in Transylvania, isn't it?' said Calamity.

'Is it?' said Mooncalf with feigned innocence.

'We did it in school for a project.'

'Who's the client?' I asked.

'Mr V. Tepes,' said Mooncalf darting a worried glance at Calamity.

'That means "impaler" in their language,' she said. 'It's pronounced tsep-pesh.'

'It's just a name,' said Mooncalf. 'Like Smith.'

'Is he any relation to Vlad the Impaler?' She turned to me and said, 'He was the original Dracula.'

'Of course not,' said Mooncalf. 'It's just a name, like Smith. If someone is called Smith it doesn't mean they shoe horses, does it? Same with Tepes. It doesn't mean you are an impaler.'

'They used a sharpened stake,' said Calamity showing off her knowledge, 'and stuck it up your bum.'

Mooncalf looked worried. 'Did they teach you that in school, too?'

'Yes. Sometimes they used a horse to haul you on to the sharpened pale.'

Mooncalf put the folder on the desk and stood up with a slightly dejected air. He clutched the briefcase close to his chest. 'Marvellous what they teach the kids these days,' he said mournfully. 'We never had the opportunities when I was young.'

After he left we both stared for a while at the empty doorway as if half expecting him to come back.

'Oh, I forgot to tell you,' said Calamity. 'There was a message for you slipped under the door when I came in. It's from Arianwen, the girl we saw out at Mrs Eglwys Fach's cottage.'

'What does she want?'

'She wants to see you about a business matter. Doesn't say what. She works in the witches' wholesaler on Chalybeate Street.'

I arranged to meet Calamity later at Sospan's and walked through town to Grimalkin's.

There was not much room in the shop, just an aisle through piles of stock rising up on shelves. On the left there were building materials: chocolate roof tiles, gingerbread bricks with marzipan cement, and a liquorice hod. Cauldrons in varying sizes hung from the ceiling; and all around there were chalices, gargoyle moulds, wands, crystal balls, candles, toadstool seeds and bric-à-brac for the altar. A sign announced familiars were down in price.

The counter, too, was an untidy profusion of wares: a display of Rune Letraset next to glass jars containing black feathers, quartz, amethyst, agate. There was a stand selling fairy traps and the injunction to bait with shiny things or children's milk teeth. For pixies, there was a larger trap with a bigger snap spring. Customers were warned not to use them for trolls, except minors. There were phials of blood in a variety of grades: dragon, bat or strangled dove. Behind the counter, through a hanging partition of amber and bloodstone beads, there was an aquarium tank in which newts stared out disconsolately and pondered their fate.

A girl stood with her back to me on a stepladder sticking up a hand-lettered sign with Blu-tac. It said: 'If you can spell it, we probably sell it.' She wore a long cloak of midnight-blue velvet surmounted by a red riding hood. Behind her were arrayed tiers of wooden drawers neatly labelled with their contents: dust of tomb, venom of toad, flesh of brigand, lung of ass, blood of infant, corpse grease, bile of ox and finger of birth-strangled babe. Everything for the weekly groceries. They sold things separately, neatly wrapped in plain brown paper; you could buy individual coffin nails in a variety of sizes and cobweb by the yard, from free-range spiders rather than the farmed stuff.

I picked up the bell on the counter and tinkled politely. The girl looked over her shoulder and smiled. It was Arianwen.

'Oh! Hello! The spinning-wheel salesman.' She climbed down the steps. 'How can I help?' She stared up into my face and smiled.

'I'm looking for a cage with a childproof lock.'

'Might I ask Sir what he intends to use it for? I must warn you, I'm very good at escaping cages.'

'Sadly, it wasn't for you. I'm trying to fatten a little boy up for eating.'

'Oh I do love a man who can cook!'

'I'm not very good at it – he doesn't seem to be putting on any weight.'

'He's probably just poking chicken bones through the bars, you know what young boys are like.'

'Where would he get chicken bones from? I'm feeding him on gruel.'

Arianwen giggled. 'You know, you really are far too handsome to be a spinning-wheel salesman.'

'Is that so?'

'You just don't look the type.'

'I was brought up to zig when the world zags.'

'And you certainly don't talk like one.'

'You're full of surprises yourself. The red riding hood is very . . .'

'Yes?'

'Provocative.'

'It's supposed to be emblematic of innocence.'

'That's what Red Riding Hood said.'

'Surely you don't doubt her?'

'I've always regarded her as a lying trollop who knew exactly what she was doing. You telling me she couldn't recognise a wolf when she saw one?'

'She was a virgin. We're easily deceived.'

'She knew what she was about, the murder of the grandmother was an inside job.'

'Men always say it's the girl's fault. Did you know, some things went missing from our kitchen about the time of your visit?'

'It was probably that blackbird.'

'Oh, of course. I hadn't thought of that. Or at least a black-hearted demon. Did you really want a cage? Or were you after a love potion?'

'What would I do with it?'

'Exactly, with eyes like that, what would you need one for?'

She picked up a pack of cards and dealt three face-up on the counter. 'Let's see what the cards say . . . Ooh, the Knight of Wands! And . . . and . . . who will our handsome knight rescue?

. . . The Queen of Pentacles . . . and the Lovers!' She looked at me, eyes sparkling in triumph. 'It is written.'

I put the note down on the counter. 'This is what I really came about.'

She glanced at it and a puzzled expression stole across her face. 'I don't understand . . .'

'You left this in my office?'

There was a pause for a fraction of a beat and then a smile replaced the look of puzzlement. A smile of sly triumph. 'Ah! Now I get it! I left the note in the office of a private detective and who should turn up but the spinning-wheel salesman! But then I always thought there was something funny about that handsome spinning-wheel salesman. In fact it looks like he was only pretending to be one. Nice try, Mr Detective! Am I right? No! Don't say, you'll only lie.'

'You got it in one, but you mustn't tell anyone.'

'Oh I won't. Have you been investigating him long?'

'Who?'

'Meici Jones.'

'Oh yes, a long time, he's a nasty piece of work.'

'He stole some things when you came round, some stamps. That's why I came to see you. My brother will be furious if we don't get them back.'

'Why don't you go to the police?'

'As if you didn't know! Snuff philately! Imagine reporting that to the cops. How much is it going to cost me to get my stamps back?'

'If you can be patient I might be able to get hold of them for nothing.'

'No payment?'

'I'm already engaged to spy on Meici Jones, it wouldn't be right to get paid twice.'

She tilted her head down and looked up through her eyelashes in a slightly awkward attempt to look coquettish. Her voice dropped in timbre. 'Maybe I could find some other way of paying you.'

'That's a good idea. Is this shop licensed by the Witchfinder?'

'Yes, why?'

'Do you know his wife?'

'Mrs Mochdre? Not very well. What's this got to do with anything?'

'You could repay me by spying on her for me.'

'Why, what's she done?'

'I don't know, that's why I want to spy on her.'

'This wasn't quite what I had in mind.'

'I know, but you didn't specify.'

Arianwen looked deflated. 'You are such a wet blanket. Or you enjoy teasing me.'

'I'm a wet blanket and I enjoy teasing you.'

'Do you really want me to spy on her?'

'Not for the time being.' I tipped my hat, thanked her. 'I'll see if I can find those stamps.'

'Is it true private detectives always seduce their female clients?'

'The big city boys do,' I said. 'But in Aberystwyth we decide on a case by case basis.'

Chapter 7

I WENT TO the office to lock up and found Uncle Vanya sitting in the client's chair. He had a bottle of vodka and two glasses on the table. The merry glitter in his eyes made it clear he had not waited for me to start. There was a copy of the evening paper on the desk folded to a story about three painters sighting Gethsemane Walters. It said they were students.

'You are a hot-shot,' he said.

'I am not a hot-shot.'

'Thirty-five years no one knew where she was, and you! Two days it took you. Even our best detectives in Hughesovka could not achieve a resolution so quickly.'

'Yes they could, trust me. She escaped.'

'Such charming modesty!'

'We don't even know if it really is Gethsemane.'

'Who else could it be?'

'I have no idea.'

He slapped the newspaper with the back of his hand. 'According to this a passer-by found her hat and handed it in. Her name was written on the label inside her hat.'

'That passer-by was me.'

'How could she be wearing her hat if it was not her? The case is almost closed. We celebrate. We drink to the hot-shot.'

'Even if it is her, we don't know how she got there, or where she has been all these years. The case is not closed, not by me anyway. I haven't earned my sock yet. Anyway, the cops are all over it now, so expect a visit from them.'

He slid his index finger across his lips to indicate that they were sealed as far as volunteering information to the authorities. 'Tonight, my friend, we drink!' he declared in a manner that would brook no denial, even on the remote chance that a denial was offered. 'Please,' he added. 'No buts.'

'OK, tonight we drink but in return you must help me.'

'Of course I will help you.'

'I want to go to the railway station buffet and speak to a man called Rwpert Valentino about this case.'

'Who is Rwpert Valentino?'

'He is a star in the TV soap *North Road*. According to the scandal sheets he hangs around the station buffet because he is in love with the girl there. He interests us because he was once in the same nativity play as Gethsemane.'

'Is he so very difficult to talk to?'

'Just pretend the case is still open.'

'Say no more,' said Vanya. 'The case is still open and tonight we drink. Tonight we test the limits of that puny vessel, your Welsh heart.'

We remained in the office for a while, and drank in silence; a mute and intense seriousness as each considered his own thoughts. For many years I had been unaware of the void in my office. It was the calling card of my trade as a crime-fighter, a caped crusader. It went with the territory along with the dents in the tarnished armour, and the liquor and the Bakelite fan. Just like Sospan had his vanilla. There had been a girl, for a while, called Myfanwy, whom all the town loved but none more so than me. She was the singer at the Moulin Club and as much a part of our town as vanilla and donkey droppings and neon and heartache. She sang of them all. And then she lost her voice and the town hall clock lost its tick. In January of this year she went away to a sanatorium in Switzerland where the doctors say she would over time regain her voice. She sends postcards, but not often. And the townspeople ask about her in ways that I find painful. I smile and say in a falsely jovial voice that she is doing well and will be back soon, but she hasn't said she will. We feel her absence almost as keenly as her presence.

I opened the drawer and took out the envelope that had contained the séance tape. I lifted it to my nose and sniffed. It was not a scent in the ordinary sense of the word, not the stuff you buy from Boots and dab behind the ears. And yet it was a scent of sorts, a fragrance from long ago that evoked an image I had seen once in my dreams: I look up from the bottom of a well, staring at blue sky framed by elm trees; the whistle of a steam engine shrieks; there is a shower of sparks and sweet smoke billows through the leaves; a woman in a cream two-piece outfit appears in the frame against the blue; she exclaims in mild dismay and says, 'Oh sugar!' She removes a spot of soot from her cream jacket sleeve. I do not know this woman but she has a young gentle face.

The level of the vodka began to approach the halfway mark. All true drinkers know that the second half of the bottle, like the second week of the summer holiday, passes much quicker than the first and this thought alone can induce a queasy form of angst. At times a summer night is a wide landscape to cross and a wise man provisions well before setting out. We walked to the off-licence on Terrace Road and I bought a supplemental bottle, this time of Captain Morgan rum.

We emerged from the off-licence with spirits buoyed by the knowledge that whatever befell us there was still alcohol. The actors in the drama of the coming night were putting the finishing touches to their grease paint, some were already to be seen emerging furtively from doorways, testing the night air with their whiskers like rats; in the orchestra pit the police cars were tuning up their sirens; already in some remote part of town there came that intimate and familiar ululation of the klaxon, denoting the first arrest or perhaps the first man carried on a stretcher into the back of an ambulance. By the end of the evening the medics would be throwing them into the back like an engineer shovelling coal into the firebox of a runaway train.

We walked along Terrace Road towards the railway station. Troops of girls, smeared with make-up, already drunk, lurched from side to side along the pavement, into the road, cars swerved and pipped their horns eliciting rude gestures from the girls. 'We have such girls in my country too,' said Uncle Vanya.

The streets cleared of the few remaining tourists, they were hurrying to their cars now, eager to return to the safety of the caravan and tonight's Ludo ration. We walked towards the railway station, that iron lung that breathed in the people fed with the oxygen of hope, and exhaled them later, bitter, soul-weary, disbelieving; and all exemplifying Sospan's assertion that belief in promised lands is defeated by the fact that we take our pain with us in our suitcase. Character is fate, as both Sospan and Heraclitus have said.

The coaches of the midnight train to Shrewsbury lay stretched out beside the platform in a maroon ribbon. Along the side were rectangles of electric light in that heartbreaking deep yellow that comes only from bulbs belonging to railway companies. Uncle Vanya beheld the train with glittering eyes. 'Ah, my friend Louie! I can never look at a train without tears. Come, we must drink!'

We went into the buffet. On the counter a tea urn shone, the array of tubes and flasks and steam reservoirs evoked the innards of a ship's engine room, or a lost property office in which had been deposited the instruments of a silver band. We took teas and sat at a shaky wooden table next to the window that looked out on to the platform. Sitting on an adjacent table was a group of actors from *North Road*. They were smoking and talking theatrical shop. Traces of foundation cream and paint still lay in the crevices of skin around their eyes. I never watched the programme but I could intuit easily enough that the young innocent-looking girl was a new recruit in the scullery and the rat-faced, grey-haired man was her master and predator. The other one, with the slicked-down hair and central parting, the big eyes and film-star looks from the 1930s studio portrait, was Rwpert Valentino. He spoke with a squeaky voice and threw his arms around in gestures that were flamboyant and self-consciously phoney. He smoked a cigarette held in a long holder and I knew for a fact there wasn't a shop between here and Shrewsbury that sold such things.

Uncle Vanya poured the last of the vodka into the tea and we drank. 'So much of my life has been spent in train compartments. Those of the Stolypin car were no bigger,' he pointed to the train. 'Ten people would share it if you were lucky; but it could be twenty or even thirty. On my way to Kolyma I spent two months in a train compartment like this, and that was by no means a record.'

'Why did they send you to the camps?'

'Which time? I was sent two times. The last time for murdering my wife. And the first time, who knows? The question is meaningless; it implies there was a "why?". There was no such thing. They threw the dice, your turn came, you went. In the early years, when the secret police came, a man might naturally ask for a reason. What have I done? But soon we learned not to ask because the question was stupid. It rested on the old-fashioned bourgeois belief that one must do something wrong to be arrested. You see? Of course, there is always a reason written down on your file, and through the endless interrogations you will eventually agree to it, whatever it is, even if it makes no sense. I was twenty, I had been working for a year as a junior card-typist in the Museum Of Our Forefathers' Suffering. And then I was denounced for being a diversionary wrecker. I got ten years. Denouncing was a very useful method of getting rid of someone you didn't like. Or who was perhaps a rival, not that I was a rival to anyone. Men were denounced by their adulterous wives in order to remove them from the scene. Neighbours were denounced so others could move into their apartment. One day someone did it to me and still to this day I do not know who, nor why. But it does not matter. I say this merely as a register of fact. I do not complain. No matter how bad one's fate, there is always someone with a worse one. Throughout my time in the camps I was haunted by the fate of a woman whose story I heard. She had been suckling her baby one afternoon when she received a visit from the NKVD. They told her to get her coat and come down to the police station to answer a few questions. She asked what about the baby, and they told her to leave the child since she would only be gone ten minutes. She tried arguing but they were very insistent; they assured her the questions were a formality and would not even last ten minutes. They refused even to let her take the baby round to a neighbour. So she put the child in his cradle and went with the policemen. In the station she was charged as an enemy of the people and shipped off to Lubyanka for further questioning. From there she joined the long rail caravans to eastern Siberia. She left her baby that afternoon in an empty apartment in Hughesovka and never saw it again. Throughout my years of servitude I meditated upon this story, and wondered: is it the most tragic of all? As a cartographer of the human heart would she have been the greatest? But who is to say? In the monastery of Slovetsky they had a crooked cupboard inside which it was impossible for a man or woman to stand up or sit down, impossible to find any position of ease or comfort; whichever position you adopted you were forced by the crooked walls and low ceiling to adopt a pose that quickly became unbearable agony. They would lock a prisoner in this cupboard overnight. In the morning he would be completely insane. How can one measure the extent of his suffering during that night? An entire lifetime of agony condensed into the space of a single interminable night. Is it worse than the unending nightmare, spread out over many years, of the little girl of eight who was so demented by hunger that she ate a grain of rye from a cowpat? Stealing from the Collective, even its dung, is a terrible crime and grievously did she answer for it: ten years' penal servitude. Is that night in the cupboard worse than those ten terror-filled years for the uncomprehending girl?'

At the table across from us the actors stood up and left, leaving Rwpert alone, smoking a doleful cigarette. We joined him and poured some rum into his cold tea. He looked at us warily and tried to lose the camp affection that had hallmarked his previous demeanour.

'If you're worried we might be two toughs looking for some fun at your expense,' I said, 'you could be right. My friend here has spent many years in a Siberian labour camp and he was denounced by an actor. He doesn't like actors.'

Rwpert swallowed hard.

'He especially doesn't like ones called Rwpert.'

'That was the name of the man who denounced me, I spit upon the bones of his mother,' said Vanya.

Rwpert decided not to ask how we knew his name but he saw clearly that it was not a good sign.

'When we arrived,' said Uncle Vanya, 'there was no camp. Just a railway line that ended in a buffer in the middle of the snow and tundra. "Where is the camp?" we cried. "This is it," they laughed. "If you don't want to die you had better build some shelter." So we did. We walked ten miles to find water and five to find wood.'

'All because of a man called Rwpert,' I said.

'I curse the bones of his mother and her mother too.'

'All the time he was in that camp, during those odd hours when he was not mining the gold beneath the frozen wastes, he was thinking of how he would revenge himself upon all the people in the world called Rwpert.'

'I spell my name with a "w"; it's a very rare form of it.'

'We know,' I said. 'The man who denounced him spelled it the same way. He was from Hughesovka which was founded by Welsh people and has the highest incidence of Rwperts who spell their name with a "w" of anywhere in the world.'

'Oh shit,' said Rwpert.

'In Siberia, during the long bitter years incarcerated with the dregs of Soviet criminal society, he learned so many ways of killing a man, so many ways of inflicting torment, that sometimes it takes him all day to decide which to use.'

'Please don't kill me,' Rwpert said softly. 'I have a sickly child. We love her very much but the expense of looking after her is difficult to meet. With me gone, I'm not sure how my wife could manage. Please, beat me if you must, but do not kill me. And if you must beat me, please not on my face. I know it's not much to look at these days, what with these accursed cigarettes, the cheap make-up and the late hours, but for all that it is my meal ticket; if you bruise my face I will not be able to work. I am sorry about the evil done to you by this other Rwpert, but please think of my child.'

I looked across to Uncle Vanya who was weeping. 'You poor man, you poor brother in suffering, I bless the sacred bones of your dear mother,' he said.

I took out the photograph of Gethsemane in the school nativity play and showed it to Rwpert. 'If you tell me about this picture we will not hurt you.'

Rwpert looked at Uncle Vanya.

'Don't be fooled,' I added hurriedly. 'He is a very mercurial man. One minute up, the next down. Soon this perception that you are united by a common bond of suffering will pass, as swiftly as a cloud passes in front of the sun, and then he will want to kill you again.'

Rwpert took the photo and brought it up to his face and peered. The look of fear and hostility on his face slowly melted, replaced by surprise and wonder. 'Yes,' he said softly. 'That's me, Joseph, father of baby Jesus. I look so . . .' He stopped. He looked so . . . what was it? A look of concentration formed, the expression of a man struggling to call to mind a vital truth. He tried again. 'You know, I was . . . I wanted . . .' He stopped again. 'I always thought that one day, I . . . I . . .' He bunched his fingers into a fist and pressed it to his forehead. 'Fuck,' he said. He began to whimper. His heart had burst, ambushed by a tumult of anguish. What was he remembering? The little boy contemplating all the great things he would one day be? Or just a gate he played on as a kid? That can do it. I would have told him, if it had not been for the tears that now glistened on his cheeks and smudged the kohl-rimmed eyes, that sometimes we cannot find the words because they are not there. Words are such wonderful things that they deceive us, we fail to see how even the simplest things so often lie beyond their reach; we can describe spaceships and translucent sea creatures that live on the floor of the ocean trench, but we have no way to describe the subtly differing currents that sweep through the channels of our own hearts. Words are brass coal tongs with which we seek to caress butterflies. When the veils of memory are torn asunder, and the raw experience is released like scent in the mind, the coal tongs snap on empty air.

'What do you want to know?' he snivelled.

'You remember this scene?'

'Of course.'

'This is you?'

'Yes.'

'The kid in the cardboard beak is Gethsemane Walters, right?'

'Yes.'

'What happened to her?'

'She disappeared.'

'We know, but where did she go?'

'I was only fifteen.'

'So you've had a long time to think about it, what do you think happened?'

Rwpert considered and said, 'I saw in the paper that she's back. Someone saw her down by the lake.'

'That's right, and someone handed in her hat.'

'Was it really her?'

'I've no idea. What do you think?'

'I think she's dead, buried in the concrete of the dam.'

'Who killed her? Goldilocks?'

'So they say.'

'What do you say?'

He pressed his wet face into his hands. 'I don't know, I don't.'

I addressed Uncle Vanya. 'Has your melancholy subsided?'

'I'm recovering.'

'Better hurry up, Rwpert. See how he flinches when I mention your name?'

'Look,' said Rwpert. 'Why not ask her mum, Ffanci Llangollen? She's back in town, I saw her the other day at the public shelter with a Tesco's trolley. She heard about the town reappearing and came back. This is her.' He pointed to the schoolteacher in the picture.

'OK, Rwpert,' I said trying to be tough. 'Forget about Ffanci Llangollen, tell us about Goldilocks.'

'I don't know. I think they were trying to nail it on him because they didn't like him, but it takes more than that, doesn't it? Even a bad guy like him is entitled to the protection of the law. That's only fair. That's what the law is for, isn't it? To protect us against spite and vindictiveness and lies and stuff. To shield us from the malice of those who would denounce us for selfish reasons of their own.'

He looked up at Uncle Vanya whose entire life had been a testament to the simple Christian truth uttered by Rwpert. They embraced as brothers.

Uncle Vanya and I stood up to leave and, on impulse, I took out a ten pound note and stuffed it into the balled fist of Rwpert. 'Hope things work out with the kid,' I said. As I walked away he called me back.

'There was something,' he said. 'The same day that Gethsemane went missing they found Gomer Barnaby, the heir to the Barnaby & Merlin rock fortune, wandering around in a daze in the streets of Abercuawg. His hair was standing on end like he had seen something terrifying, and all his teeth were broken.'

'What happened to him?'

'No one knows. But he never recovered his wits. His father has nursed him ever since. Some people said he'd seen a troll, others said the Slaughterhouse Mob had done something to him. No one knows what. I don't know if it helps.'

We walked out of the station and hovered for a while at the wrought-iron gates of Elm Tree Avenue. The night had darkened and the breeze brought scents of summer: woodsmoke, new-mown grass, creosote. But the street lights were flickering on and the orchestra of wailing police sirens was building. It was time to measure the capacity of a Russian heart against the eternal encephalograph machine of Aberystwyth Prom.

Chapter 8

A DONKEY BRAYED maniacally. His eye sockets had been filled with glowing coals. The donkey stood in the bell tower of Notre Dame silhouetted against the blood-red sunset and febrile stormy sky, braying with malignant pleasure as the bell clanged and clanged and clanged . . . Each brazen clang was a demented hammer blow against the inside of my skull, like the nauseous pounding of blood in the ears of a man raving with fever. The clapper was fashioned from bone and carved into a form that filled me with an eerie and sickening sense of *déjà vu*. I had seen this bony clapper somewhere before, long ago, in a different life, perhaps on a different world. It clanged and clanged, the donkey laughed and then the realisation broke upon me in a deluge of sweat; suddenly I knew with the withering intensity of divine revelation where I had seen the bell-clapper before: it was my head. Gingerly I undid the stitches with which my eyelids had been sewn shut and gasped in pain at the searing incandescent blade of light that slipped through the curtains. The donkey's laughter resolved into the squeaking milk sign outside the caravan site shop. A memory rose up of prisoners of war having pieces of dowel hammered into their ears; it was the ticking of my alarm clock, but louder and more exquisitely painful. The clanging of the bell was replaced by the rapping of knuckles on the tin side of my home.

I stood up and, fighting back waves of nausea, lurched as if across the pitching deck of a ship in a storm towards the place where I dimly remembered having left the door the night before. It was still there. I opened the door and saw Llunos. Despite the profusion of old wives' tales about raw egg or oysters, nothing really works against severe hangovers apart from death. And maybe even death would not take away the pain of a man who had been so presumptuous the night before as to attempt to take a sounding of that bottomless cistern, the Russian heart. But of all the things that don't work against hangovers, the one that doesn't work the most is a visit from the cops. They always have conversation on the mind and seldom of a kind likely to knit up the ravelled sleeve of care.

I sat at the table holding my head in my hands. Llunos made tea: a symphony of discordant percussion and shrill violin notes that reminded me of the atonal music they sometimes had up at the Arts Centre.

'You are a very unlucky man,' said Llunos as he placed the teapot down. He had already observed from the way I flinched each time the clock stunned the day with its vicious 'tock' that normal sounds were amplified for me this morning; or maybe he had intuited it from the alcohol fumes in the room, which, he said, made his eyes water and his head a bit dizzy. Out of kindness he lowered the teapot on to the table with the gentle controlled descent of the lunar module approaching the surface of the moon; the cups like Harrier jump jets landing vertically on to the deck of an aircraft carrier.

'One terribly unlucky man. Everyone you meet winds up dead. I need extra life insurance just to talk to you.'

I groaned.

'You're like that woman, Typhoid Mary. You should be in quarantine.'

I groaned again. He stuck a shovel into a pile of white rocks and threw them into the cauldron of tea. The god Thor lent him a spare hammer and he slammed it against the porcelain anvil.

'Oh yes, you are a voodoo man. For ten or fifteen or I forget exactly how many years you and I have been working this town, every so often I find a dead man who is somehow connected to you. Don't you find that strange?'

I groaned.

'Oh yes, Louie Knight, the undertaker's friend. It's one of your best features. But the one I really like is the way you lie; particularly to that body of people whom good citizens are required to tell the truth to, the police. You remember the police?'

I groaned.

'Course you do. Those suckers you can always ask if you want to know the time.'

He pulled out a quarter bottle of rum from his jacket pocket. My hand flew to my mouth as the urge to retch flooded over me. He laughed again and brought over two tumblers from the draining board. He filled them to the brim and slid one across to me. 'Cheers!' I looked at him in despair. 'Drink it,' he said. I picked up the glass, my hand trembling so violently the rum spilled over the rim. He took a drink, I took a drink. He took a drink, I took a drink. He took one more, I took one more. I felt better. Much better. I smiled at Llunos. He was my friend who had come to make me feel well. 'Drink,' he said. 'It will wake you up; today is an important day; we are going to see some dead men.'

I sat up straight in my chair and said . . . my face hit the table and I passed out.

I regained consciousness briefly in Llunos's car somewhere near Rhydypennau, and then once again as we drove down Penglais Hill. There was a bacon sandwich on my lap and a Styrofoam cup of tea wedged between the seat and the handbrake. It was the kindest thing Llunos had ever done for me. Probably the kindest thing anyone had ever done since I was a child. We drove along the Prom, and turned left after the castle to enter the bed & breakfast ghetto – a warren of crooked narrow streets where every second house was a Shangri-la. An ambulance and a cop car were parked outside one of the houses, with a few cops keeping the gawkers back. The cop on the door stood aside to let us through and the gawkers looked on enviously. Inside the front door it was the usual cheap seaside guest house arrangement: an occasional table with a phone and an assortment of framed photos; a vase of bulrushes stained lurid colours; framed views of Norman castles lining the corridor leading to the kitchen. Stairs led up to a landing, sheathed in russet, apricot and umber floral-pattern carpet.

At the top of the stairs, men in white paper suits were photographing and putting invisible things with tweezers into sandwich bags. A young man was sitting in a straight-backed chair next to the window, with a look of great surprise on his face, an expression enhanced by his hair which was standing up in comic-book fashion. The surprise on his face looked terminal.

'Know this kid?' asked Llunos.

'I think it's one of the students we saw painting watercolours the day we found Gethsemane.'

'Funny, you didn't tell me about the students.'

'Didn't I?'

'Must have slipped your mind.'

'Maybe I didn't think it was important.'

He made a grunt that said he would be the judge of what was important. 'His mate is in the next room looking pretty much the same. The third hasn't returned home.'

'He doesn't look very alive.'

'Died last night around midnight; the door downstairs at the back was forced. No one heard anything.'

'What did he die of?'

'Fright. Or something like it. That's what the doctor thinks. His teeth are all broken.'

A woman in a housecoat, a head scarf, spectacles with blue translucent plastic frames, and a permanent expression of martyrdom appeared on the landing. A landlady straight from central casting.

'They haven't paid this month's rent,' she said.

'It's more serious than I thought,' said Llunos. 'I thought it was just a double murder.'

'It would be different if it was your house.'

'That's right, the first thing I would think about would be the rent. You're a saint, Mrs Crogau.'

'I was banking on that money. Where will I get it from now?'

'I'll have a word with the coroner. Maybe we can let you have the pennies from their eyes.'

Mrs Crogau folded her arms under her bosom. 'I was just observing that the rent was due. There's no law against it.'

'No, but there is one against going through the pockets of dead students and stealing.'

'Who says I did that?'

'Nobody yet.'

She sniffed and began to walk downstairs, adding, 'I'd offer you a cup of tea if I didn't think you'd plant some cocaine in the sugar bowl.'

Llunos turned his attention to me. 'How come you forgot to mention the students?'

'Old age. My memory's not what it used to be.'

He scowled. It was a stupid thing to say, using sarcasm with Llunos invariably ends in tears and seldom his.

'What were you doing out there, again?'

'We just went to see the church spire.'

'Are you concealing anything?'

'No.'

'Would you tell me if you were?'

'No.'

'I don't know why I bothered, of course you are concealing something. It's habitual. If I asked you the time you'd lie.'

'What made you fetch me?'

He walked over to a chest of drawers and picked up a sandwich bag from the top. There was a Polaroid photo inside. 'Looks like they were into photography as well as painting,' he said. The photo showed me and Calamity dragging the girl from the lake. 'What was the name of your client again?'

'What client?'

He turned away. 'All right, you can go now. Don't leave town without telling me and don't walk away with the idea that I believe you.'

Mrs Crogau was standing on the doorstep which fronted directly on to the road. Her arms were folded in a defiant air that suggested Fate sending her two corpses who hadn't paid the rent was just the latest in a long series of trials. I stopped at the occasional table and looked at the photos. I picked up one that caught my eye. It was a wedding photo.

'Like weddings, do you?' she said.

'This looks like Ffanci Llangollen's sister, Mrs Mochdre.'

'That's right; married the Witchfinder. I was a bridesmaid.'

I considered the scene.

'Bit of a strange do that was,' she said.

'Strange? In what way?'

She pursed her lips. 'It's all so long ago now, of course . . . my memory, you see. Very strange it was.'

I took out a pound coin and made it appear and disappear between my fingers the way magicians do. 'Tough break, that,' I said. 'Two kids dying on you just before the rent is due. Guess it will be hard making the bingo payments this month.'

'I won't be shooting craps in Las Vegas, that's for sure,' said Mrs Crogau.

'Maybe I can help.'

She looked greedily at the coin. 'We all need help from time to time.'

'That's right. You scratch my back, I give you a shilling for the meter.' I let the sun's reflection catch the coin and play over her face.

'Where exactly is the itch?'

'I love strange stories, tell me about the wedding.'

'That coin looks awful lonely.'

'Not really, he has three brothers right in my pocket.' I put the coin on the window ledge. 'Tell me about the wedding.'

'I do seem to remember how surprised everyone was about the announcement; it was less than a week after Gethsemane Walters went missing. It seemed a bit improper really, what with her mum beside herself and that. And then there was the other thing . . . Three brothers you say?'

'That's right, three big strapping brothers who work for the bank.' I took another coin out and put it on the ledge next to the first.

'Not a very big family, is it? Are there any cousins?'

I took out a third coin and held it poised over the other two. 'What was the other thing?'

She licked her lips. 'We were all a bit surprised her marrying the Witchfinder because she couldn't stand the chap. Mrs Mochdre had always had a candle for Gethsemane's father, the balloon-folder. The funny thing was, he'd been courting them both: Ffanci and Mrs Mochdre. He couldn't make up his mind. Then Ffanci Llangollen got pregnant with Gethsemane and it sort of made up his mind for him. Some people think it was a bit convenient Mrs Walters falling pregnant like that, almost as if she trapped him on purpose, but I wouldn't know.'

'So Mrs Mochdre married the Witchfinder on the rebound?'

'Not really, it was nine years later, just after Gethsemane went missing. That was why it was so strange. He had always been sweet on her, but she would never have anything to do with him. Then all of a sudden we hear they are getting married.'

'Was she expecting?' I put the third coin down.

'That's what we all thought, but they've never had children.' She took the coins and dropped them in her pocket. 'Well, she's had plenty of time to repent her haste, hasn't she?'

'They're not happy?'

'Who could be happy married to him? That wedding bed is a torture rack, so they say.'

'In what way?'

'The usual way, only worse. He has "tastes", you see.' She gave a swift glance up and down the street and said softly, 'Conjugal beastliness. She's been a martyr to it. I won't say any more but there are those who say he only joined the ecclesiastical cops for the handcuffs.'

I wandered down through the castle grounds, past the Crazy Golf which isn't any more crazy than the way most of us spend our lives. Instinct drew me towards the ocean. The hangover had sharpened in the fierce sun and in my head a goblin beat a putting-green-sized gong with the insistent regularity of a metronome. The sun overhead pulsed in time with the rhythm. I hoped that there might be a cooling movement of air at the seafront but the water just shimmered and sighed with exhaustion. The Pier drooped.

Every case is different on the surface but underneath it every case is the same. Whatever problems bring the people of Aberystwyth to my client's chair they are all driven by the same deeply held conviction that when things go wrong they have a right of redress. Those for whom life has been a long series of misfortunes know this childish belief to be false. But others are puzzled and shocked when Life eventually knocks on the door with a bill. Carefree days have to be paid for. They are indignant, as if Life has no right to do this to them, although all the evidence suggests it is what Life does best.

Feeling unaccountably glum, I walked towards the bandstand in search of Eeyore. Was this the spiritual crisis Llunos mentioned? Did the lake really represent the collective unconscious of Aberystwyth into which, over the years, we have thrown our repressed memories along with old prams and shopping trolleys? Or maybe there is a more humdrum explanation: the reappearing spire of the church reminds the townspeople of the years of modest achievement that have passed since the last time they saw it; reminds them with sharp poignancy of the desolation that is their fate.

I found him sitting on a bench near the children's paddling pool, staring out to sea. I joined him. He pointed to the junction with Terrace Road. 'There used to be a stop over there, the number one tram. From Constitution Hill to the railway station. That's where it turned. Your mother used to be the conductress.'

'Did you ride for free?'

Eeyore looked aghast. 'Of course not! Your mum was brought up respectable.' He looked genuinely indignant for a while and then smiled and looked thoughtful. 'There would have been terrible consequences for the town if I had done that.'

'Really? What sort?'

'There would have been no Louie Knight.'

'That sounds pretty bad.'

'Her father was a policeman, you see, before the war I mean. He fell at Dunkirk. Well, if I'd taken to travelling without paying I don't think she would have thought much of me. You might never have become a twinkle in my eye.' He shook his head in mock horror at the very idea. 'Oh no, I couldn't go riding without a ticket.'

'What made you go up north to Llandudno?'

'Oh things. Can't remember now, to tell the truth.'

'That was the same summer that Gethsemane Walters went missing.'

Eeyore hesitated. 'Er . . . yes, we went the month before. As I said, I wasn't here when that fuss was happening.'

As far as I knew, Eeyore never lied to me except for the little white lies that all parents tell, about Father Christmas and the tooth fairy and all the other little hints that behind everything there is a benevolent and all-powerful hand directing the events of our lives. But last time we spoke about this I was sure he said he went up north after the affair.

'How come you never talk about mum, Dad?'

He shifted position awkwardly. 'Never know what to say. And, besides, thought it might unsettle you.'

'I don't think it would.'

'Oh.'

'But it might have once.'

'I was born when she kissed me. I died when she left me. I lived a few weeks while she loved me.'

'That's nice.'

'Bogart: *In a Lonely Place*. We went to see it together.'

Mrs Mochdre walked past and moved towards the railings, pretending not to see us. I waved and, forced to acknowledge us, she gave a curt grimace in response.

'Ffanci Llangollen's sister,' I said. 'Last to see Gethsemane alive.'

We watched her walk briskly down the Prom, hugging the railings as if they would spare her the obligation to be sociable.

'You wouldn't think so now,' said Eeyore. 'But I arrested that woman once.'

'What for? Gossiping without due care and attention?'

He laughed. 'Some daft incident at the Pier. She took a hammer to the mechanical gypsy fortune-teller.'

'Didn't she like her future?'

'You couldn't blame her if she didn't. She said the Devil had spoken to her out of its mouth. She was always hearing voices in those days; Satan, she said. Although why he spent so much time talking to her I've no idea.' He pressed the back of his hand gently against my shoulder. 'Anything wrong? You seem mellow.'

'Hangover.'

'Yes, I could smell the booze even before I saw you, but there's more.'

I sat for a while, contemplating the gong ringing in my head.

'You don't have to say if you don't want,' said Eeyore.

'I think I might be spooked by the lake. Either that or Calamity going away at Christmas. It was only for a week or so but it made me think about things. Now I keep getting this dream, I'm sitting at the bottom of a well looking up at the world. There's a steam train and some elm trees. And a woman.'

Eeyore nodded. 'Is it Myfanwy?'

'I don't think so.'

'Do you hear from her?'

'Not for a while.'

'She's probably busy,' said Eeyore.

'Sometimes I think I'm a physician treating the symptoms of an incurable disease.'

'I used to feel like that when I was a cop. It's natural. You still have to do it though.'

'Make the patient feel comfortable?'

'As best you can. Call it pain management.'

'It's always fatal eventually.'

'Of course.'

'Where does the witch doctor go when he gets sick?'

'That's why it is hard being a witch doctor, son.' Eeyore looked thoughtful. 'What you are feeling, it's not new. It's as old as the hills. It's like monks in the old days who went out into the wilderness to commune with God. Sometimes it happened that being alone there all that time they became afflicted with a disease of the soul; a terrible malaise that filled their hearts with blackness, with bleak despair. They called it the noonday demon or sometimes it goes by the name acedia. The private detective can get a similar sort of malaise, called Client's Chair Acedia. I've seen it before.'

Chapter 9

SOMETIMES IN life the only sensible thing to do is sit under a tree wearing a sombrero and sleep until the sun is lower in the sky and the shadows lengthen. I didn't have a sombrero but I had an office and a fan. I leaned back in my chair and yawned. Calamity had set up an open-reel tape deck with the séance tape. There was also an astrolabe, some tarot cards and an archive edition of the *Cambrian News* from 1955 lying on the desk. It carried the story of a bank holiday battle between cops and Teddy boys from which someone had cut out the main photo. The Slaughterhouse Mob had been involved in the fight.

'Where's the picture?' I asked sleepily.

'I don't know, it was like that when I got it.'

'What's the astrolabe for?'

'Reverse horoscopy.'

'Oh.'

'It's like a horoscope done backwards. Normally you use the positions of the planets to predict someone's future, but it's just as easy to work out what their horoscope would have been, say, last month. I thought I would run a check on this Goldilocks boy to see what he was up to the day Gethsemane disappeared. According to the news reports he refused to provide an alibi. The Feds use it a lot to check the stories of the perps.'

'I've never heard of it before.'

'Well they don't like to shout about it, you know, it's a pretty powerful technique. You get a guy in the interview room who claims he was nowhere near the crime scene on the night in question, he says he was with his auntie in Wichita the whole time, and the grumpy cop throws down the horoscope and says, "Oh yeah? That's not what The Mighty Zoroaster says: he's got you down two blocks away from the robbery on Friday between ten and twelve. And that's not all. Next day he says it's a good day financially and you could come into a little windfall. Explain that one to me, Einstein. Or do I have to check out the horoscope for your sweet little auntie in Wichita, too?" That's usually the point where the perps give it up.'

'This is daft.'

'The Feds don't think so.'

'If you believe in that sort of stuff you might as well do a reverse horoscopy for Gethsemane's dog, after all he disappeared, too.'

'That's not such a bad idea.'

'Let's listen to the tape.'

Calamity pressed down on a clunky Bakelite knob and the reels warbled up to speed. 'You have to listen hard,' she said.

Room acoustic, shuffling, whispers inaudible. Then a woman's voice, 'Is there someone there?'

A child whispering, 'Hello, Mummy.'

'Yes? Speak, spirit.'

'Hello, Mummy.'

'Who are we talking to?'

'This is Gethsemane. It's nice here. I'm having a lovely time. Happy birthday, Mummy. Bye-bye, Mummy.'

Silence, unidentifiable noises. More inaudible muttering, shuffling. Then the tape ends in a riot of knocking, clunking, banging and white noise. Calamity stopped and rewound.

'You have to listen two or three times to get the detail.' She played it again. At the end, after Gethsemane had spoken, she turned the volume up full. The hiss sounded like a swarm of angry cicadas. In amid the symphony of noise other sounds emerged, soft but distinct, a collection of tantalising sounds: high-pitched squealing, demonic laughter, a clattering sound together with a bell; and a muffled voice saying something indistinct. Calamity pressed stop with an air of triumph, we looked at each other. Her eyes gleamed.

'Any idea what the voice is saying?' I asked.

'It sounds like *quelle ee* something. I think it might be French.' She ticked off items on the fingers of her hand. 'Squealing, demonic laughter and bloke saying something in French. That's a sound signature, Louie, it's a watermark, every one of those sounds helps us identify the place where that recording was made.'

I didn't really think so, but maybe she was right. Since Christmas when her own venture failed I had been taking extra care not to dampen her enthusiasm for things. I was scared she might notice. 'Pretty tough job working it out,' I said.

'It looks like it now, I agree, but you wait till we start unpicking it. The perp. has left his muddy footprints all over this one. Those noises are a key which will help us unravel the mystery.'

'What's the next step?'

'The envelope was postmarked Aberaeron. There is only one medium listed in the phone book for Aberaeron. The chances of it being the same one are slim, but it's a good starting point. We can play it to her and ask her to tell us where the recording was made. I've booked us in for a sitting tomorrow morning. Her name's Madame Sosostris.'

'You'll need to make a copy of the tape, I promised to return it to Arianwen.' I picked up the envelope and tore the stamps off. 'Take these and send them and the tape round to Grimalkin's.' I put the envelope back into the drawer.

'Why are you keeping that?'

'It's got a smell that puzzles me. They won't mind, they only care about the stamps. What if the spiritualist won't co-operate?'

'We lean on her using the Ehrich Weiss manoeuvre.'

Calamity gave me a nonchalant look, the one that said, I know you don't know what that is but first you have to ask.

I laughed. 'Oh, the old Eric Weiss manoeuvre!'

'Do you know what that is?'

'Of course!'

'What?'

'It's when someone gets something stuck in their throat.'

'That's the Heimlich manoeuvre.'

'OK then, I don't know.'

'Ehrich Weiss was the original name of Harry Houdini. He used to expose Victorian charlatans. He had this particular trick where he would turn up at a séance under an assumed name with a letter addressed to that name in his pocket. The letter would contain all sorts of bogus personal details and he would hand the coat in when he arrived. And lo! Even though he had made it all up, the spirits would start quoting it.'

I grinned, it was impossible not to. If this was superseding the paradigm it was fun. 'And then what happens?'

'We bust her. We tell her we are detectives and threaten to nick her under the illegal spirits act or something. Then we offer to cut her a deal: we play the tape and ask her where it was made; if she co-operates we let her walk.'

Our attention was distracted by a strange clumping sound in the stairwell. There were footsteps, then a clump, then more footsteps. We listened intently, holding our breath as the sound got closer and closer. Finally an old woman appeared in the doorway, leaning her weight on an aluminium walking stick. She wore a frock patterned with sunflowers, and apricot-coloured stockings; there were bandages on both her swollen ankles. She stopped, paused to catch her breath and said, 'I'm Ffanci Llangollen.'

Evening had fallen with a melancholy so soft one could almost hear a bugle playing in a distant shire. Fog wafted in from the bay, foreshortening visibility, muffling the stars; the sea became a millpond of grey-green milk. Sospan was starting to pack up. The blackboard on the counter listed the special as Fish Milt Sundae and it was evident that the original price had been rubbed out and replaced with another more tempting one. Ffanci clutched Calamity's forearm to steady herself and stared at the kiosk with a look that suggested it had been years since she last treated herself to an ice cream; years during which, perhaps, she had assumed they were forbidden to people over the age of ten.

'Three day-returns to the Promised Land,' I said.

Sospan pulled a wan face.

'That's a tall order, Mr Knight. Taller than usual.'

'I thought it was your speciality.'

'Tickets to paradise I dispense, not the Promised Land.' He walked off to serve another customer as if the distinction was self-explanatory.

'What did she look like?' said Ffanci Llangollen. 'The man at the police station told me it was you who found the hat.'

I turned to stare at her. She had a soft face, a kind face, but one which was etched with the years of travelling and perhaps the strain of relighting a candle of hope every morning.

'She had a blue pinafore dress,' I said, 'over a white blouse, her hair was auburn, I think, shoulder length . . .'

'What about her eyes?' said Ffanci impatiently.

'I can't remember the colour but they sparkled like . . . like . . .'

'Mischievously, like an imp?' said Ffanci, and without waiting for me to answer, said, 'Yes, it's her. I knew it. Finally, I can rest.'

Sospan returned. 'Is there a difference?' I said to him.

'Between what?'

'Paradise and promised lands.'

'There's a world of difference. Promised lands are illusions, born of the failure to understand the central problem of the human condition, namely that dissatisfactions are not the result of physical geography but rather the geography of the soul. Paradise, on the other hand, is something we have lost, a happy dell from which we have been expelled, and to which we yearn to return.'

'And your ice cream facilitates a temporary return to this lost paradise?'

'Ice cream is the vehicle, but the true conduit is the vanilla. A remarkable product: an orchid containing in its flower both the male and female private parts, with a little vegetable curtain between them to prevent hanky-panky. Vanilla is from Tahiti which furnishes us with the one indisputable instance in the history of the world of men finding true paradise.'

'In Tahiti?'

'The vanilla-scented isle of dreams. The first European sailors to set foot there discovered it in a sea fog not dissimilar to the one we have here this evening. The scent of vanilla drifted to them through the fog, and they heard the sound of women singing. When the fog burned off the mariners found themselves in a bay more beautiful than any they had seen before: a lush golden-green perfumed paradise. All around them were little canoes in which stood maidens wearing petticoats of paper, playing songs on conches. Then, upon a hidden signal, they let their paper petticoats fall and revealed themselves to the men who all cheered. They spent the next month making love and all the girls wanted in return for their favours was a ship's nail.' Sospan paused in the action of serving the ice as if temporarily overpowered by anguish.

'Maybe you should go there,' said Calamity.

'Alas, Calamity, my first loyalty is to my box.'

'Have you never been tempted,' I said, 'to find a little maiden to play the conch to you?'

Sospan looked thoughtful and a distant look entered his eyes. 'There was a girl once . . . but it was not meant to be.'

'But there are other girls,' I said. 'There are lots of nice girls in Aberystwyth.'

'No, you don't understand. When a man takes the ice-cream orders, he shapes his entire life for better or ill, there is no turning back. I won't pretend that I don't occasionally dream of how it might have been; in autumn sometimes at the end of the season, when we take in the first delivery of coal for the coming winter, and the traffic at the kiosk drops off . . . I sometimes think how nice it would be to arrive home and . . . and . . . you know how it is when you open the door and smell that peculiar smell that belongs to a house wherein is found love? I sometimes picture her standing there, my girl, she kisses me and asks how my day at the box was. I kiss her back and bend down and sweep my little son into my arms and his little eyes sparkle because he loves me and especially loves my smell of vanilla.'

'I don't see why you can't sell ice cream and have a family,' said Calamity.

Sospan looked flustered. 'It's not as simple as that, Calamity, it's . . . hard to . . . one day you will understand.'

'They also serve who only stand and scoop,' I said in a lame attempt to lift his spirits. He did not answer, but stared into space wearing a pained expression.

We stopped to watch as an old man glided past pushing someone in a wheelchair. The man was wearing mustard-coloured tartan drainpipe trousers, at half mast on his legs, and a moth-eaten rain-coloured frock coat. His hair was long and white and thin, turning up at the collar in untidy curls. It was Ephraim Barnaby V, the owner of the rock emporium. His son Gomer, sitting in the wheelchair, was in his late fifties, but he did not look like a man of that age. Instead he looked like a goblin foetus: ageless, shrivelled, skinny and bonier than a kipper.

Ffanci Llangollen gasped and said in a fierce whisper, 'It's Gomer Barnaby! Went missing the same day as Gethsemane.'

'Hasn't spoken or walked since the day,' said Sospan.

Calamity and I turned to him, and, fancying himself in possession of privileged information, he warmed to his theme. 'They found him wandering in a daze among the abandoned houses of Abercuawg, his wits all gone.'

'They say he lost his teeth, too,' I said.

'All broken,' said Sospan. 'No one knows what happened, and he has never been able to say.'

'I heard he saw a troll,' said Calamity.

Ephraim Barnaby wheeled his son past the children's paddling pool and out on to the wooden jetty where the council posted the tide tables. He pushed to the very end and there they remained in poses of utter tranquillity, motionless as men turned to stone by sorcery.

Sospan, mindful that this sudden image of unmerited suffering had thrown a shadow over the sacrament of vanilla-taking, spoke to break the spell. 'So, are you going anywhere nice for your holidays?'

'We may be going to Hughesovka,' said Calamity.

Sospan nodded as if pleased by our choice. 'You must look up my cousin.'

'It's only a sort of long shot,' I said. 'We're not really likely to be going.'

'I'm sure you'll have a lovely time there, just so long as you don't try and save money by purchasing the tickets from Mooncalf.'

'Is that not a good idea?' asked Calamity.

'You know Mooncalf, he'll have you on a side trip to Romania or something. My grandfather gave me two pieces of advice when he was on his deathbed. Always polish the heels as well as the toes, he said, and never delegate your travel arrangements to Mooncalf & Sons. I have followed both these injunctions to the letter all my life and I have never regretted it.'

Calamity looked downcast. 'I'm sure it's OK now, Transylvania has changed a lot.'

'Quite possibly,' said Sospan.

Ffanci Llangollen put her hand on my arm. 'Mr Knight, won't you tell me about the case you are investigating?'

I wondered what to tell her.

'I know you will deny you are on one, the policeman told me you wouldn't say. He said you wouldn't tell him but you might tell me. Won't you tell me?'

'It's not easy,' I said.

'No,' she said distantly, 'it isn't.'

'I meant—'

'I know what you meant.'

'Let me talk to someone first, there's someone I have to ask . . . Where can I find you?'

'Either in the public shelter or on one of the benches near the bandstand. I sit there usually. I won't go far, don't worry.' She turned to leave and, remembering something, took out a letter and gave it to me. 'I found this on your mat downstairs. Hand-delivered.'

We watched her amble slowly away into the fog. I opened the letter. It was from Meici Jones, an invitation to his birthday party the next day.

Chapter 10

CALAMITY SUCKED the dregs from her cornet, threw it in the bin, and then sucked the sweetness from her fingers. 'Once upon a time in Abercuawg,' she said, 'there lived a balloon-folder called Alfred. He fancied two girls and because he couldn't decide which one he liked best he courted them both. The girls were Ffanci Llangollen and her sister Mrs Mochdre. Then one day Ffanci Llangollen got pregnant and this helped the balloon-folder make up his mind. He proposed to Ffanci. Some time later, Gethsemane was born. When she reached the age of eight she went out one morning with her auntie, Mrs Mochdre, to buy a birthday present for her mum. After lunch they returned to Abercuawg and she went out to play and disappeared. Someone saw a local hoodlum called Goldilocks burying something in his garden that night and it turned out to be one of Gethsemane's shoes. He was arrested and charged with murder. A week later Mrs Mochdre married the Witchfinder, a man she hated. On the same day that Gethsemane disappeared they found Gomer Barnaby, the heir to the Barnaby & Merlin rock fortune, wandering around in distress with all his teeth broken and behaving sort of cuckoo. He remained cuckoo for the rest of his life. A year later, someone sent a tape made at a séance in which Gethsemane allegedly turned up to wish her mum a happy birthday. Not long after that the spirit of Gethsemane turned up in Hughesovka. I guess I don't need to go into the troll bride stuff?'

'Not at the moment.'

'Thirty years later the town reappeared during a drought and two private detectives investigating a strange case of an imaginary friend in Hughesovka stumbled upon a girl who ran away leaving behind a hat with the name of Gethsemane Walters inside. There were some students painting nearby. Not long after that two of the students were found dead with all their teeth broken. The third is missing. Have I forgotten anything?'

'I think that covers everything. What's our next move?'

'We've got a busy day ahead of us tomorrow. In the morning we go to see the spiritualist and after that we do a tour of the rock foundry, see if we can talk to the typographer; they say he used to be in the Slaughterhouse Mob. Oh yeah, and we will need to pick up a present, maybe an Airfix model or something.'

'What for?'

'Meici Jones's birthday,' said Calamity.

'I don't think I'll be going to that . . .'

'Why not?'

'I don't like him.'

'That's not the point, this is business. I thought you could do some digging, you know, about the games teachers in his family.'

'Yes, but—'

'We're supposed to be superseding the paradigm, remember? It would be unprofessional not to go.'

I knew there must be a good answer to that but before I could think of it my father, Eeyore, appeared with the night mail. There was just one donkey for the last ride. The last traverse was the one that symbolically closed the shutters of the town: a gentle clip-clop of hooves that signalled the time had come to put empty milk bottles on the step, release cats for their night's mischief, and double-bolt the door against the hobgoblins of the coming dark.

'We're going to see Vlad the Impaler,' said Calamity. 'We'll probably come back with a couple of tooth marks in our necks.'

'Dad doesn't believe in nonsense like that.'

'I wish I didn't, son, I wish I didn't.'

'Oh, Dad!'

Eeyore looked sombre. 'Vlad the Impaler is no friend of those who ply the ancient trade of the seaside donkey.' His gaze became distant, but focussed as if remembering an ancient wrong done to the men of the donkeys by the old Romanian prince.

'What did he do?' asked Calamity.

'It's just make-believe, isn't it?' I said.

Eeyore shook his head sadly. 'There is nothing make-believe about the evil he did to poor Brother Hans.' He stopped and pursed his brow as if even over the distance of five centuries the wound was still tender. We paused.

Sospan was so gripped that he was leaning as far out of his box as he could without actually falling. He bored his gaze into the silent Eeyore. 'What did he do?' he spluttered.

Eeyore adopted the attitude of a story-teller who had been waiting for the prompt. 'Despite what some people will tell you, Vlad the Impaler was a real historical figure. A tyrannical prince who ruled in Walachia in the fifteenth century. Dracula was one of his nicknames, it means devil or dragon. The stuff about vampires is nonsense, of course . . .'

Sospan looked disappointed.

'Probably an embroidered folk memory of his bloodthirsty exploits. He used to dip his bread in his victim's blood which may account for the blood-drinking stories. And there are lots of bats in that region of Walachia and Transylvania, and they carry rabies. It's not unknown for someone bitten and infected with rabies to run mad and even try to bite someone else, so you can see how easily the idea could have originated.'

'And sticking stakes in the heart could have come from the impaling,' added Calamity knowledgeably.

'I thought you said they stuck them up the "you know what",' I said.

Calamity turned expectantly to Eeyore.

'Oh, they stuck them in all sorts of places,' he said. 'Regions of the body that it really wouldn't do for me to mention. In fact, given the lateness of the hour . . .' He raised an arm in a theatrical gesture towards the foggy coast in which the setting sun appeared diffused and vague, more as a bloodstain than a disk. 'I really shouldn't even be telling it now.'

'Go on,' said Sospan, 'tell us about Brother Hans. I'll give you a free ice cream.' I expected Eeyore to dismiss the offer, but surprisingly he didn't. Sospan prepared a ninety-nine and handed it to Eeyore. It looked a bit smaller than the normal ones. 'Don't tell anyone, mind,' he said.

Eeyore took a lick and resumed his tale. 'This Vlad the Impaler, you see, was an astonishingly bloodthirsty prince. He was crazy about impaling. He did it by the thousands. One time he impaled twenty thousand peasants and soldiers and sat down among the forest of pales to eat his dinner. On another occasion an invading Turkish sultan marched his army into a narrow gorge filled with thousands of rotting corpses impaled there. They had been there for months and blackbirds were nesting in the ribcages. The sultan was so appalled and dismayed that he took his army straight back to Constantinople. Vlad was truly wicked. He impaled everybody: mothers nursing infants, old men and children, he even impaled sucklings on to their mothers' breasts. Others he boiled alive, or skinned alive, or disembowelled. If he needed to send a dispatch detailing the progress of a war he would send off bags filled with ears and noses. He even nailed one man's hat to his head. All these tales were recorded in the monasteries, you see, and this is where Brother Hans, who has since become the Patron Saint of Seaside Donkeys, comes into the story. It so happened that there were three monks of the Benedictine order: Brother Michael, Brother Jacob and Brother Hans – who was their porter. For some reason or other they were forced into exile and crossed the Danube into Walachia. They found asylum in a Franciscan monastery at Tîrgovişte, which happened to be just down the road from Vlad the Impaler's palace. One day, purely by chance, they ran into Vlad and he invited them back to the palace. The funny thing was, although he was infamous throughout the land for performing these unspeakable cruelties, he was also at heart a religious man and was deeply concerned about the prospects for his eternal soul. So he questioned the monks. First he asked Brother Michael whether it would be possible for him, in spite of everything that he had done, to attain salvation. Brother Michael was only too keenly aware of the fate that automatically befell anyone who upset the prince. Who would tell the truth to such a monster? So Brother Michael said, "But of course you can attain salvation. The Lord is infinitely merciful and I can see no reason why you should not be forgiven." That was all right, as far as it went, but Vlad was no fool, he knew well it would take a brave or foolhardy man to insult him. So he put the same question to Brother Jacob and got a similar reply. Finally he asked Brother Hans what he thought. This man was made of sterner stuff than his two companions and he told him straight. "Are you nuts?" he said. "You haven't got a hope of salvation, you are the most evil, cruel, bloodthirsty tyrant who ever lived; you are so terrible that probably even the Devil won't want you, so much innocent blood have you shed." And he stopped and added, "I know you will stick me on one of your pales for this, but if that is to be my fate I ask that you do me the honour of letting me finish my tale before you kill me." And Vlad the Impaler said, "Say your piece to the end, I won't cut off a syllable and will lay no hand of violence to your person until you have done." Whereupon Brother Hans gave old Vlad the Impaler an ear-bashing the like of which it is utterly certain no one else in all his life had the temerity to address to him. "You," he said, "are the most unspeakable, cruel, barbarous, bloodthirsty, inhuman, tyrannical monster who ever defiled the sweet face of the earth. You bathe in the blood of innocents, of children and their mothers, of old and young, none of whom ever did you harm. Heaven stops its nose at your works. What right do you take to impale mothers heavy with children in their bellies, and to stick your wicked spikes through them? Answer me, I demand it of you!" And Vlad the Impaler was so astonished to hear these words, curses such as no man had ever dared utter in his presence, that he answered him. He told him, "It is not mere wanton delight in the pain and suffering that causes me to do these things, although I do admit that there are few things I enjoy more in life than to sit down and dine in a field filled with the impaled bodies of my enemies and to watch my friends the blackbirds eat their dinner at the same time, pecking the weeping eyes from the sockets. It is not mere lust and joy for its own sake but a matter of practical politics. Just as the farmer who clears weeds from his land must also take great care to pull up the roots or assuredly the weeds will return, so I, the Prince, must kill the children of my enemies or they will surely return one day to avenge themselves upon the cruel tyrant who delivered their mothers and fathers to such a wretched death." On hearing this, Brother Hans cried out, "You fool! You madman! How can you even imagine for a second that the Lord will forgive you? He will condemn you without mercy to a life of everlasting torment, a thousand times crueller than the torments you have inflicted on your victims in this life." At that point, Vlad could take it no more. He lunged out and grabbed the monk and threw him to the floor. In a bloodthirsty rage more terrible than any of the courtiers had ever seen before, he jumped on to the monk and stabbed him to death with a series of frenzied knife blows to the head. Before long the floor was slippery with the monk's spilled blood, and Vlad the Impaler lay exhausted in a heap upon the now-dead body of Brother Hans. Vlad dragged himself up to his feet, paused to reflect, and repented his quick anger. Because in so doing he had cheated himself of his one great pleasure in life: the opportunity to impale an enemy. And it was at this point, as he stood there panting above the corpse of noble Brother Hans, that he committed the crime for which he will never be forgiven, the one that will stain the clay until Judgment Day long after the blood of all the other impaled victims has been washed away by the tears and rain. He looked around wildly, mad for something to impale. And that was when his eyes lighted on Brother Hans's only possession. His donkey.'

He stopped, and we all gasped. 'It's a true story,' he said. 'Set down in the Benedictine monastery at St Gall in Switzerland.'

By the time he had finished his tale the sun had slipped below the horizon and rendered the sky of the west the colour of plum. Although the heat had not lost its edge, a strange chill passed through us, causing us to shiver; we remained for a while in silence, each privately contemplating the terrible death agonies of that poor donkey from long ago.

Chapter 11

DOKTOR GUSTAV P. Essequibo and his lovely daughter Lucrezia stood patiently at the bus stop outside Aberystwyth station. It was a hot summer day and the doktor carried his tan-coloured macintosh neatly folded over his arm; he wore a light-blue Egyptian cotton shirt, open at the neck, and beige slacks. At his feet a small cardboard suitcase bore stickers of the North Surinam Passenger, Freight and Mail Steam Packet Company as well as those belonging to the British Overseas Airways Corporation. His daughter was about sixteen or seventeen with blonde hair braided into pigtails like a member of the Cherokee tribe. She wore beige jodhpurs tucked into black leather riding boots, a crisply starched white blouse and observed the bustle of the station through a monocle. At her feet was a small box that might have been called a steamer trunk had it been substantially bigger. The doktor examined his watch with the quiet patience of a man whose life has been spent on the periphery of the world in countries where all timetables are approximations and no great significance is attached to delays of less than half a day . . .

'I've always wanted to be called Lucrezia,' said Calamity.

'I still think the monocle is over the top,' I said. 'In fact, I think everything is over the top.'

Calamity sighed. 'Yeah, I'm sorry about the disguises, they were all Mooncalf had left. He said there was a fancy dress party on at the Football Club.'

I looked at my watch. 'The buses were far more regular in Guyana.'

'That's out of character,' said Calamity. 'According to the instructions Doktor Gustav P. Essequibo is a patient man whose life . . .' She took a small instruction booklet out of her jodhpur pocket and read: '. . . whose life has been spent on the periphery of the world in countries where all timetables are approximations.'

'Not as approximate as in Cardigan.'

'You're doing research into the curative and restorative properties of ectoplasm. Remember there are only two known methods of harvesting ectoplasm. It can be found . . .' She consulted the booklet again: '. . . in the outer corpus of the genus of sea creature vulgarly known as jellyfish. And at séances.' She looked up from the book. 'Keeping jellyfish in captivity is difficult because they have no swim bladders. In the ocean they drift with the current, but when kept in tanks they tend to end up in the corner where they cannibalise each other. Can you remember all that?'

'Don't you ever get the feeling Mooncalf is laughing at us?'

'Yes, sometimes.'

A bus pulled up and the doors opened with a sigh of compressed air escaping. A wave of stuffy air, perfumed with hot plastic and the faint scent of diesel, puffed out. We climbed aboard and sat down.

'How did you get on with the letter?' asked Calamity.

I took out an airmail letter from the pocket of my macintosh. 'It's from your wretched brother, Wild Bill, who, as you know, is currently suffering the living hell of a life sentence in the cockroach-infested Demerara Institute of Penal Correction. Note the cuts in the paper, the result of a vicious knife fight which took place on the way to the posting box. Note also the letter smells of tequila, and hopelessness.'

'Wow,' said Calamity. 'Wild Bill sure got himself in a pickle this time.'

'We mustn't give up hope. For the sake of your brave mother and the agonies she suffered during her struggle with the ravages of jungle foot.'

The bus passed through the tree-enshrouded gloom of Southgate and out into the bright sunlight. To our right glimpses of pure blue translucence, the ocean, flickered through the trees, sending a secret heliograph message, sweeter than the call of sirens, about the ecstasy that awaited the traveller who forsakes the bus and dives into the cold green brine. Messages that made the heart cry.

Calamity grabbed her index finger with the fingers of the other hand. 'Item one: is there a connection between the disappearance of Gethsemane and the mystery fate of Gomer Barnaby? Item two: was it really Goldilocks who buried the shoe? Or someone trying to frame him? Item three: what did Gomer see? Was it a troll?'

'I don't think that matters so much,' I said.

Calamity continued. 'Item four: what is the meaning of the curious levitated dog?'

'What levitated dog?'

'The one in the photo Vanya gave us.'

'I forgot about that.'

'Item five: who sent the séance tape? Item six: is the hasty wedding of the Witchfinder and Mrs Mochdre significant?'

'Item seven,' I said, 'was the girl down by the lake really Gethsemane Walters, and if it wasn't, who on earth was she?'

'That's a lot of items,' said Calamity.

There were four other members of 'the sitting'. There was a man in his seventies with a bald head and big ears; he had a warm and simple smile and seemed nervous. There were two spinsters, sisters, and a woman who claimed to be a collector of antique china figurines; she engaged everyone in conversation, displaying such a degree of inquisitiveness that it was clear she had to be a plant. The man and the spinsters told her about their lost loved ones whom they were coming in search of and the maid pretended to dust the sash windows and was clearly listening intently as well. Five minutes later they were called into the other room, 'The Parlour', where a dining table was set with a green baize cloth and more tea was served.

Madame Sosostris strode in with a self-consciously theatrical demeanour, and the members of the sitting simmered with anticipation. She was in her early sixties, wore a purple dress and had a large bosom which supported a chain of heavy amber beads. She wore the stern expression of a schoolmistress who tolerated no nonsense from her girls and would equally tolerate no monkey business from the spirits at her séance.

The lights were dimmed and Madame Sosostris closed her eyes and clasped her hands; she lowered her head slightly. After a while she began to moan. The excitement intensified, meaningful looks were exchanged around the table. She began to speak in a voice that was not her own, or rather was not the one she had used when she greeted the guests. This was the voice of her personal go-between in the spirit world; for a reason not disclosed she didn't talk directly to the spirit but the information was relayed via this intermediary who was called Prince Marmion. Not much information was available concerning this prince, such as when he had reigned and where and what sort of palace he inhabited, but one of the spinsters whispered with a glint of excitement in her eye that he was a 'dark fellow'.

Prince Marmion told the two spinsters that Lucy their third sister was happy and did not resent them for abandoning her during the final years of her illness. They were told that they should not reproach themselves, the bitter terrors of a painful death which Lucy had endured alone had now been forgotten. The old man was informed that his late wife had noticed his collars were slacker than they used to be and was worried that he wasn't eating as well as he should. He ran his finger around the collar and indeed the spirit seemed to be correct. The man made an apologetic smile to us as if he had been caught out in an indiscretion. All the while, Madame Sosostris maintained her 'trance' and allowed herself to be the conduit to the prince's insights. She groaned a few more times, and then told the old man that his late wife was a bit short of cash because things were so expensive in heaven. He took out a ten pound note and passed it across the table. Prince Marmion promised to see that she got it without delay. Then he asked, 'Is there a doctor here?' It seemed like an easy guess but the two sisters expressed admiration for the acuity of the prince's vision. 'I have a message from William, he's in a terrible place,' said Prince Marmion.

Calamity grabbed my hand. 'Papa, the prince is talking about Wild Bill!'

'Hush now, Lucrezia! Let the spirit speak.'

'He is in a dark and terrible place, with lots of cockroaches,' said the spirit. 'He's not happy. And hanging over him is the shadow of the curse of the man he slew!'

There were gasps round the table: it didn't usually get as juicy as this.

'And now he broods upon his wasted life and contemplates a desperate action. You must save him, you must go and implore him not to lose faith, not to lose heart, because the dear Lord is watching over him, even in the darkest pit, even when it least seems like it.'

The old man watched the medium, entranced, the sisters nodded at the wisdom of the prince's advice because this description of the MO of the Lord accorded exactly with their understanding of his benevolence.

'But wait!' said Prince Marmion. 'There is something else . . . another person . . .'

The tension increased, people strained to hear the spirit's next words.

'A woman, the spirit of a beautiful, sad and desolate woman, a sweet lady who died young, whose little limbs were tormented on the rack of the infirmary bed, night after night on fire with the fever that started in her foot—'

'Papa, it's mama!' said Calamity.

'Isabella,' I cried, 'Isabella! Is it you?'

'Oh the poor man,' whispered one of the sisters. The old man watched, his lower jaw thrust forward in fascination.

'Isabella!'

'Oh!' cried the prince. 'She is receding, receding, receding . . .

going away into the fog. I could try to call her but she won't respond, she is going far away over the misty plain . . .'

After the séance the sitters were quickly ushered out by the maid. We retrieved our coats and returned to the parlour. We asked the maid to inform Madame Sosostris that the police would like to have a word with her. She sailed in with a slightly less regal air than before and looked perplexed and slightly anxious. I pulled out my wallet and let it fall open to show my badge the way the TV cops do. 'I'm Detective Medavoy and this is Loo-tenant Sipowicz.'

Calamity gave her a steely gaze.

I threw the bogus letter down on the coffee table. 'I don't need to ask whether you recognise this.'

Madame Sosostris's eyes widened but she said nothing.

Calamity examined her nails and spoke to them. 'Funny, I never took her for the type who would fall for the Ehrich Weiss. I had her down as someone smarter.'

'W . . . what do you mean?' asked Madame Sosostris.

'Make a habit of reading other people's mail, do you?' I said.

Madame Sosostris glanced at the letter and stammered, 'The letter just fell out of your coat . . .'

'I know, and you just accidentally read it.'

'Oldest trick in the book,' said Calamity.

'I haven't done anything,' she said.

'Keep it for the DA,' I sneered, then turned to Calamity. 'What do you reckon we got ourselves here, loo-tenant? The genuine article or one of those "gottle of geer" jobs?'

'What do you mean?' asked Madame Sosostris.

'Don't play coy with us, Sosostris,' I said.

'Prince Marmion a regular visitor here, is he?' said Calamity. 'Or just some clever piece of voice projection?'

'I'm not a ventriloquist, if that's what you are trying to imply.'

I snorted. 'What would you say if I told you Prince Marmion has been in Acapulco for the whole of the past month?'

'No!'

'I've got fourteen witnesses who can place him within two blocks of the casino. What have you got?'

'A nickel's worth of nothing,' said Calamity. 'Medium schmedium. Just a two-bit toffee apple grifter peering into the crystal ball and seeing dollar signs.'

I leaned forward, close to Madame Sosostris. 'You spent any time in the Pen recently?'

'Whose pen?'

'She thinks you're talking about a Biro, boss,' said Calamity.

'Sure she does. Listen up, Sosostris, we send you to Shrewsbury the only pen you'll hear about will be the one some cell-block big shot hammers into your ear.' I began to shout, 'Through the ear, Sosostris, so you can hear it going bang bang bang!'

'No!'

'Yes!' said Calamity. 'Last thing you ever hear: the sound of a Biro being hammered into your brain.'

'No, no, no! They would never do a thing like that.'

'Of course they would,' said Calamity. 'Why do you think they call it the Pen?'

'They put them other places too,' I said. 'Some of those felons in Shrewsbury gaol are none too refined.'

'I'll thank you not to use profanity in my house!'

'Oh you don't like profanity, huh? We'd better not send you to prison then. Make a note of that, loo-tenant, the perp. doesn't like profanity.'

'Maybe we'll send you to the Girl Guides' jamboree instead,' said Calamity.

'Play her the tape, loo-tenant.'

'What tape?' said Madame Sosostris.

Calamity took the portable cassette player out and banged it down on the table. She punched the play button the way the Feds do in the movies. She said, 'One of our guys wearing a wire caught this. We think it's one of your séances. You prove to us it's not, maybe we can ride you a little easier.' The tape began to play. 'Recognise any of this? That demonic laughter, one of yours is it?'

'No, no, he's not one of mine.'

'We think it is,' I said.

'I've never heard it before. It's not Astaroth, his voice is deeper, and it's not Caacrinolaas nor Malacoda; and the Tartaruchi never laugh; it's not Zelusrous, nor Xitragupten, nor Oulotep, and defintely not Naberius. No, it's not one of my usual ones. Please don't send me to the Pen, I don't want to die like that.'

'What about the squeals?' I said. 'I guess you don't know anything about them either?'

'No!'

'Think about it, Sosostris,' said Calamity. 'You're looking down the barrel of twenty years.'

'What for? I've done nothing wrong.'

Calamity gave a bitter laugh. 'Nothing wrong? We caught you red-handed!'

'Doing what?'

'Money laundering.'

'Don't be ridiculous!'

Calamity gave me her cynical, world-weary cop's scowl. 'They think once it passes through them pearly gates we can't trace it.'

'Or maybe that ten pound won't even get that far,' I said. 'Maybe it will end up in the cashier's pouch down at the bingo.'

'No, no, you don't understand . . . I can explain about the money.'

'Save your breath,' I said. 'We saw that money passed across the table, we caught it on hidden camera.'

'But it's not like you think.'

'It never is,' said Calamity. 'Robbing an old guy like that of his pension.'

'I wasn't robbing him, he knows it doesn't really go to the spirits. We have to do it this way, you see. That Mr Williams is a kind man, a very decent man.'

Calamity and I exchanged frowns. We hadn't been expecting this.

'Oh, what's the point?' sighed Madame Sosostris. 'You've already made up your mind, you don't care about the truth, you just want to send me to the Pen.'

'Of course we care about the truth,' I said, puzzled. 'Just tell us how it was. We saw you taking that man's money, but maybe we didn't see right.'

'Take your time, ma'am, and tell us in your own words,' said Calamity.

Madame Sosostris paused as if summoning up the strength to go on. 'He started coming to my sittings when his wife got sick. She wasn't what you might call an easy woman, Mrs Williams. No, not easy at all. She was one of those women who liked to organise everything, you see, she liked everything "just so" and woe betide you if it wasn't. She used to send him here to make the arrangements for when she went to heaven, so it would be just how she wanted.' Madame Sosostris paused and grimaced slightly as if the next bit was hard to say. 'I've never . . . I've never been a very attractive woman, I know that. But Mr Williams didn't seem to mind. He would stay for tea and, with time, when the weather turned nice and summer was upon us, we would sometimes drink pop – dandelion and burdock and on occasion, why! we might even treat ourselves to a glass of shandy. Mr Williams would take the bottles back for a refund and give the pennies to me, saying it was a little something for the spirits. That's how it started. It became our little joke. Oh! We would chat so gaily. I suppose it sounds absurd to big city people like you, but I'd never had conversations like that before, not with . . . with someone who liked me. This isn't easy for me to say but I'm afraid our friendship led us to stray from the path of righteousness. There were consequences. A child. A little girl called Maddy. This was fifteen years ago, Aberaeron was different then – there was no way we could even think of keeping her. Mrs Williams was still alive, you see, and despite having made very elaborate provisions for her accession to heaven she didn't show any great impatience to finish the job. So we decided to give Maddy to my sister in Gwent who would bring her up as her own.' Madame Sosostris clenched the tablecloth in her fists. 'I've never been very good with words, so I won't even try and say how that felt, giving her up, the fruit of the only episode of happiness I had ever known. Such a harmless thing, happiness, and yet we always seem to end up being punished for enjoying it. Mr Williams never saw her after that. I mean he never met her, although I do suspect he goes away sometimes and watches her through his binoculars. He goes on birdwatching trips, you see. But for fifteen years now he has given me anything he can spare for her. This is his way. A little money slipped across the table to be passed on to the spirits. That way the gossips round here will be none the wiser and he goes home happy that his daughter will have the occasional treat.' A shiny tear fell on to the tablecloth. 'May the Lord have mercy on us both. We were weak, led astray by laughter and summer days filled with gaiety and shandy, in a life that had always been as dour as the cover of a Bible. Was it such a sin? Life is so hard sometimes, so hard . . . so . . . cruel.'

I pulled out a handkerchief and handed it to Madame Sosostris. She accepted it without looking at me, and squeaked in acknowledgement like a mouse.

'I think the loo-tenant here might be thinking of making a cup of tea,' I said.

Calamity stood up. 'Sure, boss.'

'Tell the maid,' said Madame Sosostris. She dabbed her eyes with the handkerchief. 'I'm sorry for making a scene, I . . . I don't know what I would do if you sent me to prison. I don't know how I would cope.'

'No one's going to send you to prison,' I said softly, eaten up with shame. 'It's all been a terrible mistake. We were given wrong information. We're truly sorry, I would like to ask you to forget this meeting ever took place.'

She looked up, eyes glistening, and squeezed my hand. 'Please don't worry about it. Policemen are human too.'

Calamity came back with the maid, who carried a tray. As she stirred her tea, Madame Sosostris said, 'I don't think that tape you played was made by anyone at a séance. The demonic laughter sounds a bit artificial to me; and that squealing in the background sounds like seagulls; and the other sound, the clattering one with the bell, it reminds me of a tram. If you ask me the recording was made in Aberystwyth, somewhere on the Prom.'

As the bus circled the village green before heading back to Aberystwyth Calamity turned to me and said, 'That story about Mr Williams, I guess it had to be true?'

I looked at her and said nothing.

Chapter 12

ONCE UPON *a time a man called Caxton transformed man-kind's destiny for ever by forging letters out of iron. Later the iron was replaced by molten lead. Thus were born those epistemological coal tongs we call printed words, and with them our ability to catalogue the contents of that mansion of infinite floors, the human heart. Our thoughts and dreams, our memories, the anguish of love, our inexpressible bafflement at the antinomies of space and time . . . all that had once been unnameable intimations were brought within the scope of the coal tongs. In those sturdy iron squiggles, all could be written down and communicated, not only to the living but to people who had not yet been born, to people who might not be born for many centuries to come. But, as we know, a cruel and pitiless contingency characterises our fate. We are chaff in the wind and the cup of life which, sooner or later, all must drink to the lees, is often more bitter than gall. And so to prevent this brute and inescapable fact from casting its shadow upon our summer holidays, it was ordained that the epistemological coal tongs in Aberystwyth would be fashioned from sugar. And men would call it Rock. In scarlet crystalline sweetness thereafter would all human thought be extruded. Or, as a very clever person once said, 'Whereof the rock cannot speak, thereof one must be silent.'*

At least that's what it says in the free guidebook. Calamity read it with a frown creasing her forehead as we waited in the queue.

Barnaby & Merlin's rock foundry occupies the southern wing of the Old College on Aberystwyth Prom. It is built from warm yellow blocks of stone in an eclectic architectural mixture of Teutonic castle, monastery, schoolhouse and St Pancras station. On the tower at the end is a mosaic of Archimedes, the man credited with having worked out in the second century how many grains of sand there are in the universe. For his reward he stands immortalised in little coloured stones, looking out upon a beach on which there isn't a single grain of sand, only grit and smooth pebbles. They say the mosaic is not opaque, it just appears so from the outside, and in reality it is translucent and behind it sits old Barnaby counting his money. That's what they say.

There was a queue of around ten or twelve holidaymakers. We followed them, up the steps and into a neo-Gothic foyer: stone spiral staircases, pale sandstone banisters, arched windows and circular skylights with stained glass. The floor was laid out of shiny red tiles. An old stone griffin stood sentinel and the building hummed, a sound that seemed to come from all sides and also from nowhere. The same sensation is experienced by people in the engine room of ships. At Barnaby & Merlin work continued round the clock throughout the year; in winter the rock was stockpiled like hay. The pink smoke never stopped belching from the modest chimney.

'I've been looking into the troll bride angle,' said Calamity. 'It seems that a number of girls have gone missing from the area around Abercuawg over the past century. The old folk reckon they were sent to the trolls. Usually they got rid of unpopular girls, slatterns who gave the village a bad name. That's what they say.'

'I see.'

'Traditionally it was the Witchfinder who organised it.'

'That's interesting.'

Mr Williams, the man who conducted the tour, seemed neither surprised nor disappointed at the small turnout; indeed he seemed to consider it reasonable. The decline of an entire way of life could be read in his resignation. The world had forgotten about rock, they had forgotten why they needed to eat it, and that was not difficult because there was no reason. People ate it because it was one of those things you did at the seaside, one of the things everyone else did. It answered no great need. If all the seaside rock in the world disappeared tomorrow, the seaside holiday which itself had all but disappeared would not be greatly diminished. The same would be true if the donkey rides disappeared because sitting on a donkey is not particularly essential; and the same would be true of eating hot dogs, and bingo, and countless other things. The experience of the seaside holiday would not be diminished if any of them disappeared but if they all did there would be no seaside holiday.

Each of the slim pink alabaster-smooth rods of confectionery was made in strict accordance with a secret recipe invented by founder Ephraim Barnaby and his partner Merlin who didn't exist. Ephraim Barnaby had been a man with an acute understanding of Victorian business practice and knew that you couldn't get anywhere in those days without an ampersand. It was universally acknowledged that B&M rock was superior to all other seaside rocks and this was the result of a secret formula that was passed down from father to son on his twenty-first birthday in a sealed envelope.

When the time came, the elder Barnaby would take his son for breakfast at the Belle Vue Hotel. There, amid the shining silver and the crisp white linen spread on an alcove table commanding a kingly view of the Promenade and Cardigan Bay, they would dine on dry toast and tea without milk and the young son would intuit from this that the meal embodied a moral about those twin cheats, triumph and disaster. After breakfast they would take the Cliff Railway to the summit of Constitution Hill and spend the morning discussing matters of business. The culmination of this ritual would be the handing over of the envelope that contained the secret formula. There would be a pause on top of that hilltop with its dramatic vista of Cardigan Bay and the boy would then open the envelope and read its contents, having first given his father a solemn undertaking, sealed with a handshake, to strive to make his life worthy of the legacy being entrusted to him, and also to take pains to bring into the world a son into whose care he could entrust the same legacy in a similar scene on top of Constitution Hill in years to come.

The boy would read the letter containing the secret formula and return from the mountain, like other prophets before him, with an expression composed in equal parts of astonishment and fear. The torch had been passed on this way for five generations without mishap until the current one when young Gomer Barnaby lost his wits the same day that Gethsemane Walters went missing. After this, the elder Barnaby became a recluse in the turret of the rock foundry and devoted his declining years to caring for his broken son and focussing his energies on the betterment of mankind by developing a better type of placebo. It came to be known as Ampersandium and people swear by it.

Mr Williams hurried through the first three halls because he knew from experience that no one cared. We rushed through a warehouse and unloading bay where the main ingredients, sugar, water and pink colour, were unloaded. We passed a kitchen in which people wearing hats and masks supervised steaming saucepans the size of small swimming pools. Inside the pans, constantly stirred by automatic spoons, was the hot mixture. At some point that was not disclosed the secret formula would be added from a glass phial by Ephraim Barnaby V personally; and some time after that would come the peppermint flavour and the pink colour. Lesser brands of seaside rock use a variety of artificial colours but B&M's was a traditional firm and only used one. This was a mildly interesting discovery: the scintillating red of the letters, the pink of the outside and the white middle were all products of the same sugary dough. It was beaten and pulled and slowly aerated, a bit like bread, and the more it got aerated the lighter it became. Pulled and pulled and pulled until finally it was white. Along the way, a scarlet lump would be broken off for the letters, and further on down the line the pink casing would be set aside.

No one was interested in any of this. There is only one part of the tour that people care about, the typographer's room; and only one question dominates all thought: how do they do it? How do they put in the letters? In keeping with the air of profound mystery that surrounds the letters passing through the rock we expected something equally impressive in the room where the rite was enacted: an enchanted grotto filled with bright shiny cogs and wheels and levers and all manner of fantastic machinery, but there was nothing: just a long table and tubes of the red, pink and white sugar-dough. But most importantly there were men. No machine can put the letters in seaside rock. There were three typographers, and a superintendent who I could tell was the ex-con from the Slaughterhouse Mob.

How do they do it? What is the great secret that baffles all those who have ever bitten into or just sucked a stick of seaside rock? Jam sandwiches are the secret. This is the visual analogy which will unlock the puzzle.

Imagine you have a jam sandwich, a square sandwich rather than one that has been cut into triangles for arranging on a plate. Look at it end-on and you will see a layer of red in between two layers of white. Now imagine that the white is not bread but white rock, and the filling is not jam but red rock. There you have it: this is your building block. All the lettering is created out of these sandwiches.

All the letters are in upper case and in Helvetica, or at least a sans serif face. This is because it already takes twelve years to teach a man to write A B E R Y S T W Y T H and that time would be even longer if he had to learn to do lower case as well with all its extra curves and flourishes. On its own, without need of any embellishment, a jam sandwich gives you the letter 'I'. Put another one on top and you have a 'T'. Add two more branches to the tree and presto! You've got an 'E'. Already after six sandwiches you have the word 'TIE'. Add two more sandwiches and you have 'TILE'. In between individual letters you put spacers of white, which are sandwiches with no filling. Slightly more difficult are the ones where the cross-beams are diagonal: A, W, Y, and these require a certain degree of jiggery-pokery with your sandwiches, but nothing insurmountable to an enquiring mind. And that brings you to the tough ones, the ones for which the rock master spends twelve long years learning the craft: the ones with curves. But the principle is the same. Consider the letter 'S'. To make this, first imagine wrapping the jam-filled sandwich around a tube of white, like a Swiss roll. Looked at from the end you will have a circle of red. Now bisect the circle with a knife to form two half circles. Move one up and you find you have an 'S', and it takes little skill to see how this arrangement can be adapted to make a 'D' and a 'B'. All that remains is the Cellophane and a specially blurred, washed-out photo of Aberystwyth.

The tour petered out in the gift shop and we were free to wander round. Calamity went back to the office. I followed the chief typographer out into the yard and sat on a bench next to him as he had a smoke. I took out a brown paper bag that contained tongue lubricant without which in Aberystwyth the engine of detection grinds quickly to a halt.

I said, 'Lovely day, isn't it?'

He didn't answer.

'I guess you don't get to see much of the summer, working inside all day.'

Still no answer.

'Apparently this building was originally built by the railway company as a hotel, but no one came. Makes you think, doesn't it?'

Apparently it didn't.

'Is it hard getting the letters in?'

Finally he spoke, without turning to look at me. 'Ask a lot of questions, don't you?'

'I just like to talk.'

'No, you like to make other people talk, I know. Spotted you the moment you walked in, knew straight away you were either cop or snooper. Spotted the brown paper package too. Cops don't come bearing gifts.'

I let the top of the rum appear through the paper. 'You mean this?'

'That's what I saw. You intend drinking it all alone?'

'Would it be a bad idea?'

'Drinking alone is the thin edge of the wedge, I generally advise against it.'

'Know anyone round here who could help shoulder the burden?'

'I'm not busy at the moment.'

I unscrewed the cap, took a drink from the bottle and handed it to him. He tried not to look too eager but his hand was shaking.

As he drank, I said, 'I like a nice conversation when I drink.'

The typographer swallowed a third of the bottle in a series of glug-glug sounds. He let out a long gasp of satisfaction and held the bottle away from him and examined it as if he had never seen such a wonder before. He said, 'I can get downright chatty when there's liquor around.'

'They tell me you used to be a member of the Slaughterhouse Mob.'

'Yes, I was a bodyguard.'

'Did you know Goldilocks?'

'You could say he and I were acquainted.'

'Story goes he escaped from prison while awaiting execution.'

'I heard that story too.'

'How did he manage to escape?'

'By magic.'

'Oh.'

He took another swig. I waited. He took another swig. It was one of those silences.

'By magic, you say?'

'Yup.'

'Just like that.'

'Yup.'

'A mystery.'

'Sort of.'

'Care to throw any light on it?'

'What sort of light?'

'You know, the stuff made of photons.'

He nodded. 'Oh that.'

I sighed.

'Dewi Stardust,' he said. 'Conjuror to the mob. It was the Christmas party and he went to give the prisoners a little show. He was going to make someone disappear and needed a volunteer. Since Goldilocks was on death row he was the obvious choice. We all thought it was really funny. Dewi Stardust had a big animal cage on the stage and Goldilocks went inside; they shut the door. He threw a drape over the cage and waved his wand and stuff. Then there was a bang and a flash and that was quickly followed by the bark of a dog. He whipped off the drape and it seemed Goldilocks had been turned into a dog. Well, they all cheered and clapped thinking it was a pretty good trick.

'Then at the end, when the show was winding up, Dewi tried to change the dog back into Goldilocks and it wouldn't work. He tried and tried, using all the magic words he knew, but nothing happened.' The ex-con paused for lubrication. 'That was the last anyone ever saw of Goldilocks.'

We sat in silence for a while as I contemplated the story. 'What happened to the dog?'

'They put it in his cell for a few days, on the off-chance that it might change back spontaneously. After that, they gave it to the cook to look after. The dog was happy about that, was better fed than any of the prisoners, and was enormously popular around the cell block. The dog is the one character who ends up happy in this story. He was called Nipper.'

'And no one ever saw Goldilocks again?'

'Nope, or at least no one that I know of.'

'How did you end up working here?'

'I did old Mr Barnaby a good turn and he gave me the job.'

'What did you do?'

'I saved his son's life.'

'Most folk say you got the job because Barnaby must have lost his marbles.'

'Most folk don't know anything. They think the Slaughterhouse Mob tortured the son and broke all his teeth. I'm the one that took him to hospital.'

'Why did they do that to him?'

'Who?'

'The Slaughterhouse Mob.'

'Who said they did anything?'

'You did. Or you implied it.'

'My friend, I told you what folk say. I don't take a position on it. About the only reason I am still alive, unlike every other member of that mob, is I don't take positions on things. It's not healthy. I found Gomer Barnaby wandering around in a daze, with his hair standing on end and all his teeth broken. I don't know what happened to him, and nor did he. I thank that particular piece of shared ignorance for the long life that I have enjoyed.'

'A little knowledge is a dangerous thing.'

'Round here especially.'

'This was the same day that Gethsemane disappeared, isn't it?'

'That's right.'

'Are those two things connected, do you think?'

'Probably, but I don't know how. I don't take positions on that neither.'

'Was Goldilocks as bad as they say?'

'Depends on how bad they say.'

'I guess you wouldn't care to take a position on it?'

'I'd say he was more misunderstood than downright bad. They say he got his sister pregnant as soon as Ahab the father left, but it wasn't like that. He was the one protecting the sister from the drunken father; him and his brother. That's why his big brother Shadrach got sent away. He came home and found the old man messing around with the sister and went for him. Nearly killed him, but not quite. He got sent to a mental asylum where he spent his days in a straitjacket. Goldilocks used to go and visit. Wasn't supposed to, but he just went. Hitch-hiked. Then one day the father ran off and left Goldilocks and his sister alone. I don't know what became of the sister. But she always said Goldilocks never laid a finger on her and I believe it.'

'What happened to the mum?'

'Disappeared one Christmas. Ahab put her shoes in the pig pen to make it appear like they'd eaten her. Goldilocks couldn't have been more than ten or eleven when that happened. Some people reckon that's why he went to work at the new slaughterhouse; get his own back on the pigs. Me, I don't believe it, but they do say he loved killing those animals.'

'What really happened to the mum?'

'I don't know. Maybe Ahab did her in, maybe she just couldn't take it any more and ran away. Maybe Ahab lost her in a card game. Nothing would surprise me.'

'Did Goldilocks kill Gethsemane?'

'I don't know.'

'Have you got a theory?'

'Everyone's got a theory.'

'I haven't.'

He took another drink. 'This stuff is good!'

'It doesn't seem to be having much effect.'

'It's working fine, you are just too impatient.' He paused again, and this time the silence was longer. I could see him thinking about it all, those days of long ago, a young man on the threshold of his life, filled with the hot-blooded lusts and desires that torment all young men. His memory insisted that the spotty youth of long ago was him, but it must have been hard to believe. 'I don't know whether he did or not, but I always found it strange that he would bury one of her shoes in his own garden. You'd have to be pretty stupid to do that and he wasn't dumb.'

'Of course if you wanted to frame him that's exactly what you would do. I guess we'll never know.'

'There is one person who knows. The Witchfinder.'

'Why him?'

'While he was on death row the kid asked to see a priest. Said he had a confession to make. They sent the Witchfinder along. I guess they thought there was no point finding a real priest for a wretch like him. He made his confession and shortly after that he escaped. Something has always puzzled me about it. Strictly speaking, the Witchfinder was required by the seal of the confessional not to divulge what he heard. At the same time, if the kid had said on his deathbed that he was innocent, then the Witchfinder could hardly let that remain secret, could he? So it was sort of understood that if the kid was guilty the Witchfinder would say nothing, but if he was innocent he would make it obvious without actually saying it in words. Well, he said nothing, which sort of confirmed what everybody thought, that the kid was guilty. But, if that was the case, why didn't he say where the body was? Why would you take the trouble to confess and not give up a detail like that? Always puzzled me, that.' He finished the bottle of rum and handed it back. 'Much obliged.'

I stood up and then remembered something. 'So how did the kid escape?'

He held out a bunched fist. 'This hand is Aberystwyth gaol.' He held out the other hand. 'And this is Aberystwyth. The question is, how to get from the one to the other, right?'

'You seem to have outlined the problem with great economy.'

'Exactly. Now, imagine it was a coin in one hand and you were a magician, how would you get the coin from one hand to the other? That's the way to think of it.'

'Maybe I should ask Dewi Stardust.'

'That wouldn't be easy. Dewi Stardust is not taking calls at the moment. Shortly after the escape he did a little disappearing trick of his own. A permanent one.'

Chapter 13

EICI JONES eased the car out into the traffic flow. We drove along Pier Street and followed the one-way system through town to Southgate. I sat hunched in the small seat, cradling on my lap a plastic shopping bag containing the gift-wrapped Airfix model which Calamity had bought on my behalf. As traffic slowed to a standstill on the Penparcau Hill Meici turned to me and said, 'Look, Louie, I really appreciate you coming to my party. I just want to say . . . I just want to say I'm sorry about what happened.'

'What do you mean?'

'When we were at Mrs Eglwys Fach's house, I was short-tempered with you. The thing is, I've had my eye on Arianwen for quite some time now.'

'Think nothing of it,' I said. 'She's a lovely girl.'

Meici flinched.

'Not my type, though,' I added hurriedly. 'And anyway, you saw her first.'

He looked comforted. 'Yes, I did, didn't I?'

We picked up speed and drove on. The heat rising from the tarmac vaporised the world and made it dance.

'You're a good bloke, you are, Louie.'

My body tensed involuntarily. Remarks like that, made so early in a relationship, are seldom the overture to a good afternoon. I resisted the pressure to respond and the unreturned compliment hung over our heads like a bad spell.

'No, you are. Really,' said Meici. 'A good bloke. You can be my friend, if you want. Would you like that?'

'Yes,' I said without enthusiasm. 'That would be really good.'

Meici looked pleased. He became expansive. 'Mam's always telling me to bring a friend home for tea, but . . . just between you and me, Lou, I don't have any. It's not easy making friends is it?'

'No,' I agreed. 'It's not.'

'You're a good bloke you are, Lou, a damn good bloke.'

'Please don't call me Lou. Where does your mum live?'

'Not far from Bwlchcrwys.'

'How many people are coming to your party?'

There was no answer.

After five miles free of traffic we found ourselves reduced to a crawl by a group of escaped sheep trotting down the middle of the lane. Meici hit the horn but, unusually for creatures who are normally easily spooked, they didn't seem concerned. 'I'm glad I let you be my friend,' said Meici. He took a slip of paper out of his shirt pocket and proceeded to unfold it one-handed. 'I 'spect you know a lot about book-learning and stuff,' he said. 'Don't you?'

'Yes,' I said. 'A lot.'

'Thought so, you can tell. What's this mean?' He handed me the slip of paper. The word 'serenade' was written on it.

'Serenade?'

'Yeah, what's it mean?'

'It means to court a girl by singing outside her window.'

'Ah!' said Meici. 'That explains where I went wrong. I thought it was a drink.'

'They're easily confused. Where did you come across it?'

'That would be telling, wouldn't it?'

The group of sheep divided and darted to either side, back on to the high green grass bank. We picked up speed and drove on, an awkward silence left hanging in the car by Meici's last remark. After a while he spoke. 'You see, I got myself into a bit of a fix by telling mam that Arianwen was my girl. Mam keeps on at me to bring her round. So I've been doing one of those correspondence courses about how to talk to ladies and stuff. I'm not sure if you noticed but a lot of my patter is straight from the book.'

'*The Old Black Magic?*'

'That's right. Have you read it?' He dug me in the ribs with his knuckles. 'You'll never guess what?'

'What?'

'I've bought one of those condoms. It's hidden in my room for when she comes round.'

I changed the subject. 'So, near Bwlchcrwys, you say?'

'Not that close. Maybe five or six miles. We used to live in Abercuawg before they built the dam.'

'That's the town that reappeared because of the drought.'

'That's right.'

'Quite eerie, isn't it?'

'Yeah,' said Meici. 'It is. Gives me the willies.'

'Did you know the girl who disappeared?'

'I wasn't born then, but mam knew her.'

'What about the boy they accused of murdering her?'

'Goldilocks? She knew that family, too. She'll tell you some stories you wouldn't believe. The father was a lay preacher, called Ahab; always drunk. The mother ran out one Christmas.' He turned to me. 'You know what the father did? He put her shoes in the pig pen and told the children the pigs had eaten her.'

It was a small cottage built from the grey local stone. Meici turned into a rutted farm track and stopped the car. He got out and fetched a bag from the boot. He took off his trousers, rolled them up and put them on the back seat, then took a pair of short trousers out of the bag and put them on.

'They were cut down from my granddad's Sunday best,' he explained. 'I'll cop it if I don't wear them. I'm not allowed to wear long trousers. Mam says maybe next year when I'm thirty-five.'

I took the present out, a gift-wrapped, rectangular slab. 'Happy birthday!'

Meici looked at me and smiled uncertainly. It was as if the meaning of the ritual escaped him but he did not want to let on. I pushed the present towards him, against his chest. 'It's for you.'

'What is it?'

'A present, of course.'

He blinked and then a smile began to spread across his face. 'A present? You mean like in *Pollyanna*?'

It was my turn to look puzzled.

'That's a book I'm reading. It's ever so good. It's about a little girl who always sees the bright side of things. When things go wrong she plays the Glad Game. Like one Christmas she had a present, but it was a pair of crutches. Instead of getting upset she played the Glad Game and said she was glad because she didn't need crutches. I play it too, sometimes.' He clutched the present in both hands and stared in wonder. 'I didn't think real people got them.'

'Maybe you should open it.'

He unwrapped the gift with hesitant, unpractised fingers, taking great care not to tear the paper. Finally, he held the box out at arm's length and admired it. 'A model plane,' he said, eyes brimming with tears of joy. 'I've seen them in the shops.' He paused and then said, softly, in a reverie, 'Best to keep it in the car. If mam sees it she might . . . she might . . . well, we don't really have much room for it at home.'

We drove on and pulled into a hole in the hedge and parked in front of the cottage. In the space of a twenty-minute drive from town Meici's confidence had drained away; now he seemed nervous and unsure. As we approached the cottage his stature diminished, helped perhaps by the short trousers, and he started to tremble like a dog who has fouled the lounge carpet and knows what is coming. He walked past the front door which was clearly only used 'for best' and round to a kitchen door that hung on one rusty hinge. Many years ago it had been painted green but almost all trace of that paint had gone. Meici pressed down the latch with his thumb and walked in. I followed. The kitchen smelled of camphor and anthracite smoke, stale bacon fat and unwashed flesh turning sour with age. His mum sat with her back to us, ram-rod straight at a simple kitchen table that had been set for tea. She wore black with her grey hair spread across the shoulders. She made no attempt to turn round. We walked round to one side, still she stared straight ahead. She was thin and bony with sallow skin and a bitter expression on her face. The atmosphere was frosty and even without knowing either of them I could sense something was seriously amiss.

'Mam,' said Meici, 'this is my friend L . . .' his tongue froze as he noticed something unusual about the supper scene. There was a condom lying with mute accusation on his plate. He gasped.

Meici's mum articulated her sentence slowly and trembled slightly with repressed fury as she spoke. 'What is this filth I found in your room?'

Meici opened his mouth to answer but nothing came out but a puff of air, the ghost of a sigh.

'Answer me directly, boy, or it'll be the worse for you.'

He stammered the beginnings of a word but could get no further. He pressed his thighs together and thrust his backside backwards in the posture a child adopts to control its bladder, but which I had never seen deployed by an adult before.

'I'm waiting,' said his mum.

'It's a French letter,' he said finally.

'It's an engine of Satan,' she corrected him. 'Explain how this abomination came to be in this house.'

'I . . . I . . . Louie gave it to me,' said Meici, 'I didn't want it.'

His mum considered. The progress of her cogitations were revealed by a slight clenching of her cheeks. 'A likely story! Do you remember what I told you would happen if I caught you messing around with harlotry?'

'Yes,' said Meici almost inaudibly.

'Speak up, boy!'

'Yes.'

'Bring me my stick.'

'No, please, Mam. Please.'

'Fetch me my stick and go into the shed.'

'Please send me to bed instead.'

'You'll go to bed directly.' She turned and looked at him, her eyes glinted with anger. The look crushed all further protest and Meici went out. His mum gathered herself and rose slowly, and, still affecting not to notice me, walked out. A minute passed and I heard swishing sounds followed by yelps. When Meici came back in he was wiping tears from his cheeks with his sleeve and snivelling. His mum followed and said, 'Now get to bed, and take Esau with you.'

Meici looked at me with an expression of desolation and took my hand. 'Come on, Lou. We have to go upstairs.'

I had hoped to ask his mum about Gethsemane and Goldilocks but I found myself instead following him up the dim stairs to a little bedroom at the top. We trooped in and sat on the single bed, covered in a patchwork quilt coverlet. Underneath the window there was a little table covered with a cloth like a small altar. A photo of Arianwen was propped up and next to it were some hair slides.

I wondered what happened next. During my years as Aberystwyth's only private eye I had been involved in some strange adventures but this was the first time I had been sent to bed without my supper.

'Bugger,' said Meici. 'How on earth did she find it?'

'Mums have a sixth sense for this sort of thing,' I said.

'She thinks you are my brother Esau. He died when I was three. We slept in the same bed. I woke up one day and he was stone cold. They called him Esau because he was born very hairy.' He slid off the bed and kneeled on the floor. He looked under the bed. 'Phew!' he said. 'At least she hasn't touched my correspondence course.' He pulled a book from under the bed and handed it to me. It was a textbook with a cover bearing a photograph of a suave-looking man wearing a jacket and polo-neck sweater, holding court to a group of attractive and admiring ladies. The title said, *The Old Black Magic: From Dumbo to Don Juan in Four Weeks*. He pulled out another book.

'This is one of the set texts you have to read to build up your vocab. *Pollyanna*. Remember me telling you about it?'

'What did he die of?'

'Who?'

'Esau.'

'He was smothered in the night.'

'Who by?'

'I don't know. A goblin. They never caught him.'

'A goblin?'

'Yes. That's what the policeman said. The front door was locked but goblins have magic keys, you see. They found Esau next morning in my arms, cold as stone. Mam has never got over it – honestly! The way she goes on about it sometimes anyone would think I'd done it.' He nudged my arm with the back of his hand. 'You should read this, it's ever so good. You'd like the Glad Game. Do you want to have a go?'

'No.'

'Don't be like that. There's no use crying over spilt milk. Come on, we'll play the Glad Game. It'll cheer you up in no time. It goes like this: I'm sad that mam sent us to bed but I'm glad she didn't send us to the cow shed.'

'OK, I'm glad we had no supper because it helps us have compassion for the starving children around the world.'

'Hey, you're good at this. I'm glad we got sent to bed because I get to talk to my new friend Louie.'

'And it's good, too, because we don't really have to go to bed.'

Meici looked puzzled. 'What do you mean?'

'It's not like we have to put pyjamas on or anything, is it?'

He examined my face for a hint that I might be pulling his leg. 'Are you mad?' he said. 'Of course we have to go to bed.'

I stood up and walked downstairs and out through the front door. As I crossed the smear of grit that passed for a garden path my muscles stiffened in anticipation of a challenge from Meici's mum. But none came. I relaxed and cast a brief look back. In the upstairs window Meici's face was pressed to the glass, eyes gleaming with awe or fear at my act of treason. Or maybe it was the sharp gleam of spite and the dim vestigial memory of a crime he committed on the threshold of his life; one so terrible they had to pin it on a goblin. I fumbled with the latch on the gate, hands shaking like those of an alcoholic reaching for the first drink of the day.

Chapter 14

I T WAS a long walk to the bus stop and Calamity had gone by the time I got to the office. Eeyore had left a book open on my desk. It was Llewellyn's *History of the Welsh Stylite*, with a passage referring to the spiritual malaise called acedia underlined. It said, 'And when this has taken possession of some unhappy soul, it produces dislike of the place, disgust with the cell, and disdain and contempt of the brethren who dwell with him or at a little distance . . .' This must be the sickness that afflicts the private detective in the lurid electric-blue desert night, the neon wilderness of Aberystwyth.

I took the envelope that had held the séance tape out of the drawer and smelled it. I explored the feeling of disquiet that had taken up abode in my heart.

Had the reappearance of Abercuawg made everyone aware of the void in their lives and the stratagems they employed to conceal it? Faith, ice cream, arresting people . . . Each chooses his own road. One man makes Ampersandium, the world's greatest placebo. Others set sail for promised lands such as Patagonia, Hughesovka . . . Ffanci Llangollen, they say, has wheeled a shopping trolley around the coast of Britain in search of the daughter she lost. Vanya, too, had filled his life with a quest, and yet I got the impression that he did not seriously expect it ever to be resolved. The important thing was the quest.

I left the office and walked down Terrace Road. The cries of children from the beach became discernible as the light slowly changed hue; there was always a subtle change in the children's voices at this time of the afternoon, as if in a recess of their hearts they were registering the subliminal decline of the sun, the soft, barely perceptible transition from a hot summer day to the edge of evening. The ability to perceive it is innate, the way the knowledge of the river of birth is hardwired into the soul of a salmon.

All seaside towns are in a state of permanent autumn. This is evident in the ruins of the former great civilisation that once built Aberystwyth: a scar in the hillside beneath Pen Dinas too smoothly curved to be the work of nature, it turns out to be the cicatrice of a lost railway line. If you consult an old map you discover with a shock that it was built long ago to Milford Haven; you can't even get a bus there now. Other archaeological relics left by this vanished race of super-beings include the bandstand which now has a padlocked concertina door like an old garage. Once it had its own silver band, in a town that boasted two orchestras, one at the Pier and one at the winter gardens on top of Constitution Hill. Now no one even knows what a winter garden is. I don't. Is it really a garden or does it mean just a park of some sort? According to the old guidebooks, the ones that tell you to eat kidneys for breakfast and give advice about buying your fishing licence, there used to be a winter garden on Constitution Hill. But you will look in vain for any trace of it now.

Nowhere is the emptiness more acutely symbolised than in the institution of the pleasure pier where no pleasure is to be had. Originally piers were functional constructions, built to tie boats up to, boats that once plied the main with big smokestacks and restaurants and children in sailor suits or miniature frock coats; but the boats have gone and the projections into the sea remain like those towers they built to enable passengers to alight from Zeppelins in the early years of the twentieth century. The forlorn holidaymakers still walk to the end and back, partaking in a ritual whose meaning escapes them, unaware that there had once been a purpose to this two-hundred-yard walk out to sea. In the absence of anything else to do they buy ice cream or spend money in the amusement arcade and after a while this becomes the point.

The spiritual befuddlement that dogs the man of Aberystwyth at every turn is thus an unavoidable part of his fate because it is written into the very stones of the town in which he dwells. Other talismanic cities of the world such as Timbuktu, Troy and Gilgamesh grew out of the imperatives of trade and commerce or war but, like Babylon, and the towns of the American gold rush, Aberystwyth grew as a town of pleasure. A town in which human felicity was perverted into the singing, carousing, giddy tarantella, the vertiginous stovepipe hat debauch.

When I reached Sospan's stall there was a sign saying, 'No specials until further notice'. Uncle Vanya was there, looking worried. Sospan wore the face of a man whose hour has come.

'What's wrong?' I said.

'Something's happened,' said Vanya.

'Something?'

'Oh, Mr Knight,' cried Sospan. 'Something terrible, something awful, the worst, the absolute worst thing that can befall an ice-cream man has befallen me. I may have to leave town under an assumed identity.'

'Oh dear. And no specials today either?'

'No specials. It may be that there will never again be specials.'

'Not even a Fish Milt Sundae?'

'Yes, mock me in my hour of need,' said Sospan. 'The Fish Milt Sundae was the cause of my downfall. As you know, it was not exactly popular; possibly the most despised flavour I have ever served. But there was one customer who liked it. A very devout and religious woman of advancing years, not normally given to levity, who came every afternoon for three weeks to eat my special Fish Milt Sundae.' The ice man paused and exhaled in despair. 'Today I have received news that she is pregnant.'

I said, 'You can't get pregnant like that . . . can you?'

'Mr Knight, I will be frank with you. I assumed that you couldn't. But, as you know, biology is not my strong suit.'

'There must be another explanation,' I said.

'She is not the sort who would be mistaken about such a thing. She used to work for the St John Ambulance Brigade.'

'Maybe she got pregnant by the conventional route.'

'Impossible.'

'Who is it?'

'That I cannot tell you.' He put a plain vanilla cornet on the stands in front of me. 'On the house. I might as well use up the stock before I leave town.'

'Are things really that bad?'

'What can I do?' he replied. 'What would you do?'

'If it was me,' I said, 'before I made such a drastic move I would first demand a paternity test. And then, if it was established that I was the father—'

'I've spoken to her doctor, there is no doubt about it.'

'I'm not doubting her condition,' I said. 'Just the cause. Sospan, sometimes in situations like this even respectable ladies do not always tell the truth. It is not unknown, for example, for a lady of good reputation to fall victim to the sugary lies of some passing Don Juan and later when her belly gets big she seeks out a decent and unworldly man such as you, in the hope of deceiving him into believing it is his.'

'You mean,' said Sospan, 'like Mary and Joseph?'

'That is an extreme example of the phenomenon. Far more humdrum examples are to be found in the *Cambrian News* every week. Although the Fish Milt Sundae routine is new. You definitely ought to check if it is yours.'

Sospan stared out at the sea, surrounded by the shattered fragments of his world. 'And if I do that and it turns out to be mine?'

'Then you should do the honourable thing,' I said.

Vanya and I took our ice creams to the seaside railings and watched the slow drift of people packing up on the beach. At some point, once the heat loses its edge, a chill breeze can arise that throws a soft shadow over our joy.

'Things are far worse than I expected,' said Vanya gloomily. 'I saw Calamity in Great Darkgate Street, she has told me everything.'

'What has she told you?'

'About the troll brides.'

'I wouldn't pay any attention to that, it's not serious.'

'Do you think my worries can be so easily dismissed?'

'You can worry about anything you like but I wouldn't waste time on troll brides.'

'This is a bitter blow. Of all the fates that I imagined might have befallen the child whose spirit possessed my daughter this is one I did not consider.'

'I'm sure the ones you did consider are far more likely.'

'My grief is not so easily assuaged. To become the bride of a troll is a fearsome fate, especially for a child. The Portuguese have a word for this heaviness in my heart, *saudade*. In Hughesovka we call it *hiraeth*, a Welsh word, I believe, which denotes a form of spiritual homesickness.' He pushed himself up and away from the railings. 'Come, we must drink. There is no other remedy.'

The sky in the west had turned the colour of geraniums and Aberystwyth began to unfold like a rosebud in time-lapse photography; a sick rose whose innards have been eaten by a worm. The air turned sultry and the breeze of the summer night wafted over the Prom heavily laden and moist. A rich assortment of smells were intricately intertwined in the sensual tapestry: vanilla, dead mollusc, seaweed, aftershave, suntan lotion, spilled ice cream, soiled nappy, stale sweat, the electric ozone smell of the machines in the amusement arcades, take-away curry, fried onions, chips, hot dogs, testosterone, salty breeze, fish milt and, of course, prowl car, handcuff grease and the unmistakable sour fumes of police sarcasm.

Vanya produced a bottle of vodka from a bag, took my arm in his and we ambled along the Prom. The shift changed, the decent folk began to scurry away to their chalets and caravans, and the dance began; the giddy jig. The hustlers and the hoods and fixers, the druids in their sharp Swansea suits, the girls in the stovepipe hats and dreams of making it sparking in their eyes, the drunken brawling sailors, the morose fishermen and melancholic tradesmen, the lonely and the damned, the haunted and the hunted and the exiles all converged on the electric-blue Prom to sweat away the night.

Vanya breathed in deeply and exhaled with appreciation. 'Bignoniaceous,' he said. 'The word is bignoniaceous.'

I gave him a puzzled look.

'Yes, my dear friend Louie, bignoniaceous. There is a word for everything and for this experience too, there is a word.'

'What does it mean?'

'It describes a type of plant with trumpet-shaped flowers adapted for pollination by bats. Did you know that? I have great respect for this mammal. Few animals are quite so unfairly slandered as the harmless and affable bat. Their sonar is so good they can use it to catch fish; their sense of smell is far superior to that of the bee. All that the rose needs to do to attract the noble bee is give off its hot vapour to the summer breeze, and yet what is the scent but that of the rose? The rose smells of its own essence, which is a feat we all manage, and counts as no great achievement. But the bignoniaceous plant, faced with the challenge of attracting the attention of the far more discerning, though unloved, bat has to try harder. Bignoniaceous plants smell of cabbage and mice. Did you know this?'

I confessed that I did not.

'I have come to the conclusion this is the same trick repeated every spring by the old courtesan Aberystwyth. She cakes on the all-concealing foundation, and stands at the back of the chorus line, where the shadows are deeper, hoping that her faded charms will last another season, while the leg-kicking strumpets at the front twirl petticoats that flash and blaze like fireworks in the hot footlights. Is it not so, dear Louie?'

'I've never heard Aberystwyth described like that before but it captures her perfectly.'

He examined my face to see if I were in earnest and finding that I was said, 'The vodka is good.'

A thought flashed across my mind like a swallow through a barn. I realised a simple truth: I loved Vanya, although I was not sure why.

We reached the end of the Prom beneath Constitution Hill and we each placed a single foot upon the railing in accordance with a ritual whose origins are lost in the mists of time.

Vanya spread his arms and exclaimed, 'Yet the bat is generally disdained by poets, even though bat-pollination is responsible for one of the greatest gifts from animals to mankind, namely tequila. As an analgesic for the soul it is far more effective than the breathless rose-scented summer night. In fact, it is precisely this quality of the summer night that tequila can cure. But the crowning glory of the bat-pollinator's art is the durian fruit from Southeast Asia. It is something of an acquired taste. A Victorian traveller once described the experience of eating it as that of eating strawberries and cream in a public convenience. This is because the odour has a faint whiff of carrion about it. To which is added notes of civet, sewage, skunk spray, turpentine, caramel, onions, custard and gym sock.'

We turned and walked back, towards the bandstand. It is not likely that anyone would have eaten strawberries and cream in the convenience in the public shelter on the Prom, but as we passed it by an old woman emerged eating jam tarts. She pushed a shopping trolley across the zebra crossing. It was Ffanci Llangollen. In her trolley was a dirty woollen coat, black-and-yellow-hooped football socks, mitts and a fake sheepskin hat screwed up into plastic shopping bags from which all the lettering had worn away.

'I love the old Prom,' she said. The words weren't really addressed to us, nor anyone, but said simply to the night. She had long ago learned not to expect a response.

I said, 'We all do.'

Uncle Vanya offered her the bottle of vodka and she looked grateful and surprised. She took a drink and patted her chest as she registered the invigorating effect of the medicine. 'Your smell reminds me of my time in the Stolypin car,' said Uncle Vanya. 'I do not mean that unkindly,' he added quickly. 'That was the greatest event in my life. We seek happiness with an insatiable hunger, like plants seek the sun, and yet it is the dark times in which we gain our real insight into the mysteries of life.'

Ffanci, whose entire life had been spent exemplifying this philosophy, did not deem it worthy of comment and took another drink. Vanya took Ffanci's trolley and wheeled it over to the shelter. I left them and walked over to the Spar on Terrace Road to buy more bottles. I sensed it was going to be another of those nights. An old man in a charity shop suit stood by the door and asked me for the price of a cuppa. I gave him a fiver and told him not to waste it on tea or any other type of soft drink. He thanked me for the advice, and waited discreetly for me to leave before going in to buy something to slake his thirst.

When I returned they were absorbed in Uncle Vanya's life story.

'In the camps men would play cards and because they had nothing to wager they would stake your life. And you would not even know it until the moment came for the gambler to pay his debt. You could be in the same room and remain unaware that they were playing for the privilege of murdering you. This was the way of the two men Yuri and Ivan. They befriended me and showed me great kindness and I was too naïve to understand that no good could come from their solicitude. Instead, I was touched. No one had ever shown me kindness before. Perhaps the kindness of the wolf is better than nothing to a lonely man. The other inmates perceived this and watched in silence, striving to keep the mocking look from their faces as Yuri and Ivan gave me extra rations. They told me they were going without food themselves in order to help a fellow Christian soul and I was deeply touched. Of course they were not going without at all, some other poor wretch was. Since the food in the camps was never more than barely enough to keep a man alive, then it follows that the extra food they fed me must have led to the death of another man, and his death still weighs heavily on my conscience. But I loved these two men deeply because they fed me, which is the greatest act of love you can show to a man in the camps. They also used their power to get me an easy job as a clerk in the office, and that too meant the difference between life and death. If it was not for those two criminals I would surely have perished that first winter. I loved them, for how could I have known what they had in store for me? How could I have known that on the day of my arrival in the camp Ivan won me in a card game?

'As winter approached its end they informed me they had an escape plan and I was invited to go along. Even then I was too ignorant to understand their scheme, to understand what evil, what horror these men had planned in their wicked hearts. We climbed over the wire in May at the first hint of spring. Escape was virtually impossible and successful escape, almost unknown. It is so far — thousands of square miles of empty tundra where even the wolves struggle to survive. There is no food and finding fuel is difficult. The local people if they catch you will turn you in. In the past it was not so; in the time of the Czars, there was a tradition that they would leave milk and bread out on the doorstep overnight to help escaping prisoners, because Siberia has always been the land of exile. But under Stalin those who aided or gave you succour would end up in a camp themselves; even for failing to report having seen you was enough to get them a ten-year stretch. The task was truly hopeless. But some there were who preferred to die trying rather than serve their twenty-five years of hell. Many were the times during that journey when it seemed that Death had finally come for me and each time some miracle intervention by my two companions stepped in to snatch me from the edge of the precipice. Each time they saved me, my love for them grew deeper. We crossed a frozen river and the ice cracked beneath us and I fell in; those two men, those two evil merciless murderers, both risked their lives to save mine. Then later we were attacked by wolves and this time I was surely done for, but my two friends fought them off with fire. Another time we were attacked by a bear and they drove the bear off with rocks. Thus in the company of these two scoundrels I crossed the vast frozen wastes of that land and also traversed the inner continent of the human heart. There I discovered the darkest wisdom ever to be found in such a vessel, far down in the deepest, dimmest cistern of the heart where only lunatics visit. I began that spring the journey that would bring me here to the Promenade in Aberystwyth, I discovered the terrible wisdom and became the most celebrated, most famous cartographer of the human heart, second only to the woman whose fate haunted me the whole time, the mother forced to abandon her suckling child and entrain for Siberia.' His voice acquired a croak and we could tell without looking that his face was creased with pain. 'Perhaps I shall not finish this story tonight.'

Ffanci put her arm round him and reassured him. We left the shelter and walked slowly along the Prom, taking turns to drink from the bottle. At the Pier Vanya suggested we go dancing. I expected the doorman at the Pier to create difficulties with regard to Ffanci but it appeared that Uncle Vanya had already befriended this man during his short stay in town. 'He is a great bear of a man,' explained Uncle Vanya, 'and so am I. We have an understanding.' We walked down the carpeted corridor with windows overlooking the blackness of the sea, towards the dark smoky cavern at the end. Disco balls twirled and threw flashes of light on to the corners and niches where couples hid. A man in a penguin suit holding a small flashlight showed us to a table near the back. The tables were set in a circle around an empty dance floor; it was not yet midnight, still early. Some druid wise guys were seated near the front with young girls eager to make an impression sharing their table. Here and there, dotted around, there were members of the cast of *North Road*, the grim ritual of determined drinking saying more eloquently than words that being a soap star was not much of a career to aspire to. Here and there too were waiters and chefs from the hotels' grills, dressed up as far as their meagre wages would permit; and there were a few isolated souls, men drinking alone in a way that suggested they could no longer remember a time when that had not been the case.

I took Uncle Vanya aside and suggested it might be kinder not to bring up the reason for his being in Aberystwyth, about the quest. He agreed and went to the floor to dance alone, completely oblivious to the impression he made. Ffanci ordered a brandy and Coke and said, 'There used to be proper dancing when I was young. Waltzing and things.'

'I hear you used to be quite a famous singer.'

'Oh yes, back in the forties. Skegness, Scarborough, Weston-super-Mare, I did them all, all the lovely old piers, the lovely old songs . . .' She began to sing in a frail soft descant:

> It's a lovely day tomorrow
> Tomorrow is a lovely day
> Come and feast your tear-dimmed eyes
> On tomorrow's clear blue skies . . .

The words faded out.

I said, 'After that you became the schoolteacher?'

'It was just a little school I ran for a while . . . all the children, I loved them all. But after Gethsemane was . . . after she went away, they stopped coming to my school. I had to close. Then I went on my travels. When it rains I wonder if she is getting wet. When I'm cold I wonder if she is cold too. When I buy new shoes I wonder what sort of shoes she wears. Sometimes I get a new dress from the charity shop and I wonder what sort of pretty dresses she likes to wear.' She turned to look at me. 'I've spoken to Llunos. The girl they found by the lake wasn't Gethsemane, it was an actress. Some students paid her as part of a rag stunt.'

'That was a wicked thing to do,' I said.

Ffanci made a half smile that seemed to dismiss the significance of the event when set against the broader canvas of her life. 'I suppose they thought it was funny . . . How could they have known what I . . . They wouldn't know. They are so young.'

A waiter brought two more drinks and Ffanci moved her hand holding her drink in time to the music with the simple side-to-side movement of a puppet.

'Is it true you and your sister were courted by the same man?'

'It wasn't . . . Alfred wasn't like that, I don't care if he was just a balloon-folder, he had dignity. All the girls were sweet on him. Including my sister, but he never requited it, that was just her jealous imaginings. He used to drive the tram for a while, when balloon-folding times were lean. I know what they say, that I . . . you know . . . when I fell pregnant, those gossips said I did it on purpose to trap him. It's not true. I would never have dreamed of doing such a terrible thing, it just happened the normal way these things do. He loved me, you see. That's what my sister could never forgive. I don't blame her for that, we're all human and jealousy is as human an emotion as love in a way, isn't it? You can't stop yourself sometimes, I know that. But you have to make the best of it, don't you? We all do. Why she had to go and marry that Witchfinder, I really don't know. It's not like she didn't have suitors. And she had made it quite plain she couldn't abide the chap. Then she goes and does that. It's almost as if she did it to spite me, to punish me the only way she could, by punishing herself.'

A body came between Ffanci and the glittering ceiling lights and a shadow passed over her face. I looked up. It was Arianwen. I stood up, she stepped forward and kissed me on the cheek. She whispered something into my ear but I couldn't hear what she said in the noise. I bent down over Ffanci Llangollen and pointed to Vanya. 'That man there is my client,' I said. 'You can ask him about Gethsemane. I wasn't going to tell you; I wanted to protect you, but I realise I don't have the right.'

Arianwen and I left by the exit at the back and emerged on to the iron walkway that led out to sea and ended in an iron precipice where the end of the Pier had long ago been blown away. Flashing coloured bulbs lit up her face and cast it again into darkness.

'You are so amazing,' she said. 'You returned the tape and the stamps.'

'Think nothing of it.'

'Wasn't it dangerous? Meici Jones must be in with some bad people.'

'It wasn't dangerous.'

'He's been following me. Or at least I think it's him. Someone is anyway.'

There was silence for a while except for the sigh of the surf on the rocks twenty feet below us. We stood separated and joined by an unresolved tension.

'Why don't you like me?' she said.

'What makes you think I don't?'

'You're not interested, I can tell. They tell me you used to go out with Myfanwy.'

I said nothing but flinched softly in the dark.

'She's in Switzerland, isn't she?'

'Yes.'

'Do you miss her a lot?'

'I was born when she kissed me. I died when she left me. I lived a few weeks while she loved me.'

'That's lovely. I wish you'd say that about me.'

'It's Bogart, *In a Lonely Place*.'

'It's still lovely. They say she isn't coming back.'

This time she felt me flinch.

I said, 'I don't care what people say. They don't know anything.'

'Yes, people always say horrible things, they pretend they want the best for you but really they want bad things to happen to you so they won't feel so upset about their own lives.'

We returned to the disco but Vanya and Ffanci had left. We walked out too. 'Will you walk me to the cab rank?' she asked and then suddenly her face flashed with scorn. 'Well of all the . . . You see! I told you he was following me.' I followed the direction of her gaze and saw Meici Jones standing next to the hamburger van.

'Go and make him leave me alone, Louie. Please, he gives me the creeps.'

I strode across to Meici Jones. His face was a sea of desolation.

'You're a dirty double-crosser!' he cried. 'I ought to smash your face.'

'Don't bother, it's not worth the effort.'

'I saw her first.'

'We were only talking. Other people are allowed to hold conversations.'

'You must think I'm stupid.'

'I do actually.'

Over the past hour my spirits had sunk lower and lower and I no longer had the energy for pretence. I turned to go and said, 'Just leave her alone, OK? She wants me to tell you, she's not interested in you. She never was and she never will be. So forget it and scram.' I was ashamed of how good it felt. It was like pulling the legs off a spider.

'You're a dirty double-crosser!' he cried again.

I looked round. 'What are you so upset about? Why don't you play the Glad Game? I'm sad that Arianwen is talking to Louie but I'm glad for her because he's better looking than me and I'm a creep.'

'Just you wait! I'll get you!'

'What are you going to do? Smother me in the night like you did to Esau?'

For a second he wore the expression of a fawn startled by a noise in the undergrowth. And then a different expression, one of astonished revelation, crept across his face. It was a vile sight. I realised with a sick feeling in my stomach that he had never known, had never suspected the reason why his mother hated him. He gasped twice, choked once, spluttered once, and then clutched at his heart with hands contorted to talons. He spun round and fell to the floor and lay there convulsing in pain. People crowded round him and I told the bouncer to call an ambulance. Arianwen stood next to me resting her head on my shoulder as we waited for the medics to arrive. It wasn't long. We watched them load Meici into the back of the ambulance. He had an oxygen mask strapped on and his two eyes bulged on either side with hatred or heartbreak; two eyes that were trained the entire time on Arianwen. Then they closed the doors.

The next afternoon an anonymous package was delivered to the office. It was addressed to 'Louee the dirty double-crosser' and contained the broken shards of an Airfix model and the charred remains of a correspondence course, *The Old Black Magic*.

Chapter 15

T WO DAYS later, as I drove through Borth at lunchtime, I saw Mrs Mochdre waiting at the bus stop. I stopped and offered her a lift. She hesitated, torn between the agony of putting herself in my debt and the equal displeasure of waiting for a bus. She got in, squirmed in the seat and grimaced an expression of gratitude. I drove off.

'I heard an interesting thing the other day,' I said with a false note of cheeriness in my voice. 'About you and your sister Ffanci Llangollen.'

'Oh yes?' Mrs Mochdre peered up at the clear blue sky and claimed to see a cloud. 'Looks like it might be changing, finally. It will be nice for the garden, bit of rain . . . I expect.' She sounded unsure and continued watching the sky with a mixture of anxiety and distrust as if the vagaries of summer weather were designed to spite her personally.

I said, 'I heard you and your sister used to court the same man.'

Her face froze but it was difficult to see whether at the impropriety of the suggestion or because of the tender memory I had brutally dragged up.

'I don't know where you heard—'

'He was the balloon-folder, wasn't he? He couldn't choose between you and then whoops-a-daisy! Ffanci Llangollen gets pregnant.'

Mrs Mochdre stared fixedly ahead, glaring.

'Some people might think there was something a bit quick and convenient about it, almost as if the chap was being given a helping hand to make up his mind.' I peered across at her, she kept her head fixed staring forward, wearing a face of stone. 'Perhaps if she wasn't the prettiest—'

'My sister was always the pretty one—'

'Well sometimes it's not about that, is it? Not always. Maybe if he liked the pretty one but there was something about her elder sister that was . . . was . . . deeper, something he liked and satisfied him and touched him deep down in his soul, well, I can see how the elder one, even if she wasn't the pretty one, in fact especially if she wasn't . . . She knew she wouldn't get many offers in her life, while all through her teens and early twenties she sees the boys rolling up at the door courting her sister and never one for her and all along she has to wear that face of bright airy joy and pretend she is just happy for her fortunate sister . . . that could get a bit wearing after a while. In a situation like that I could see how the elder one might feel aggrieved . . . might feel as if the chap was a worthless chap after—'

'Don't you ever say a word against Alfred Walters! Do you hear? Don't you ever!'

I was stung into silence by the venom of her response. If I was a cop this would be the point where I smiled inwardly and thought, 'Gotcha! I've found the button to press.' But I didn't feel like that. I wasn't a cop, and I never wanted to be. I never wanted to feel triumphant at a moment like this. I said no more and we drove on in awkward silence. Mrs Mochdre had pressed her knuckle into her mouth and remained staring fixedly at the sky. As we drove up towards Commins Coch I shot a glance across. Her eyes were wet. She saw my look and said, 'Some busybodies oughtn't to poke their noses into things they don't understand.'

There was a man and a dog sitting side by side on the beach, facing the waves. I went to join them. It was Uncle Vanya and Clip the stuffed sheepdog from the museum on Terrace Road. The sky was filled with shredded cloud; a strong breeze churned the sea to foam, the surface dancing with seams of gold in the bright late-afternoon light. The breeze was scented with vanilla and stewed tea, and seaweed and vodka. An empty bottle lay at Vanya's feet and a half-full one stood erect between the paws of Clip. Vanya's hair was wet.

'My friend Clip has been explaining everything to me,' said Vanya. 'I understand it all now. I see what a terrible waste my life has been. Clip doesn't say much but the things he says strike home.'

'Isn't he cold without his glass case?'

'Sometimes, Louie, your comments perplex me.'

'Why did you steal him from the museum?'

'He wanted to come, I didn't steal him.'

'Why is your hair wet? Have you been for a swim?'

'The man who owns the rock foundry, the one whose son is in a wheelchair, I helped him.'

'Was he in trouble?'

'He fetched an ice cream for his son and while he was away the boy dragged himself out of the chair and down the steps to the beach. He crawled on his belly into the sea.'

'You saved him?'

'Yes.'

'That's a great thing that you did.'

'Mr Barnaby gave me something very precious as a reward: a phial of his panacea Ampersandium. Would you like some? I poured it into the vodka. It makes the taste of life less bitter on the tongue.' Vanya passed the bottle across. I took a small drink to be sociable, but I could see this afternoon he was far advanced along a road that I had no wish to take myself, the one that always ends in tears. 'We must drink, my friend, because it may be we will not meet again for a long time.'

'Are you going away?'

'Yes, I have an urgent journey to undertake.'

'The case isn't closed yet.'

'It is for me. I will send you another sock as an indication of my complete satisfaction with the services you have rendered.'

'I don't need any more socks, the first one was enough. I would prefer you to stick around until I can finish the case. It's still full of mysteries.'

'But I am the client and I have learned enough to satisfy me.'

'What have you learned?'

'Under the searching and intelligent gaze of Clip, all mysteries have evaporated.'

I said, 'You talk of leaving and we still have not found out what happened to Gethsemane.'

'The answer to the mystery is to be found in the Museum Of Our Forefathers' Suffering in Hughesovka. It took dear Clip to make this apparent to me. As soon as I saw him I knew the truth: it was never intended that my life would end with the happy consummation I sought. Some men are born broken, never to be fixed. The moral of my tale is contained in the dark wisdom of the camps.'

'What happened after you escaped with Ivan and Yuri? You never finished that story.'

'I am finishing it now, on this beach with the help of Wise Clip who has been kind enough to corroborate for me the essential truth it contains.' He put the bottle to his mouth and threw his head back as if gravity unaided was too slow a method of bringing the drink into his gullet. 'At some point during our terrible journey,' he said, 'I sprained my ankle and could not walk. Ivan and Yuri took it in turns to carry me. This piece of bad luck put an intolerable strain upon our fellowship. My two friends began to quarrel and then one night there was a terrible fight and Ivan slew Yuri. I will never forget how the blood stained the moonlit snow. I said that we should bury him as best we could, but Ivan was indignant and said, "Why on earth would we want to do that?" I said, "Because it is the Christian thing to do." He scoffed. "You don't want to bury him?" I said. And he said, "Why waste good meat?" It took me a while to understand his meaning. "Surely," I said in horror, "you do not mean to eat him?" "Of course I do," he answered. "If we do not we will surely die." "But he's your friend," I said. "There is no way I would ever eat Yuri." Ivan laughed in a way that chilled the marrow, a laugh that would have shamed even Satan, and said, "You won't eat Yuri? Now that, my friend, is ironic."' Uncle Vanya stopped sadly and made a small wave of his hand, a gesture that somehow was meant to sum up the contingencies of fate. 'This is the dark wisdom of the camps. There is only one way two men can escape and hope to survive. They must invite along a third man, preferably a chubby one, who does not yet know the dark wisdom of the camps.' He emptied the vodka bottle and reached into a bag lying next to Clip and pulled out a third.

We both sat for a while, as the clouds gathered and took away the light, raising goosebumps on flesh and flooding the heart with anguish. He offered me a drink, but I turned it away. There are times when you have to face the terrors naked. Vanya spoke staring straight ahead, his words both for me and for all the ghosts who reside in the deep waters of the sea, slowly putting on incorruption:

> I close the book;
> But the past slides out of its leaves to haunt me
> And it seems, wherever I look,
> Phantoms of irreclaimable happiness taunt me.

We continued sitting there for a while; Vanya in a place somewhere that I couldn't even begin to imagine, and me robbed of meaningful things to say. 'I don't pretend to understand any of this,' I said. 'But I respect the fact that for you it has a deep personal meaning . . . And I understand, too, that there are things in my life that would be mysterious to you but which are of vital significance for me. But . . .' The words trailed away into the empty air.

Vanya broke off staring at the sea and turned to me. 'You remember I told you about a story I heard in the camps, the story that haunted me all my life: about a poor woman who was arrested while she suckled her child, who was taken away that afternoon and never returned, never saw her child again. To tell you truly, Louie Eeyoreovitch, I did not hear that story in the camps. I carried it with me. That child abandoned was me. My whole life has been haunted by the tantalising prospect that I might one day find her again, but now I see this for the vain and futile self-deception that it is. Only in heaven will we be reunited. I am a failure, Louie Eeyoreovitch, everything I touch turns to dust. Even the fragile and short-lived bliss I had with my wife and child I managed to destroy. I am like my namesake in the play by Chekhov who failed in everything, even in his attempt to kill himself.'

We sat in silence, drinking slowly, each tending his own thoughts. The goosebumps became fiercer, the hairs all the way up my arm curling into the wind like ears of corn. Far off, the children could still be heard playing with laughter that at this distance sounded forlorn. Vanya began to speak, words not so much addressed to me as to the sea or all the people he had passed on the road over the years.

'A wise man once said there are three ways to find a fool. He is a fool that seeks that which he cannot find; he is a fool that seeks that which being found will do him more harm than good; he is a fool that, having a variety of ways to bring him to his journey's end, takes that which is worst. These have been my ways and the way of all the men I know. Dreams, illusions, faith, even love are flaming brands we pull from the fire and wave against the night, to keep the wolf at bay. Eventually we re-consign the charred stick to the flames. Sit on this beach in the late afternoon, dear Louie, when a strong breeze is blowing, and absorb the lesson. See how the wind whips the back of the sea; the sky is full of torn clouds that scud across the surface of the blue. The sun is fierce and laces the bubbling waters with veins of gold. You squint ahead into the crashing watery fire, ears filled with the roar. A transcendental feeling of loveliness floods your being, and then a cloud passes across the sky, the heart contracts like those deep-sea creatures that retract their tentacles at the approach of danger. Even in that moment you hear the pale far cry of the wolf. More clouds drift by, slowly they fill the sky with grey, and colour drains from the land, the gold that seamed the surface of the sea turns to stone; it gets chilly. The throbbing golden sea now looks cold, forbidding. You walk into the fierce waves, soon you are out of your depth, and the strong wind blows. You swim for the shore but you notice a strange thing: the shore recedes. You swim more strongly, and thrash against the mighty sea with all the power of a bobbing cork. This is all you are: a cork on a stormy sea. The waters no longer sparkle with shifting silver, they are dark and dim, and underneath the current grasps and pulls you towards the deep ocean with a force that mocks the puny efforts of your arms. The water is deep, and cold and alien, and bitterly salty: you have passed the boundary of the familiar, of ice creams and suntan lotion and sand in wasp-tormented sandwiches, of gritty towels. The figures on the beach grow small, the town retreats from view, and floats unreal like the view of town in the dim dish of the camera obscura. You gasp to catch your breath and instead of air you swallow a lungful of sea water; you choke and gasp, choke and gasp. Water is heavy, oh so heavy! It is like cement that fills the natural buoyancy chamber of your lungs. But it tastes good now, it works like morphine, the pain diminishes along with the subsiding world. The shore on which you left all your troubles recedes so gently, the way it does when you stand on the stern of a ship, of the ferry they sent for you alone. You watch the receding shore, perplexed by your sense of detachment. You recall vaguely it was fun there mostly and there were laughs, there was fellowship and dancing and there were tears. But both the laughter and the tears seem unaccountably unimportant. What was it that made them matter so much? It feels strange to leave this way, but no stranger than the way you arrived: immersed in salty water with a far-off drum-din pounding in your ears.

'This was how your mother brought you to the shore, years before with the stars fading before the growing dawn. Soon there will be nothing left to see of the town, just a V-shaped wake trembling into nowhere. You scan the coast. There, on a headland maybe fifty miles away, is a field still shining fire-green, one field picked out by a single beam of sunlight. A delirium of envy convulses your heart as you perceive the bleak truth: that field belongs to your past. You drink a little more morphine, just a few more mouthfuls to take away all pain . . . This, my dear friend Louie, is the dark wisdom of the sea, which we all must drink one day.'

Chapter 16

A CENTURY or two later I was shaken awake by hands too gentle to be cops'. I opened my eyes. I was alone on a bench on the Prom. Vanya and Clip had gone. I looked up into the face of a monk. He had wispy white hair, shaved into a tonsure, and was wearing a cowl the same colour as the stormy sky.

'Louie, you mustn't sleep here,' he said. 'It isn't right. Why don't you come with us, we're going for a cup of tea.' And then, while the fog cleared in my mind, he grasped my hand softly and said, 'I'm John Nepomucene, the Patron Saint of Silence.'

Another man stepped out of the shadows and said, 'Yes, come with us, Louie, you can't sleep here.' He wore a plain dark suit that had seen many years of wear, with an old-fashioned shirt from which the collar had been detached. The studs still hung in the eyelets at his neck, pressing against his Adam's apple. His throat was scrawny and had the soft blush on it of a man who had shaved before coming out this evening, and had done so every evening of his adult life in a ritual involving a badger-fur brush, and unperfumed shaving soap smelling lightly of municipal toilets. His hair was white, but neatly trimmed, thin on top. He smiled at me, his face was wrinkled but suffused with health. It was the kindest face I had ever seen. His hands were resting on the bar of a shopping trolley similar to the one belonging to Ffanci Llangollen and in the trolley, lying on top of the plastic bags, was a bowler hat and a violin case.

They set off. I fell into step behind, with John Nepomucene. I said, 'I don't think there will be anywhere open. The cafés close fairly early.'

'Maybe we'll be lucky.'

'How did you get to be a patron saint?'

John Nepomucene chuckled. 'Oh! thereby hangs a tale. I was working at the court of King Wenceslas, preaching, converting, that sort of thing. Trouble was, old King Wenceslas had a short fuse and I was taking the confession of his wife. Take my advice, Louie, never get yourself into a situation like that. Naturally he wanted to know what his wife had been getting up to. If you knew his wife, you wouldn't blame him. How do you handle a situation like that? He had me tied to a wheel, set on fire, and thrown into the Moldau. Even now my skin comes out in goosebumps when I recall how cold the water was.'

'What was the wheel for?'

'I've no idea; he didn't say. I can tell you from personal experience that it doesn't add anything of any great significance to the displeasure. Seven stars appeared above the town after my death, which was a nice touch.'

The man in front turned and said, 'We'll try the café on the Pier.'

I said, 'There isn't one.'

'O ye of little faith!' said John Nepomucene.

When we arrived at the Pier, the video shop had been replaced with a café. It was a humble affair of bare wooden floorboards, tables and chairs, a jukebox and a Formica counter. On the counter there was a silver tea urn and a glass case containing custard slices. I had seen it before somewhere long ago but I couldn't remember where. Although I was pretty certain it wasn't in Aberystwyth. The café was empty and we walked in and sat down at a table. The old man excused himself and walked off towards the sign saying 'Gents'.

'Your friend doesn't say much,' I said.

'He's one of those guys that speak softly and carry a big stick.'

'Who is he?'

'Don't you know? It's the Big Guy. The Boss.'

'Of the café?'

'Not just that. Of everything. The world.'

'Not God?'

'He prefers to be called Jehovah.'

I absorbed this new information. 'What's He doing in Aberystwyth?'

'It's like Hitchcock, you know how he liked to appear as an extra in his own movies? Nothing special, you know, just a fleeting glimpse of his face in a crowd shot. It's like that.'

God came back and sat down. I looked around at the empty room.

'I really like silence,' I said. 'It's the best thing you did.'

God smiled warmly, but with a hint of tiredness in His old watery eyes. 'That's kind of you to say, Louie, but the truth is, that is about the only thing in your universe that I had no part in. It was there when I started.'

'Oh.' I was keenly aware of having said the wrong thing. 'But of course that's not the only thing I like.'

'Please don't feel bad,' said God.

John Nepomucene yawned and rubbed his eyes. 'I'm worn out, the sea air always does this to me. Is it OK if I . . .?'

'Sure,' said God, 'you go.'

John Nepomucene shook my hand and disappeared into the night.

'He's a good guy,' said God simply. He took out a stick of rock and unpeeled the Cellophane. He began to suck thoughtfully.

I played with my teaspoon for a while and then said, 'I have to ask.'

'I know.'

'You probably get sick of being—'

'Just say it, Louie.'

'Why do we have to suffer so much?'

He examined the stick of rock, held it an inch away from his chin, lost in thought. The silence lasted a whole minute. He took a deep breath and said, 'It was a mistake. It was my first attempt, I got it wrong.'

'Attempt at what?'

'A universe.'

'Oh.'

'They told me suffering would give it "depth".'

'Who did?'

'The other deities. They didn't want me to win. They saw my stuff: Kilimanjaro, new-born lambs, lapis lazuli, Polynesia, Saturn, bluebells. They knew it was good. They said it needed more dark stuff to set it off, more light and shade – like a chessboard.'

'You mean it was a competition?'

'Yes.'

'You entered the universe for a competition?'

'That's right.'

'Did you win?'

In answer, God gave me a look of such desolate sadness it pierced my heart. He took a quiet suck of the rock and added, 'It was my human condition that let me down.'

I gave him an encouraging squeeze on the shoulder.

'My later ones were much better.'

I said, 'I've never been to this café before but it seems strangely familiar.'

'I took it from *Brief Encounter*,' said God. 'You remember that movie set in the railway station café?'

'Of course.'

'It's one of my favourites. Do you know the one thing they really loved? The one thing I made that really tickled the other deities?'

'No idea.'

He held up the stick of rock. 'This.'

'They liked Aberystwyth rock?'

'Rock they liked. Doesn't have to be from Aberystwyth. The stuff I showed them said Eden. It really tickled them, though. They kept looking at each end and professing in wonder, "The letters go right through! How on earth do they do that?" And I said, "I don't know, it's a mystery. One of the profoundest mysteries of my universe."'

'Surely not quite as profound as time and space and stuff?'

'Those things are not so very mysterious to me.'

We wandered out into the night to look at the summer lightning, a phenomenon for which long ago God had got top marks. We walked through the darkened castle past St Michael's church and on into the castle grounds. At the war memorial we stopped and sat on the steps. The breeze was warm and salty, summer lightning pulsed in the sky. Sometimes it flickers like a faulty neon tube, and sometimes it is like pinball in the sky, but tonight it had a soft creamy quality. There was no thunder and, unheralded by any noise, different parts of the sky would flare up, bright as the moon, and for a split second invisible thunderclouds would become incandescent like heads of spectral coral swimming in the ocean above us. I looked up at the statue: a naked girl in bronze reaching into the sky above us. Her breasts were full and uncovered, her hair wild and luxuriant like the figurehead of a windjammer; everything about her bespoke vigour and lusty sinews and glory; a cruel falsehood cast in bronze. They should have a statue of a mother holding a telegram from the War Office and weeping.

God stared up at the statue for a while, lost in melancholy, his kind old features creased with a pain that might have been guilt. Then, as if overcome by a sudden weariness, he rested his head against the stone. 'You know, it's part of my essence to be forgiving, but sometimes it's hard. Sometimes the ingratitude really . . . I mean, I don't expect "thank you" letters or bouquets of roses or anything, but some basic appreciation . . . an understanding of . . . of . . . what I did would be nice. Have you any idea how chuffed I was about the horse?'

'Which one?'

'Any one, all of them . . . just horses. Of all the beasts, don't you think they are possibly the most lovely?'

'Off the top of my head I couldn't think of a more wonderful creature.'

'Don't you just love the way they take apples from the palm of your hand? The way their big black noses peel back to unveil those big choppers, and so gentle . . . they could bite your arm off but they never do. And those big dark lake-sized eyes. I worked for ever on the detail. Horses were my special gift to man. And what did he do with them? Sent them to the Somme. It's the little things that haunt me, you see. Not the poison gas nor the stupidity of the generals, but the whinnies of the horses as the shells landed among them.' He closed his eyes and whispered, 'My lovely horses.' The wind blew strands of white hair softly across his brow as he rested his head against the stone column. 'You know,' he said, 'when the fighting finished and the troops went home, the War Office was too cheap to buy return tickets for the horses and sold them all to French butchers.'

We both sat in silence for a while, listening to the wind. I said, 'I read, in a magazine, an article about Hiroshima. There was this little girl, would have been about two or three at the time, I forget her name.'

'Sadako, her name was Sadako. It means chaste.'

'Ten years later she got leukaemia. They called it the atom bomb disease, and they knew they couldn't save her. But she got it into her head that if she somehow managed to fold a thousand origami cranes she would be saved. So she spent the last months of her life in hospital folding cranes.'

'Yes,' said God quietly.

'Folding, folding, folding.'

'Yes.'

'Even used the labels off her medicine bottles for paper. She reached the target, and went past it, and then she died.'

God nodded.

'I mean, what were you thinking?'

'It's difficult to describe.'

'You must have known, right? When she was doing it, you must have known it wouldn't work?'

'It's not as simple as that.'

'Isn't it?'

'What would you have done, Louie?'

'If it wasn't going to work I wouldn't have let her have the idea in the first place.'

'How do you know it wasn't going to work?'

'What does that mean? Did it depend on the cranes? She just didn't make them nice enough?'

'No, not like that.'

'Could it have worked?'

'I don't know. Maybe.'

'A thousand and fifty cranes.'

'One thousand two hundred and seventy three. I counted every one. They were beautiful.' He paused and said softly, 'Louie, I must leave you now. Try and . . . have faith.'

'But I don't believe in You.'

'I know. It's the ones who don't believe who need faith; it's easy for others. Goodbye, Louie, I'll be watching over you.'

I held his hand. 'Why did you come to Aberystwyth?'

'I came to collect Vanya.'

Chapter 17

L LUNOS CAME round to my caravan next morning to tell me the news. Vanya had been fished out of the harbour shortly after midnight, dripping brine and vodka with some barbiturates in his head. On the shore, in the shadow of the Pier, they found a stuffed dog, a neatly folded museum curator's uniform and, in case the barbiturates failed to do their work, an old revolver, loaded but not fired.

When I got to the office it smelled strongly of rum. There was a witchfinder sitting in the client's chair. He was smiling and the rum – which was usually kept in the desk drawer – was now slipping down the U-bend of the sink in the kitchenette. The empty bottle was standing up-ended in the bin.

He was an old man, in his seventies, with long grey greasy hair down to his collar and a bald pate. His nose was sharp and in his eyes there burned the flames of zealotry and on his lips there played that particular smile of moral rectitude possessed by religious fanatics and the criminally insane. He wore the customary outfit of the ecclesiastical cops: a dark blue serge policeman's tunic over a plain shirt and dog collar. Ecclesiastical cops have disappeared from the towns but still exist in the country in a state of uneasy truce with the regular police, their jurisdictions overlap with unclear boundaries and conflicts of interest. They deal with social problems that blight village life in the hinterlands beyond Aberystwyth, chastising strumpets, loose-tongued women and common scolds.

I nodded as if I had been expecting a bad start to the day and here was confirmation. 'My two least favourite people in one: cop and holy man.'

'The servants of the Devil abhor the sight of blessedness twice over.'

I picked the empty bottle out of the bin and put it on the desk for no good reason. 'I hope you've got a warrant for this.'

'No warrant is needed in commission of the Lord's work.'

'I bet they said that at Nuremberg, too.'

'Alcohol is an abomination unto God.'

'You've obviously never tried it.'

I slumped down in the chair opposite and scowled. He had also saved me the trouble of opening the morning mail. He threw a letter across the desk. It was from Vanya. 'As his last act upon this earth,' said the Witchfinder, 'your friend sends you a sock. The Lord will cure him of his levity.'

The envelope contained the matching half of the Yuri Gagarin sock and a note explaining it was to cover the funeral expenses. 'The truth about Gethsemane Walters is more terrible than even I could have imagined,' he had written. 'There is no point going on. Goodbye, Louie. Your dear friend, Vanya.'

I read the letter and looked up. 'Talking of God, I spoke to Him the other day, he was in Aberystwyth . . .'

The smile on his lips expanded a fraction. 'That really is an unwise way to begin a sentence.'

'Is it a crime to talk to God?'

'I will enjoy humbling you.'

'What do you want?'

'I have information that you recently visited Grimalkin's in Chalybeate Street and placed an order for some "flesh of brigand".'

'I was going to make a sandwich.'

'Ah! The wisecrack, the favoured artifice of the snooper and reprobate.'

'Or maybe I was going to use it as fish bait.'

He raised a polite eyebrow. 'Or Devil's bait?'

'He certainly turned up.'

The smile faded.

I said, 'Actually I was hoping you'd come round, I needed to see your face when I asked you how much they paid you to set Goldilocks up.'

'I don't remember doing that.'

'You probably repressed the memory. That's known as psychology.'

'Who are these people who allegedly paid me?'

'The villagers at Abercuawg.'

He smiled the smile of a man who knows you've got nothing on him. 'My memory is shocking.'

'The way I see it is this: Goldilocks would have been insane to bury Gethsemane Walters's shoe in his garden, even if he did kill her. But someone who wanted to see him hang might have done it. That someone was you. The villagers wanted to get rid of him and you buried the shoe and got one of them to report seeing Goldilocks doing it.'

'Please go on,' said the Witchfinder. 'I'm really enjoying this. Why do you think I set Goldilocks up, as you put it? I tried to help him. I went to see him in prison.'

'Yes, wasn't that an act of pure Christian charity! In that sacred communion between a priest and a condemned man when each man tells the truth of his heart he told you that he had never laid hands on Gethsemane Walters and he begged you to intervene on his behalf. And you said yes, of course you would, but really you had no such intention. You already knew he was innocent because you knew what had happened to the girl. And you knew the buried shoe was a phoney because you buried it.'

'And what did happen to her?'

'I don't know.'

'Why did they want to get rid of Goldilocks?'

'He found out.'

The Witchfinder looked genuinely intrigued. But not worried. 'Found out what?'

I didn't know. I knew nothing. I didn't know who did it and I didn't know what it was I didn't know they did. I just knew he was mixed up somehow in something that wasn't nice.

'He found out that his mum didn't get eaten by the pigs. She disappeared because Ahab the father sold her off as a troll bride and you arranged it.'

Like most shots in the dark it hit nothing. The smile returned. 'These are grave charges,' he said. 'Selling women to trolls, you should pass all the evidence you have on to the police. You do have evidence, I presume?'

I gave him a steely stare, one that attempted to convey smug self-confidence but which really said I was a busted flush. I knew it and I knew that he knew it. He rested his elbows on the desk and leaned forward. 'I've been reading up on you. Your mother was a trollop, a common tram conductress. Did you know your parents never married?'

I picked up the phone and dialled the hospital. 'Yes, 22/1B Strydy-Popty, can you send an ambulance, an old man is about to fall down the stairs.' He stood up hurriedly and walked out and left me wondering about the reason for his visit. There could be only one: he wanted to find out how much I knew. No wonder he left with a spring in his step.

I put my feet on the desk. There was another, quarter, bottle of rum in the drawer that the Witchfinder had overlooked. It seemed a pity to waste it. I leaned back and closed my eyes, drinking languorously from the bottle. First thing in the morning is not generally a good time to drink hard liquor but it's not every day you receive a sock from your dead client. I understood now the nature of the strange bond that had been forged between us: it was the story he told of his lifelong quest to find his mother. I knew now what the scent was on the envelope. It was the scent of my mother. How did I know this? I just did. And the image that had appeared to me of the world seen from the bottom of a well was really the world viewed from the pram. The long-buried memory of a time suffused with unfathomable contentment gathered like honey from the months spent floating serenely through the world. I now understood the nature of this sweetness: it is a residue of God's original purpose, of how he intended life to be for us, and would be in those other, brighter, more perfect universes he worked on in his later years. They say artists frequently produce their greatest masterpieces late on, those who understand these things say Beethoven's late string quartets were the sublime pinnacle of artistic achievement, and so it must have been with the later worlds. The one we inhabit is the work of the young God, a piece of audacious but flawed genius, showing early promise, but which would come to be disregarded by scholars as juvenilia.

Sospan's kiosk was closed and a scrappy sign, hastily hand-written, was Sellotaped to the outside: 'Closed until further notice'.

'Sospan has left town,' said Calamity who was leaning against the empty kiosk. There were tears in her eyes.

'Calamity, what's wrong?'

'I killed him, didn't I?'

'Who?'

'Uncle Vanya.'

I gasped. 'No, sweetheart, you didn't!'

Sobs engulfed her. 'I did. If it hadn't been for me superseding the stupid paradigm . . .'

'But Calamity, it was nothing to do with that.'

'It was. He saw the cuttings about troll brides, that's why he killed himself.'

I took Calamity in my arms and hugged her. I said nothing for a while, just let the weeping subside. When finally it did, I said softly, 'Calamity, Uncle Vanya's death had nothing to do with you. I think . . . I think he always meant to do it, I don't know why. I just never got the impression he intended . . . I mean, I think he always knew he would die in Aberystwyth.' I eased her away and held her face in my hands. 'OK?'

She snivelled and nodded.

'Where did Sospan go?' I asked.

Calamity shrugged. 'No one knows.'

The abandoned box stood sadly, like the shell of a crab that has moved on. Already seagull droppings disfigured the illuminated fibreglass cone on the roof. A piece of newspaper gusted against the padlocked door.

'I think now is definitely the time to go to Hughesovka,' said Calamity. 'We could use the money left over from the sock.'

'And what would we find when we got there?'

'The solution to . . . to . . . everything. Why Vanya killed himself, what happened to Gethsemane. They are linked. He virtually said it, didn't he? Told you the answer to the mystery could be found in the museum. Something he saw in those cuttings about troll brides broke his heart. If we go to the museum there we can find out . . . I don't know . . . something.'

I leaned back wearily against the box. I twisted my head round to face Calamity. 'You really want to go, don't you?'

'I loved Uncle Vanya,' she said simply.

'I did too.'

'Don't you remember, Mooncalf said we could go cheaply if we agreed to act as couriers and take something to his client in Romania. It's not like we don't have a few days to spare, is it? I think we owe it to him.'

The voice of the paper boy drifted down the Prom. He was shouting something about a girl and Talybont and murder. Calamity ran up to the boy and bought a paper. She glanced at the front page and returned, handing it to me without a word, her face ashen. A girl had been found in an alley behind Woolies. She had been bludgeoned to death. It was Arianwen.

I peered at the story with unfocussed eyes. Beneath the article there was an ad for a gift shop in Pier Street that showed one of those glistening plasma globes. I've stared at them in the shop window. Tender filaments of lightning dance and fork like animated trees, retracting and exploding softly against the Perspex like the spume crashing against the sea wall, or the violet tentacles of jellyfish shimmering in the sea. This vital dance, these concatenations, is what we are; it crushes the heart to think of how precarious it is, how frail. The dance only has to pause for a second and everything goes dark. Concatenations smeared on the sole of a shoe.

'Call Mooncalf,' I said. 'Tell him we need two tickets to Hughesovka.'

Two days later I stood across his counter. He handed me a smart travel folder printed with a montage of old travel posters and suitcase stamps: The Grand Hotel, Luxor. The Eastern & Oriental, Penang. Raffles.

'The route is straightforward: Orient Express from Paris to Istanbul, with a small detour to deliver this letter to my esteemed client Mr Vlad Tepes in Romania.' He handed me an envelope marked simply Mr V. Tepes, Sighişoara. 'You will take the local train from Brasov to Sighişoara where Mr Tepes, or someone representing him, will meet you at the station. You will stay for dinner and overnight as a guest and in the morning you will catch the train to Bucharest and continue with your journey to Hughesovka. At your destination you will be met by a member of the Welsh Underground who will make all necessary arrangements.'

'They have a Welsh Underground?' I asked.

'It's just a formal expression, nothing to worry about.'

'Something in your voice tells me there will be plenty to worry about by the time we reach our journey's end.'

'You jump the gun, Mr Knight. Did I say there was nothing to worry about? In respect of your errand to Mr Tepes, there is nothing to worry about, but with regard to the journey on the whole there is plenty. Hughesovka is not a typical tourist destination. In fact, in the fifty years that Mooncalf Travel has been operating we have only ever sent one party of tourists there, the Talybont and Environs Ladies bowls team.'

'And how did they enjoy themselves?'

'I have no idea. They never came back and all efforts to inquire about their fate via the British Consulate in Kiev were rebuffed on grounds of State security. But I am sure you will not go wrong so long as you remember to observe the two cardinal rules of travellers to Hughesovka, to wit: never utter a syllable in disparagement of its revered founder John Hughes, whose tomb and mausoleum you must as a matter of unavoidable courtesy pay homage to at your earliest convenience; and, secondly, on your way to Hughesovka, beware of honey-traps.' Mooncalf finished his sermon and looked at me enquiringly, as if there might be any part of it that was not clear.

'Why would I need to beware of honey-traps?'

'Because every traveller to the Ukraine does. It's not a personal thing, it's like telling someone not to drink the water or to take precautions with regard to mosquitoes.'

'But what reason would they have to entrap me?'

'They don't need a reason, they do it as a matter of routine in order to compromise you at a future date should it prove necessary.' He took out a small pamphlet and put it on to the desk. It was a cheaply printed A5 booklet bearing an image on the cover of a lady in silhouette unpeeling a stocking in a hotel bedroom together with a skull and crossbones warning symbol such as you get on bottles of poison in cartoons.

'Everything you need to know is in here, familiarise yourself. The only other point to cover is the matter of your incognitos. I presume you would be happy to go as a spinning-wheel salesman?'

That night Calamity and I caught the midnight train to Shrewsbury.

Chapter 18

A LIGHT SUMMER breeze blew across the rooftops of Mont-
martre, around the eaves and garrets from where candlelit
artists mailed off ears to ungrateful lovers. It blew through
the iron trelliswork and removed someone's hat and sent it rolling
along the platform to stop at my feet. It was a stovepipe hat. I bent
down to pick it up and straightened up to look into the face of a
pretty young girl of about seventeen with blonde ringlets and high
Slavic cheekbones. She was wearing Welsh national dress. She
smiled, took the hat with a '*Merci, monsieur*', curtsied and ran back to
her suitcase that was being held by the porter. I checked my watch,
and waited for Calamity to return with her postcards. I thought it
was a little too early in the journey to send them but Calamity had
never been further than Shrewsbury before and my words were
useless.

With a few minutes to spare she arrived and we walked in the
direction of the train. Lights began to flicker on and the braids of
intertwisting track out beyond the platform's end turned gold in the
setting sun. The carriage was a deep lustrous midnight blue, imprinted
in gilt with the world's most romantic stencil: Compagnie Interna-
tionale des Wagons-Lits. At the carriage end, next to the door, there
was a smaller removable enamel sign that said: Orient Express: Paris–
Munich–Vienna–Budapest–Bucharest–Istanbul (with connections to
the twice-weekly steam packet to Hughesovka). The last sentence was
written in tiny print like the bottom line of an optician's chart.

We climbed aboard and found the guard sitting in a little office
next to the shower and WC. It was no more than a cubby hole with a
small desk, a lamp giving off a yellow glow and suffused with a smell

of Pernod. He examined our travel documents and his face lit up with pleasure or surprise, or some emotion that suggested few people ever ventured as far as this fabled Shangri-la. A faraway look glimmered in his Pernod-stained eyes as he said, 'Hughesovka. Ah yes! There was a time . . . a time long ago . . . when I too might have . . . ah! But whatever became of those years? Kept in the same place as the snow from last winter, no?' He handed the tickets back with a melancholic smile. 'Light-fingered life steals the dreams from our pockets while we are busy watching the parade, is it not so?'

'That's exactly how it is.'

'Compartment 4a, and 4b for Mademoiselle Calamity. *Bon voyage!*' And then he added, 'Monsieur Mooncalf is a great man.'

The door to my compartment was ajar, a man stood with his back to the door, peering into a mirror inset in the aged wood veneer of the compartment. He seemed to be taking his own pulse but once my eyes became accustomed to the light given off by the dim bulbs in blue-velvet, tasselled lampshades I saw that he was in fact adjusting his cufflink. Opened on a small shelf beneath the mirror was a gentleman's travelling kit containing brushes, combs and manicure devices. From this he took out a set square and checked the precision with which his cuff was aligned to the central axis of his shirt. I coughed politely and he turned round and said, 'If you are looking for Edgbaston he's gone. Killed himself. Good riddance, too, he was a liar. He deserves no pity from the likes of us.'

'I don't know Mr Edgbaston.'

'You're looking at him now, or rather at the husk that once contained the impostor known as Edgbaston.' He reached out a hand to shake. 'Stanley. Stanley Edgbaston. I would give you one of my cards but I burned them all.'

'Louie Knight.'

'What do you do?'

'I sell spinning wheels.'

'I was in extruded aluminium. Hard to believe, isn't it?'

'What are you in now?'

'Now? Now I inhabit a different world, one where a man scorns to have his soul bend to the crude arbitrage of such labels. The man who for thirty years submitted to that yoke is gone.'

'Was he your brother?'

'He was a Judas. He wore these clothes, he wore this face. For many years he drove a Vauxhall Cavalier with the same registration number as mine up the M69 every morning and ate my breakfast at the Heston Services. He slept with my wife every night and he dandled my little ones. But he is gone now and with him the falsehood he called a life. His wife and children beg for crusts, and his little one asks each morning, "Mummy, when is daddy coming back?"' He finished with the cuff, and grabbed the knot of his tie and rammed it into his Adam's apple. 'Spinning wheels you say? What sort?'

'Oh you know, the usual: Sleeping Beauties, Cinderellas, full Saxons mostly and a few semi-automatics, nothing fancy.'

He nodded. 'You'll have to tell me about it.'

'Most of my work is secret: for the government.'

He mouthed a silent 'ah' in acknowledgement as if this was just as he'd suspected.

We dined with Edgbaston and the girl in Welsh national dress who was sharing the compartment with Calamity. Her name was Natasha and she was returning to Hughesovka from her finishing school in Caerphilly. When I arrived, Edgbaston was talking about the day he killed himself.

'For twenty years we had been telling our customers that plastic was no good, that aluminium was the only suitable material for replacing a wooden door. We preached it every day, from morning to night, like Jehovah's Witnesses. It was a mission. They used to come back at us and say, "Ah yes, but aluminium sweats doesn't it? You get condensation, don't you, which you don't get with plastic?" And they were right, of course, but then we confounded them by thermally breaking our aluminium. You probably don't know what that is but it means joining two sections with a seal of resin so that the heat can't transfer. It was a masterstroke. Suddenly you get the strength and resilience and good looks of aluminium combined with the thermal properties of plastic. The bloke who thought of that should have got the Nobel Prize. That was in 1981. There was no stopping us then, or so we thought. And then one day we were all called in to a special sales meeting and the marketing director gave us the news that we would be selling plastic alongside aluminium from now on. He even had the gall to suggest that it would be a boon to us, an extra string to our bow. Not a nod to the fact that we had spent all our lives insisting it was no good. Our universe fell apart. We weren't spivs, you see, we were honest guys. People think salesmen are all full of shit, but it's not true. Most of them find it easy to do their job because they believe what they are saying. Selling doors might not be heroic like being a fireman or something, but we can't all be firemen and there is a quiet satisfaction that comes from knowing that you've been persuading people to buy your product because it is genuinely in their best interests. You've been telling them the truth. And then you find that you've been talking a load of crap all your life like some cheap sit-com parody of a travelling salesman . . .' He stopped and lowered his head as if once again reliving the pain. Natasha looked moved and squeezed his forearm as if to say that no matter how black things got he must not give up. When he spoke again it was in a distant voice, as if addressing someone from his burned up past.

'When we raised this point in the meeting, the point about our shattered credibility, they said, "Oh, now we've addressed that. We've been working on this plastic system for three years in close partnership with the Swedish manufacturers and we've ironed out all the problems." But you only had to take one look at the suite to know the truth: it was just a cheap off-the-shelf system hastily branded with our name and brought in from the continent to stem the haemorrhage of sales figures to plastic. And because it was a cheap off-the-peg system it had all the problems we had been descrying for years, in spades. Plus a few more we had never thought of.'

'And so you burned your business cards,' said Natasha sadly.

'What else was there to do?'

'But what about your little children?'

He looked up and now there were tears in his eyes. 'Leaving them was the hardest decision I've ever had to make. But what sort of father would I have been to them if I had continued living that lie?'

Silence engulfed us for a while. On the other side of the window a group of ghostly *doppelgängers* dined, served by transparent waiters. A tiny moon raced alongside, gently bobbing up and down like a stone skimming the surface of a lake; trees and copses swooped past like diving birds.

I said to Natasha, 'You must have loved Caerphilly, the pleasure pier is wonderful.'

'Yes,' said Natasha, 'although I didn't spend too much time there, the sea makes my tummy queasy.'

'Don't be daft,' said Edgbaston, 'Caerphilly is thirty miles from the sea.'

Natasha gasped. 'Oh!'

'And there's definitely no pier there, I know that because I've been.'

'There's a nice castle,' I said. 'It looks a little like a pier from a distance.'

She thought for a second and then exhaled as if defeated. 'I'm such an idiot. I told them I could never hope to fool a guy like you.'

'Told who?'

'Them.'

'Who?'

'I can't tell you.'

Edgbaston and Calamity and I exchanged automatic glances, empty of meaning.

'Please don't ask me about it . . . Oh, this is all so . . . all so . . . so horrible!' She flung her napkin down and threw her face into her hands and emitted the sounds of muffled weeping.

'Steady on, miss,' said Edgbaston.

'No! Don't! Please . . . please don't say anything.' She stood up and rushed away in the direction of the sleeping carriage. The waiter observed through half-closed eyes and gave out a studied yawn, expressing the deepest imaginable ennui.

'Women!' said Edgbaston. 'Can't live with them, can't bury them beneath the patio . . . oops! What have I said!' He gave me a bone-chilling wink.

During the night, to the soothing background sound of clanking wheels and creaking wood, France turned into Germany. Periodically the hypnotic rocking of the train would subside, imperceptibly, until it had gone completely and a tingling silence remained. At such times I would crawl to the end of my bed and peer out through the gap between the edge of the blind and the window frame at an unknown station, bathed in yellow electric light. No one would be around except perhaps a station master somewhere cradling a cup of coffee, listening to the radio, his presence sensed rather than seen. Moths swarmed round the lights, and far away other lights flickered green and red. By dawn we had reached Munich. I ate breakfast alone, neither Stanley, Calamity nor Natasha turned out. I took out the photo of the invisible imaginary friend holding the levitated dog. What did it mean? Assuming the imaginary presence of Gethsemane Walters did not really have corporeal form, it meant somebody must have rigged this shot up. But to what purpose? And was it really possible that the spirit of Gethsemane could have travelled to Hughesovka?

The next day dragged by, we skirted alpine foothills and entered Austria. Vienna arrived and four Austrian policemen boarded the train and took Edgbaston away. They saluted me and called me 'sir' but didn't say why they were taking him away and I knew cops well enough not to waste time asking. Stanley avoided my gaze.

The sky filled with cloud, the light dimmed, the waiter was replaced by a plumper, less supercilious one with a moustache. Dumplings appeared on the menu and Budapest station slid past the window. It was nice being alone in the compartment. I examined the letter Sospan had given me to deliver to Mr Tepes. It seemed improbably light considering its contents were somehow of such moment that they were paying for our travel expenses to Hughesovka. I obtained a flask of boiling water from the dining car and back in the compartment I steamed open the letter. It was empty. I was a courier for an empty envelope.

That evening, Natasha was late for dinner and missed the soup course. Calamity read through the itinerary. 'We need to get the local train to Sighişoara and then look out for Igor. He's got a walleye. We deliver the envelope . . .'

'Which is empty.'

'Which is empty. We deliver it to the Count and dine tonight as his guest. Tomorrow we get the milk train back to Brasov and pick up the Orient Express from there.'

'Are you sure he is a Count?' I asked.

Calamity looked mildly irritated. 'Of course he is! He's directly descended from Vlad the Impaler. That makes him a count or something like it.'

'It just says Mr on the envelope.'

'He probably doesn't like to give himself airs.' She considered for a second and then said, 'So, how much of the fare does this side-trip pay for?'

'All of it. Our entire trip to Hughesovka is being paid for by the Count.'

'That's a bit strange, isn't it?'

'Considering the envelope we are delivering seems to be empty, that's very strange.'

'Maybe he likes Welsh envelopes.'

'That's possible but for a man of such means there must be easier ways of satisfying his craving.'

'Maybe he likes visitors from Wales.' Calamity scraped her soup spoon in random circles across the base of her dish, her brow furrowed by the intrusion of a new thought. 'So who do you think killed Arianwen?'

'The Witchfinder.'

'Why do you think that?'

'Well, who do you think did it?'

'The Witchfinder,' said Calamity. 'But I don't know why. Just because I think he's insane. Do you think he killed the students?'

'Yes.'

'Why?'

'I don't know. I just do. He's mixed up in all this, but I'm not sure what all this is. The bit where he goes to see Goldilocks on death row is the giveaway.'

'Only if Goldilocks was innocent.'

'He was innocent. No one kills a girl and buries her shoes in his own garden. Or at least, some people might but not someone from a criminal gang.'

'We haven't got much to go on, have we?'

'No.'

'Are we doing this to try and nail the Witchfinder for killing Arianwen, or to find out what happened to Gethsemane or because we really liked Uncle Vanya?'

'All of them, I guess. But really because we owe it to Vanya. We have to try and if it doesn't cost us anything . . . we have to try.'

The waiter cleared the soup dishes and asked if Mademoiselle Natasha would be joining us. Calamity explained that she had a slight headache but would be along shortly. After he went, she said, 'I think you need to watch out for Natasha.'

'What do you mean?'

'Honey-trapper. I've got a hunch.'

'What do you know about such things?'

'I've been reading the book. It's all to do with the psychology. First thing they do is tell the guy he is different. Every man secretly thinks he is different.'

'Haven't you got better things to do than read such nonsense?'

'It's not nonsense. We can adapt some of the techniques in our own investigations.'

'Somehow I doubt it.'

'Then comes the saviour routine. All men dream of saving a damsel in distress. So the girl pretends to be in some kind of trouble and doesn't know what to do. It sounds corny but men can't resist it. Then there is some mushy stuff about the poor little sisters and brothers starving by the empty hearth at home.'

'What happens if the guy guesses it's a honey-trap?'

'The girl just admits it and burst into tears. She tells him she has broken the cardinal rule of honey-trapping and fallen in love with the John. Works every time.'

A moment later Calamity kicked me under the table to warn of the arrival of Natasha. 'Hi,' she said looking up and speaking in that artificial tone of voice that indicates you have just been talking about the person arriving. 'Hope your headache is better.'

Later, as Hungary faded unseen and Romania fused with it somewhere, Calamity made the excuse of tiredness and returned to her compartment to read more of her book. Natasha grabbed my hand and begged forgiveness for the performance of the previous night.

'I'm so ashamed,' she said, although I was not sure why. 'Dragging you into all this.'

'Into all what?'

'No, no, no don't! It's my problem.'

'Are you in trouble?'

'Please don't make me say! Let's get drunk and forget all our pain and woe. The night is still young – waiter! Waiter! Another bottle of wine, please!' She emptied the one already on the table into our glasses, filling them to the brim and spilling the dark ruby wine on to the tablecloth. She gulped back half a glass and forced me to do the same. She did it again and again and soon we were drunk. I asked about Hughesovka and she told me about the mausoleum in which they kept the embalmed body of John Hughes. I said it sounded wonderful. I talked about the challenges facing someone in the spinning-wheel trade. Midway into the third bottle of wine the conversation dropped and she looked sad. There was silence.

'What's wrong?' I said. I grasped her hand across the table.

'Everything, everything, it's all so . . . so . . . horrible.'

'Tell me about it.'

'I can't, oh God! I should never have dragged you into it. You're such a good, decent, kind man . . .'

'Tell me about the trouble you are in. Maybe I can help.'

She stroked my hand and smiled through tears welling up. 'It's kind of you but what can a . . . a guy who sells little wheels do against . . . against them?'

'But—'

'Oh Louie, you are so sweet! A sweet old, dear old, salesman who spends his days looking at treadles and yarn and never even dreams of the sort of problems girls like me get into.'

'Girls like you?'

'You see! Two days and you still haven't guessed. You're such a sweetie.'

'What are you saying?'

'Oh Louie, don't look like that, it's not a criticism. I like you being innocent. It's so funny. That other gentleman knew straight away.'

'What other gentleman?'

'The one who murdered his wife and kids. Mr Edgbaston.'

'Who told you he did that?'

'The guard.' She looked away bashfully. 'He knew my game too.'

'Are you saying you are a prostitute?'

She gasped in horror. 'Louie, how dare you! Of all the . . . well . . . I . . .'

'I'm sorry, I'm confused, it's the wine. I didn't mean it . . .'

She smiled. 'Yes, now it's me being silly. After all, there's not a lot of difference, really, is there?'

'Between what?'

'You know, a girl like what you said, and what I do for a living.'

'What do you do?'

'I'm a honey-trapper, silly!'

'You are?'

'Yes.'

'Who you trying to trap?'

'Why, you of course!'

I blinked in astonishment.

'Oh, you look so funny. Your face!'

'But why?'

'To pass my exams, why else? You see, I haven't qualified yet, I'm still learning.'

'But why on earth are you dressed in Welsh national dress?'

'Because you're from Wales. They told me it would turn you on.' Her face fell. 'But of course if you don't think I'm pretty it doesn't matter really how I dress, does it?'

'But you are pretty.'

'That's exactly the sort of sweetheart thing I would expect you to say. That's what I like about you, Louie, you're different.'

'No I'm not.'

'You see! Every other man I've said that to has been secretly flattered.'

'So you've said it to lots of men, have you?'

'Only in class. This is my first . . . practical.'

'I'm touched.'

'As I say, it's my first time, so don't expect the earth to move . . . except outside the window, ha ha!' She gave a shrill drunken laugh at her feeble joke.

'But we're . . . we're not going to . . . you know. Are we?'

'You don't want me?'

'Of course I want you, but it feels all wrong. You just offering it to me like a butcher giving me a steak. A man needs to . . . to . . .'

'You need to woo me, don't you? I should have known. It's my inexperience, you see. I've blown it. Now I'll never get the job . . .' Her face twisted in anguish. 'Oh Louie!' She squealed and grasped my hand with fervour. 'Can't we just do it and forget about the world and everything in it? Just one night, that's all. Oh please, Louie, please make love to me. Think of my little sisters starving in Hughesovka, don't you want them to have a life too? Do you want to condemn them to spending the rest of their lives travelling on the Orient Express dressed in stovepipe hats? Is that what you want? Don't they deserve to have a life too? Don't they deserve to see the beautiful trees and flowers and walk under the stars just like you?'

'This is just crazy.'

'Think of little Lizaveta and Tanya, Louie. Think of their little hungry tummies and the pain in their uncomprehending eyes as they sit next to the cold fireplace.'

'They won't starve . . .'

'Oh but they will, they will, you don't know how it is in Hughesovka. Do you think I would be doing this if I had any choice?'

'That makes it even worse.'

'No, no, I mean of course I want to do it with you but . . .'

'Why don't we just pretend we did it. Who's to know?'

'My teachers would know when they developed the film.'

I groaned. 'Look, Natasha, how old are you?'

Frustration creased her features. 'Does it matter?'

'Yes.'

'Eighteen.'

'No you're not.'

'I will be soon. Honestly, don't worry about it. Girls in Hughesovka lose their virginity when they are twelve.'

'That's not the point.'

'But, of course, I'm not like them, if that's what you are thinking. My father was ever so strict. All through my teens he wouldn't let me out from under his eye.'

'What did he say when you took this job?'

'He locked me in my room, so I escaped.'

'You see!'

'Oh Louie, don't worry about silly old papa, he's so old-fashioned!' She paused and her brow clouded. 'What's wrong?'

'Natasha, I want you to stop all this honey-trap silliness and go back to your father.'

'Oh Louie!'

'I've never had a daughter so I can't pretend to know exactly what your father must be going through but I do have my partner Calamity. She is about the same age as you, and . . . look, don't ask me to explain.'

'I understand,' she said softly, with a deflated air. She drew back across the table. She wrapped her arms around herself. 'Brrr! how cold the night is!'

I took off my jacket, walked round to her side of the table and put it across her shoulders.

'I've been a complete idiot,' she said. 'I've really put my foot in it.'

'Forget it, it's nothing.'

'You don't understand. I've made a terrible mistake, the one mistake you must never make. The one they all warn you about. What a fool I am!'

'What mistake?'

'I've fallen in love with you.'

Chapter 19

A SHORT HAIRY man called Igor with a walleye and saliva permanently dripping from the corner of his mouth picked us up in a buggy from the station at Sighişoara. We drove at great speed through the town as the setting sun festered like a crimson wound in the Transylvanian sky. Igor thrashed the backs of the horses mercilessly with his whip and flung curses at the nags in the ancient Bohemian tongue of his ancestors. Peasants leaped aside and crossed themselves as we passed. We thundered down the cobbled streets, through the main square and on towards a hill overlooking the town upon which stood a gloomy castle. It looked like a collection of organ pipes carved from the bones of a giant upon which had been placed in a variety of sizes some witches' hats made of red tile. From time to time ravens swooped down off the battlements and rose again in lazy arcs to stain the face of the setting sun. A wind picked up and Calamity drew herself against me for warmth. The road twisted up the face of the crag and along the way we passed groups of peasants carrying torches who waved their fists at us in a strange greeting.

Igor cast anxious looks at the progress of the torch-carriers and cracked the whip even more, hurling ever fiercer imprecations at the horses. We crested a rise and clattered over a wooden drawbridge as Igor sitting above us suddenly ducked. Even so, the ragged tooth of the lowering portcullis almost parted his hair.

Our bags were carried away on the backs of two dwarfs in servant livery and we were shown into a hall the size of a modest cathedral. Igor assured us that the Count would be down shortly. The heads of animals hunted long ago watched us balefully through glass eyes that gleamed like the embers of a fire. Suits of armour receded into the gloom like Russian dolls, and torches pinned to the bare stone walls threw a dancing illumination that left much of the hall in shadow. Tapestries depicting ancient scenes of the chase through the forests of medieval Carpathia fluttered above our heads, and set against walls built from single blocks of stone the size of wardrobes were pieces of oaken furniture that seemed designed for the people of Brobdingnag.

Calamity gazed at everything in wonder and said, 'You know this letter we are delivering to the Count, is there any reason why Mooncalf couldn't have posted it?'

Two servants, formerly hidden behind stuffed bears, strode forth and opened two iron-studded doors. The Count stepped through to greet us. He had fine aquiline features, swept-back silver hair, and was dressed in a black Jesuitical frock that encased him from throat to floor.

'Mr Louie and Miss Calamity!' he said. 'How good of you to come. Welcome to my humble abode.' He gave a dismissive wave as if to apologise for the modesty of his living arrangements. I handed him the letter from Mooncalf and he took it to one side to read in the flickering light of a torch. He opened the empty envelope, paused for a second, and then cried out in theatrical delight. He threw the envelope with a flourish into the flames of a roaring fire. 'Mooncalf is a great man,' he said.

A wolf howled.

The Count explained that dinner would be served in an hour's time and entrusted us in the meantime into the care of his house-keeper Frau Folterkammer, whom, he said, we must not pester with questions because she had no tongue. Frau Folterkammer led us to our chambers in the south wing carrying before her an iron candelabrum with seven tines. The corridor was a vortex of conflicting draughts and the flames of each candle twisted in agony as if each one was a virgin being consumed by the fire of the Inquisition. The floor was flooded with silver fire that was the moon cut into slices by the leaded lights. We passed an old dame sitting on a wooden settle and counting her rosary with rheumatic fingers. A door was open to our right and inside the dark chamber we caught the unmistakable outline of a spinning wheel. We paused and peered in; we saw no one but heard the sound of a girl weeping. Frau Folterkammer waved her hand angrily in front of my face and urged me to move on. I apologised for my indiscreet curiosity. It was a Semi-Saxon horizontal with the sheathed bobbin and slip-backed flyer. Old, but still good.

Frau Folterkammer stopped outside a door and indicated it was Calamity's room. She handed me the candelabrum. As she went to open the door our attention was drawn to a sound coming from the room opposite – children's laughter, and a music box faintly playing 'Für Elise'. Instinctively we turned towards the sound whereupon Frau Folterkammer waved her hand in a dumb show meant to indicate the room was out of bounds. She ushered Calamity into her room. The fire was made up in the grate and, the casements open, heavy velvet drapes wafted gently in the night wind. Frau Folterkammer went to close the windows. In the centre of the room was a four-poster and Calamity's suitcase had already been laid at its foot. I agreed to meet Calamity later for dinner and followed Frau Folterkammer to my own chamber next door.

Evening dress had been laid out for me and there was a small en suite bathroom attached to my room. I showered and dressed for dinner. There was a knock on the door. It was Calamity.

'I just want to tell you that the eyes of the portrait above the mantelpiece follow me round the room.' I grinned but a look of consternation furrowed Calamity's features. 'I'm not joking. And my wardrobe is full of bridal gowns in my size.'

'How do you know they are bridal gowns?'

'They look like it.'

'They probably belong to someone else. It's not your room, after all.'

'My name is written inside the collar.'

'It's probably some sort of local national costume which you are expected to wear for dinner. You should be grateful to the Count for being so thoughtful. Look, I've got evening wear for dinner, isn't that something?'

'I'm just telling you, that's all. Here, take one of these.' She held out a tin containing garlic capsules. 'Just in case.'

'Now you're being silly.'

She took two from the tin and put them in the breast pocket of my jacket. 'Maybe.'

Calamity went back to her room and ten minutes later she knocked again. 'There's a mob carrying torches outside my window, across the moat.'

I pulled a face and Calamity told me to go and have a look. I peered outside but couldn't see anything unusual. 'It was probably the gardeners,' I suggested. 'Stop worrying about that and change for dinner.'

'You really think I should wear one of those dresses?'

'I think it would be very rude not to.'

She emitted a loud sigh and returned to her room.

Ten minutes later there was another knock but this time it was not Calamity. An old woman stood in the doorway in great distress. She wore a long flowing nightdress and her grey hair fell in untidy skeins from beneath a traditional night cap. She had been weeping and carried a candle. 'It's the twins,' she cried. 'We must help them, I smelled burning . . . come . . . come . . .' She grabbed my hand. At that moment, a man, similarly dressed, appeared at the other end of the corridor.

'Anneliese,' he cried. 'No, no, no! Come back.'

Anneliese pulled my hand and dragged me after her. 'The twins, we must help them, oh the smoke, the smoke!'

'No, Anneliese,' shouted the man. 'No! Stop!'

'The smoke, oh the smoke! We have to help the poor twins!'

'Sir, sir, stop her, I beseech you!'

The man was old and ran towards us with a feeble gait. Anneliese dragged me to the door across the corridor from which earlier we had heard the sound of children's laughter and the music box.

'No, Anneliese, no!' cried the man.

'The twins, the twins . . . oh the burning . . .'

The old man was almost upon us but arrived a half-second too late. Anneliese opened the door to the room and gasped. She stood trembling violently on the threshold and her hands flew to her face; she wept. The man caught her in his arms and comforted her. I looked into the room. It was a child's bedroom but one that had evidently not been used for many years; white drapes were spread over the furniture and the air had a stale, musty smell. On the mantelpiece there was a photo of two children in Edwardian sailor suits. The room also had a faint smell of smoke. The man led the weeping woman away.

We were shown to a modest hall and seated at a long table beneath shields emblazoned with lions and stars and griffins, and cross-hatched in red and white chevrons like military sentry boxes. Calamity looked ill at ease in a dress that did appear to be very much like a Western bridal gown. The Count arrived accompanied by his three daughters and Monsieur Souterain, their lute tutor. The children were nine, ten and eleven years old and wore richly brocaded and pearl-studded gowns in white taffeta. They were skinny and gaunt, with dark intense gazes that stared out from the violet shadows of their cheeks. They introduced themselves with slow languorous curtsies. Salome, Porphyria and Medea. The lute tutor bowed politely and the Count glanced at Calamity with a look of mild surprise that seemed to be directed at the dress. 'In our country we normally wait until the big day,' he said. And then, mindful of having committed a minor offence against etiquette, hurriedly changed the subject. 'You must tell us all about Aber-ystwyth.'

We talked for a while of the Pier and the bandstand and Clip the stuffed sheepdog in the museum, but although the Count interjected now and again with polite enthusiasm it was clear our efforts failed to ignite a fire of interest in his dark eyes.

'The camera obscura is the biggest in Europe,' said Calamity.

'How interesting,' said the man whose family had invented an entire Hollywood movie genre.

'Yes, and on a clear day you can see Snowdon. And we've got a nice castle . . .' She looked up at the stone eagles and griffins and escutcheons and swords, the chain mail, the old masters and tapestries depicting hawks and riders galloping the flower-embroidered plains of medieval Europe and said, 'It's not quite like this, though.'

'I'm sure it's delightful,' said the Count.

'Do you know the people in the town crossed themselves when they saw us?' I said.

The Count scoffed. 'It's just a joke, they do it because of our family's history. They find it funny. I suppose it is in a way but one does get tired of it.'

'Are they still unhappy about the impaling?' said Calamity.

The Count shrugged. 'The impaling thing is rather overdone if you ask me. It was just a normal part of keeping order in those days. There have to be laws otherwise there is anarchy.'

'We heard your ancestor once impaled a donkey,' she said with a regrettable lack of tact.

The children emitted gasps and the atmosphere froze. The Count threw his napkin down in disgust, causing the knife to rattle against his plate. 'You know, that, if you will permit me the observation, is such a tiresomely British thing to say. My ancestor impaled an estimated ninety thousand people in the early fifteenth century, not to speak of countless other atrocities, and yet the one crime we are never allowed to forget is the damned donkey. I know you have a reputation as a nation of animal lovers but this is absurdly sentimental.'

I felt the cold moist swab of a lizard's tongue on the back of my hand. I looked down with a slight shudder. Porphyria was rubbing my skin with her fingers in the same way that a buyer in an Arab bazaar checks the quality of cloth. She made a soft gurgling sound. I jerked my hand away. She stared deep into my eyes, her gaze filled with a mocking glint of corruption, and incanted a ditty:

> . . . and all her hair
> In one long yellow string I wound
> Three times her little throat around,
> And strangled her. No pain felt she;
> I am quite sure she felt no pain.
> As a shut bud that holds a bee,
> I warily oped her lids: again
> Laughed the blue eyes without a stain.

Conversation around the table died as she spoke and the last words were said to a hushed audience. There was a pause and then Monsieur Souterain raised his hands artificially high, to the level of his nose, and clapped in counterfeited enthusiasm. 'Bravo! Bravo!' he cried. It seemed to me, in the absurd exaggeration of his applause, that he lived in daily fear of some terrible fate that fell in the gift of the children to visit upon him. Porphyria twisted her head up and around, throwing the tutor for the briefest fraction of a second a sniff-encased look of withering contempt. The clapping stopped, the final cycle arrested in mid-air by that heart-piercing look. Robbed of their purpose, his fingers fluttered like those of a concert pianist playing Paganini and then retracted into the palms of his hands. He lowered them and stared with a chastised air at his cutlery.

Porphyria eyed him briefly and said to her vanquished tutor, 'Phwee!'

There was a pause.

'I need to go to the little girl's room,' said Calamity.

The Count flashed in anger. 'Who told you about that? There isn't one. It's a lie!'

'I mean, the you know . . .'

'Papa!' said Salome. 'She means the water closet.'

The Count smiled. 'Oh yes, of course. Forgive me. It's at the top of the stairs, next to the nursery.'

Calamity turned to offer her thanks but the girl poked her tongue out, quickly, while the Count was looking elsewhere. Monsieur Souterain caught the gesture but, instead of offering admonishment, made a forlorn attempt to ingratiate himself in Salome's favour by offering complicit glances and feigning mild shock at her naughtiness. Salome disdained the offer of an alliance and in a move of exquisite cruelty gave the tutor a long-drawn-out quizzical look that directed everyone's attention to the odd face he was pulling. His spirit crushed, Monsieur Souterain returned his attention to his turbot and for the next few minutes the silence in the room was broken only by a tinny Morse code as the fish knife in his trembling hand rattled against bone china.

We ate in silence. Porphyria started rubbing my flesh again. I took out one of the garlic capsules and put it in my mouth. I bit and breathed at her. The result was dramatic. She jumped back and began coughing violently. Her hand flew to her mouth as if she was about to be sick and the other hand sought furiously in the folds of her heavy dress; she found her purse and snapped it open, taking out an asthma puffer. She drew deep and long breaths on the inhaler, interspersed with agonising groans.

'It's nothing, do not be alarmed,' shouted the Count trying to restore calm. The tutor took the girl to the window and opened the casement. She continued to cough and gasp.

'Just a little childhood asthma,' announced the Count.

Calamity returned and whispered into my ear. 'There's a rocking-goat in the nursery.'

I inclined my head and hissed, 'A what?'

'Rocking-goat.'

'Is everything OK?' asked the Count seeing us confer.

'Absolutely wonderful,' I said. 'Calamity was just complimenting you on the . . . porcelain of your bathroom.'

He smiled and in that diplomatic smile could be seen generations of breeding that had perfected the art over the years of concealing disbelief, of smiling while plotting to stab. Calamity smiled back, equally false, but without the advantage of generations of breeding. She said, 'Actually, I was just telling Louie that there appears to be a mob carrying torches outside my window.'

The Count dismissed her remark with a slight wave of his hand. 'If you are concerned about them keeping you awake, I really shouldn't worry. They soak their brands in tar, you see, which means they usually go out after about forty minutes. Once that happens the men tend to lose motivation and retire to the inn.'

'Are they angry about something?' I asked.

The Count gave a weary sigh. 'Angry? Of course they are angry, they are serfs, they live in a permanent state of choler.' He raised a goblet of wine and then thrust it back down on the table, causing the wine to spill. 'I mean, it really is too much sometimes. They are an ungrateful lot in the village, they really are. They moan incessantly about the excesses of my ancestors and yet half of them have turned their hovels into boutique hotels to accommodate a tourist trade that wouldn't exist were it not for the excesses they so loudly condemn. If it wasn't for us they would still be eating turnips and swedes. You see them carrying medieval torches above their heads but half of them drive Volvos. But they forget, you see; that's the trouble with serfs, they have very selective memories.' He turned to his man-servant who was standing at the fireplace. 'Igor, what are they moaning about this time?'

'Easter 1393, my lord.'

The Count made a choking sound in the back of his throat that signified exasperation and said, 'Oh, for Pete's sake!'

'What happened at Easter 1393?' asked Calamity.

'Oh just a bit of harmless tomfoolery,' said the Count. 'One of my ancestors needed a new castle in a hurry, you see, so he organised an Easter party for the villagers. They all turned up in their Sunday best and there spread out before them were tables heaving under a feast the like of which they had never seen before in their sweaty lives. There was roasted ox and venison, chickens and partridges and all manner of dainty fowl, milk-fed veal and suckling pig, hedgehog pie and rabbit pâté, squirrel soufflé and pan-roasted field mouse, carp from their lord's ponds, and real *blancmanger* made with lamb and almonds and for afters there was Turkish delight made with the tears of a virgin. All day they filled their red pox-scarred faces with my ancestor's finest Burgundy; they danced and sang and partied and burped until sundown at which point they all learned a rather painful truth about there being no such thing as a free lunch. At an order from the Count they were all surrounded by soldiers while the blacksmith went from each to each putting fetters upon wrist and ankle. Then, still wearing their party clothes, the entire village was force-marched fifty miles north to a desolate windswept rocky promontory where they were told to start building a castle. As I say, it really is a rather droll tale. They worked from before dawn till late into the night, and were given just enough food to keep daily funerals in the single figures and ensure that work was not interrupted by excesses of weeping. Travellers who passed through the region nine months later related wonderful tales of seeing these workers slaving away almost naked because their clothes had rotted to rags and fallen quite away.'

'Did they ever return to their village?' I asked.

'You know,' said the Count thoughtfully, 'I really can't remember. I think they all died during the construction of the castle but it is possible the Count had them put to death. He would have been quite justified in doing so since the workmanship was appallingly shoddy. In fact, when the Count saw the finished castle he refused to set foot in it and used it instead to store his hosiery. But the moral is one of rank ingratitude: seven hundred years later and the locals still bang on about that castle but not one of them ever mentions the lovely party that preceded it.'

There was a short silence after the Count had finished his story, and the servants poured the coffees. The Count stood up and said, 'Porphyria, take Miss Calamity off to play with your toys after dinner. Mr Louie, you will find port and cigars in the library. You must excuse me, I rather fancy an early night, we have a great day ahead of us tomorrow, is it not so?'

'Yes,' I said. 'I was meaning to ask you about the arrangements. We need to catch the early train to Brasov.'

A mild confusion creased his brow and then he burst into a wide grin. 'Ha ha ha! Early train to Brasov! Yes very good, very dry. Your sense of humour is apt to catch one unawares.' He raised his glass. 'And now, before I retire, why don't you all join me in one last toast to our patron and provider, the great Mr Mooncalf!'

Later, as I sat on a wine-coloured chesterfield enjoying the Count's port, Monsieur Souterain appeared looking flustered.

'Where is Mademoiselle Calamity?' he said.

'She's playing with the children.'

'Oh no! No, this must not be! You must leave this place tonight.'

'But we've only just arrived.'

'You must flee, you are in great danger, you must flee tonight. And take me with you. I have arranged everything. A carriage will wait by the scullery door tonight at nine. From your room, follow the corridor away from the great hall and take the first left after you pass the triptych depicting the Impaling of the Mother and Child. There you will find a staircase that leads directly to the scullery. Look out for the maid with webbed fingers, she will show you to the carriage . . .'

'Souterain!' a voice rang out along the cold stone corridors. His eyes opened wide with fear. 'I must go. Please, I beseech you, find Calamity, nine o'clock, remember!' He ran away looking back. 'Remember!' he cried. 'Nine o'clock.'

'Webbed fingers,' I shouted.

A few seconds later Porphyria appeared.

'Have you seen Monsieur Souterain?'

'No, not since dinner.'

'I thought I heard voices.'

'Yes, it seems to be a peculiar property of this castle; we heard children's voices just now from an empty room.'

'Those would be the little twins.'

'Will we be meeting them?'

'I hardly think so. They died in a fire ninety years ago. Do not be alarmed, the appearance of this particular apparition signifies good fortune unless accompanied by the sound of a music box.'

'Have you seen Calamity?'

'I last saw her in the nursery admiring the statue of Pan!' She walked off giving a silvery laugh. Moments later I heard her shout, 'Souterain, on your knees, you dog!'

I abandoned my port and went to find Calamity. I wandered along the many corridors calling her name, but I saw no one. The nursery was empty and my attention was drawn to the sound of a commotion outside. I walked over to the casements. The mob of villagers beyond the moat had gone but within the grounds of the castle there appeared to be some form of chase involving men with dogs and torches, in pursuit of a man running across the ornamental lawns. I returned to my room and found Calamity changed back into jeans and T-shirt, packing my case. 'We're leaving,' she said. 'Igor has told me everything. I'm due to marry the Count tomorrow.'

'There must be a misunderstanding,' I said.

'Why? How do you think Mooncalf got the tickets so cheap?'

'He's got contacts in the trade.'

'You can say that again. Did you take a look at the doll's house in the nursery? One of the rooms in it has the charred corpses of two little babies in bed.'

'What's that got to do with anything?'

'We're leaving.' She looked at me, her eyes sparkling with fear. 'Please, Louie.'

From outside the noise of the chase grew suddenly louder. The barking of dogs rose to a pitch of intoxication that suggested their snapping jaws were only inches now from the tailcoat of their quarry; and rising above their incessant yapping there came the loud clear call of a man falling followed by what sounded like a splash.

I changed back into my travelling clothes, picked up the bags, and we ran. In the scullery, we were met by a girl in a ragged dirndl carrying a small shovel and box of cinders. There were sooty smears on her cheeks. She smiled, put the shovel down and splayed the fingers of her hand before us. They were webbed. She led us through the kitchen and out of a side door to where our coach was waiting. The mob of villagers stood on either side holding their torches aloft. When they saw us they cheered and rushed forward to guide us into the carriage.

'What about Souterain?' I cried.

'It is too late for him,' a voice answered. 'There is no time to lose.'

The coach door was slammed and the whip cracked in the night. We were jolted forward and the villagers cheered again. As we raced off into the night, lightning flashed in the night sky. High above us, on a grassy slope falling away to the moat, the servants of the Count were gathered, and seemed to be dragging something wet and heavy and man-shaped from the moat. Just then lightning flashed once more and picked out three little girls who burned like Roman candles in their gowns of taffeta. They stood erect, and proud, like marble statues unmoved by the pitiful scene being enacted before them. Three little girls who would not be having lute lessons the next day.

Chapter 20

CALAMITY RETURNED from the samovar with two glasses of black tea. 'We still owe the *provodnitsa* three gryvnia for the bowl of cabbage soup we had at breakfast,' she said. 'That was good soup.'

'It sure was. Of the fifteen bowls of cabbage soup we've had on the ferry and this train, this *provodnitsa*'s was definitely the best.'

I warmed my hands round the hot tea. This morning had started quite chilly, and the carriage had still not warmed up. Last night's soup had been in Odessa, and the five bowls before that had been on the Black Sea ferry from Istanbul.

'I can't believe Mooncalf would promise me as a bride like that,' said Calamity.

'We don't know for sure that he did.'

'That's what Igor said.'

'It might have been a misunderstanding, English isn't his first language.'

'Oh sure! What about the wedding dress, and the empty envelope? And . . . Monsieur Souterain.'

'That was a terrible accident, I don't see what that has to do with Mooncalf.'

'We ought to report him to Llunos.'

'He'd just say Transylvania was outside his jurisdiction.'

'Yeah, he'd say it served us right for going there, and for leaving our travel arrangements to someone like Mooncalf.' Calamity looked at me and brightened as the truth of that remark sank in. We both knew that was exactly what Llunos would say, and he would be right. 'I'm sure Hughesovka will be a lot better,' she said.

'That's right, even Mooncalf wouldn't try and marry you twice.'

Calamity grinned and punched me on the arm and we both gazed out at the countryside flowing by. The gently rolling farmland of the Western Ukraine slowly gave way to the outskirts of that longed-for Eldorado, Hughesovka. Some people said it didn't exist, it was just a far-off, remote, hopeless land of dreamers, where every home was an ice-cream castle in the air for romantics and fools. We were about to find out.

A man wearing a plain grey two-piece suit stood on the platform staring intently at everyone who stepped down. He was holding a sign saying 'Louie and Calamity. Croeso i Hughesovka'. When he saw us, his face burst into a grin, he put the sign under his arm and rushed forward to greet us. 'Mr Louie and Miss Calamity! I'm delighted to meet you; I'm Jones the Denouncer. You are just as Mr Mooncalf described you.' He stopped and peered up the platform beyond our shoulders. 'But where are the spinning wheels?'

'They are being sent on,' I said.

He took us through the main ticketing hall, down the steps into Ploschchad John Hughes, and across the car park to a battered Lada. The buildings in the vicinity of the station had an impressive faded grandeur. Directly across from the station was the ornate portico with winged angels of the Hughesovka Ballet. Next to that there were the golden onion domes of the church. And in the centre, where the trams pulled up to turn around, there stood a statue to the great Welsh steelman who had made it all possible. Jones the Denouncer told me the streets had originally been laid out according to the street plan of Merthyr Tydfil.

We drove down Bulvar John Hughes, the main boulevard, flanked by chestnut trees and with a central reservation of trees and grass where young lovers and old ladies in head scarves sat on benches. The avenue terminated at the steps of the Hughes Mausoleum, a large building fronted by Doric columns. There we turned into Vulitsya Kreshchatyk and again into Prospekt Bakunina by which time we had left the centre and were entering the suburbs. The buildings got smaller, the tram lines ended, and we found ourselves in a wasteland of featureless modern apartment blocks.

'Wow! It's just like Penparcau,' said Calamity for whom all new experiences were a source of wonder.

'Where is that?' Jones the Denouncer shouted above the din of the engine.

'It's a housing estate in Aberystwyth.'

'You must write it down for me, I am thirsty for all knowledge about the Motherland.'

We stopped and got out at one of the tenements. The lift was broken, the common areas stank of urine. We climbed a dark, graffiti-covered stairwell to the fifteenth floor and were let into a barely furnished apartment: tattered linoleum floor, a few religious icons on the wall, a table covered with an oilcloth set with food. The table was laid with glasses and chipped, floral-patterned china. There were hard-backed chairs and no soft furnishings. There was a large group of people waiting and when we entered they cheered and ran forward to hug and embrace us. Music started up and Jones the Denouncer said, 'Louie, you will be staying with the consumptive student one floor up and Calamnotchka will be staying with the public prosecutor's clerk's daughter. I will take you there in a while, but first we must celebrate.'

We ate slices of pig fat with chillis, gherkins, caviar, black bread and vodka. Jones the Denouncer introduced us to the company. Evans the Swindler, Morgan the Enemy of the People, Williams the Betrayer of the Proletariat, Jones the Deviationist heretic, Edwards the Fascist Wrecker, and Lewis the Pedlar of Nationalist Opiate under the banner of Proletarian Literature; together with their wives. It was difficult to keep track of all the names.

'So this is the Welsh Underground.' said Calamity.

There was an awkward silence after she said this. Edwards the Fascist Wrecker explained, 'We don't normally talk about our . . .

our nature quite as openly, but, yes, I suppose that's as good a term as any.'

'What do you do?'

'We meet when and where we can, in safe houses mostly. We also print our own samizdat . . .' He pulled out a tattered and tightly rolled-up mimeographed pamphlet. It was called *Hiraeth* and bore on the cover an illustration of Barry Island pleasure park. A woman dressed in a dowdy red peasant dress and a sleeveless pullover stepped forward and spoke with a certain fiery passion that indicated that she and Edwards the Fascist Wrecker were engaged or married but she tired of his slow dithering ways and regretted that he could not apply himself with more fervour to the cause.

'Our aim is to return to the Motherland for which we all ache so terribly in our hearts. But, of course, the authorities will never allow such a thing. And so we try to gather what scraps of information we can. Your visit to us today is a great and longed-for honour. Occasionally we organise an escape. But the authorities are cruel and cunning and thwart us at every turn.'

'What do they do?' I asked.

Lewis the Pedlar of Nationalist Opiate under the banner of Proletarian Literature replied soulfully as if he bore the pain of all the failures in his own heart. 'They intercept our escapers and arrest them. We don't see them for many months. What happens to them is not clear but we believe they are taken to a special psychiatric institution where they are re-educated. The doctors at this place are without mercy. They erase entirely the memory of the re-education and implant in its place the false memory of having reached Aberystwyth and found it a great disappointment. After the treatment they are released back into life in Hughesovka but they are not the same as they were before. They avoid their old haunts, shun their old friends and contacts. After many months, quite by chance, one of us will run into one of them in the bread queue or something, and say, "Hi, Boris, what are you doing here, I thought you'd gone to Wales?" And he will refuse to answer, look away and mumble something sheepishly, some absurd story about how he travelled to Wales and decided to come back because he didn't think it was all that good.' The people in the room scoffed in disgust at the absurdity of the notion.

'So far,' said the girl in the red peasant dress, 'not even the strongest among us has been able to withstand the brainwashing technique.'

A hubbub of conversation broke out as they discussed their oppression. Edwards the Fascist Wrecker spoke up. 'But tell us, Louie Eeyoreovitch, you have seen how we live here, you see how we ache and groan under the yoke, and you have seen the blessed town of Aberystwyth, is it possible that a man who had sampled the delights of which we read, such as Sospan's ice-cream kiosk and the automated fortune-teller in a glass case in the Pier amusement arcade . . .'

The mention of the mechanical gypsy drew gasps of wonder.

'And the kiosk selling whelks freshly scraped from the rocks on the beach,' a voice piped up. More voices added their opinions:

'And the funicular railway that shoots up the face of Constitution Hill at giddying speed . . .'

'And the train of mules that offer rides to sick and weary children along the seafront . . .'

'And bingo, the working man's chess . . .'

'And the rocks that line the seashore, many millions of years old, which are inlaid with a strange red mineral in configurations that some say resembles lettering . . .'

'Some people even claim it spells out the name of Aberystwyth . . .'

'And though many scoff at this notion, yet they cannot explain whence came the letters . . .'

The hubbub rose again as each turned to his neighbour to discuss this latest marvel. Edwards the Fascist Wrecker hit a glass with his fork to bring the room to order, and turned to me: 'Is it really possible that a man having seen such things would willingly return to Hughesovka?'

I scanned the eager faces waiting breathlessly for confirmation that the myth by which they lived their lives was valid. 'No, it is not possible,' I said. 'Only a madman would return.'

My words whipped up the party spirit and more vodka was handed out and many toasts were drunk including one to Comrade Mooncalf. And then they asked me about our business here and I described the case of Gethsemane and the strange photo of the imaginary friend and the levitated dog. The company expressed great excitement and demanded to see the photo. I reached into my jacket pocket but inexplicably the photo was no longer there. I apologised that I was not able to show them. 'This is really strange,' I said. 'I had it on the Orient Express.'

'Someone must have stolen it,' said Williams the Betrayer of the Proletariat.

'Honey-trap,' said Calamity knowingly. I avoided her gaze.

Fortunately my description of the photo rang a bell in the mind of Evans the Swindler. He went to the bookcase and brought back a catalogue; it looked similar to the one Mooncalf had used to evaluate the market price for the Yuri Gagarin sock. He skimmed through to the right page and opened out the book. One page listed Yuri Gagarin socks, worth only a few pence apparently. Not the thousands of pounds Mooncalf had offered us. On the other page was a reproduction of the photo of the levitated dog which could, it said, fetch many thousands of pounds at auction. Mooncalf must have noticed it as he searched for the Yuri Gagarin sock and realised its worth. Then he feigned interest in the sock while really it was the photo he wanted. But had he arranged the honey-trap to steal it as well? It was baffling. Evans the Swindler explained the significance of the photo.

'This image of the levitated dog is the work of a famous retoucher who worked for many years for the security apparat, in a basement across the street from the infamous Lubianka Prison. His job was to help in the re-writing of history by altering photographic evidence to fit the new version of events. This photo was his suicide note. He was given twenty-five years in a camp and died of pneumonia.'

'But what does it mean?' asked Calamity.

'The dog is not really levitating, it is held in the arms of a person but the person has been removed from the picture. His orders were to retouch out the person, remove her from the historical record, which is what he did; but in an act of suicidal impudence he interpreted his directive literally and removed only the person, leaving the dog suspended seemingly in mid-air. This piece of photographic retouching became thereby an act of counter-revolutionary terror. It is impossible that he could not have been aware that in performing this act he was signing his own death warrant. It was a futile anguished cry from the heart rebelling against the compassionless inhumanity of the system. A man who was an artist and should have used his gifts to bring joy and enlightenment to the human race wasted instead the best years of his life and his rich store of talent falsifying history, turning lies to truth, giving false benediction to the tyrant.' He paused and took a breath.

'What exactly is retouching?' said Calamity

The people in the room, who had gone quiet as Evans the Swindler spoke, now turned to him with gazes that urged him to speak. He walked up to Calamity and lowered himself, bending at the knees to be nearer her level. 'Picture the cow grazing in the field,' he said in a bedtime-story voice. 'The cow that goes "moo"; picture her coming to the end of her days. She is old and cannot see or hear very well any more; she has lost her teeth and cannot chew and because she cannot eat she loses weight and grows thin and feeble. Sometimes in the morning, she cannot even get up. Picture the cow that comes to the end of her days.' Calamity was frowning and broke off the gaze of Evans and turned to me. I put on a broad happy idiot smile and nodded as if to encourage her to pay attention. Evans continued. 'Her meat is sold to man, the entrails minced up into dog food, the horn turned into buttons that the prisoner in the lonely depths of winter sometimes boils up for food and gnaws for the ancient echo they contain of a summer meadow. And the old cow's bones may be turned into glue, or by some exquisite alchemy may render us a gelatine so pure, much more so than the variety we find in our cakes and dainties, that it is made into a photographic emulsion containing crystals of silver halide.' He paused and raised his arms to the heavens in adoration. 'Now imagine the sun, the big yellow sun with a happy morning face: he sends us a photon and this little photon arrives on earth and bounces off the first thing it touches and then is refracted down the lens of a camera, and in the belly of that machine it impacts the silver halide which releases an atom of silver. This is the ink of God. Suspended in the gelatine that had once been a cow the atoms of silver preserve a record of the latent image of the world and the deeds done under the sun by men. The history of man is thus written in the incorruptible ink of light and silver. This is called photography. And though silver and gold have traditionally adorned the heads of kings, yet did the humble cow play her part too in this celestial chemistry. This is a thing of wonder! Light, that most elemental of things, the first that God made on the first day, light which fills our hearts each dawn with hope and the strength to carry on in the face of all our difficulties, light that was sent by Him to illumine our world both physically and metaphorically, this same wondrous light exposes our deeds and also records them in the spectral shadow of silver upon celluloid. Here written in light is Truth. The record of our passing, of our joys and sorrows, never to be erased or altered. And herein lies the seeds of wickedness: the tyrant takes this joyous gift and perverts it to his twisted purpose. Through photographic retouching he insults the Creator and impudently undoes His handiwork; he changes and alters, he lies, he turns despots into heroes and erases our suffering, reduces and expunges it, and fills our tears with mud. He brings injustice to birth. All this did the great retoucher understand and against this wickedness set his seal even though it would, he knew, be mortal for him.' Evans the Swindler wiped a tear from his eye and apologised for being over-emotional. The great retoucher was, he said, his father.

'So,' said Calamity with the air of one patiently separating wheat from chaff, 'there used to be a person holding the dog and the authorities airbrushed her from history, but the guy left the dog in the picture.'

Evans the Swindler agreed but looked saddened to have it all presented in such bald outline.

After lunch, Edwards the Fascist Wrecker drove us round Hughesovka. We visited Uncle Vanya's house but it turned out to be a fire-gutted shell occupied only by vagrants. They told us no one had been living there for many years and they had not heard of Vanya. But they were very kind and, while we waited, one of them fetched an old crone who had been living in the area all her life. She told us Mrs Vanya had been murdered in 1957 by her husband. She remembered the date well because it was the same year that Laika had passed in orbit above their heads and filled all their hearts with hope for a while. The school for remote viewing which Vanya's daughter had attended was now a paper wholesaler's. The Museum Of Our Forefathers' Suffering was closed. A thick chain held the door fastened and it was clear that for many years now, the only visitors had been State spiders.

When we returned to the car, Edwards was in a state of nervous agitation. 'I've received a message,' he said. 'Something has happened. We must get back.' He drove as fast as the old Lada would go through the backstreets of Hughesovka and pulled up outside the apartment block. There was consternation in the apartment.

Jones the Deviationist heretic explained what had happened. 'You've been denounced.'

'Denounced?' we both said. 'Who by? What for?'

'We're not sure, but no one has seen Jones the Denouncer since this morning. Quick, there is no time, you must prepare.'

Someone handed us our suitcases. 'There is bread inside and biscuits.'

A girl handed me my jacket: 'I've sewn on cow-horn buttons. In lean times they can be eaten.'

'Are you crazy?' said Williams the Betrayer of the Proletariat. 'He could be killed in the camps for those buttons.'

Someone advised us to avoid becoming unwittingly staked in a card game. 'You should try and get a job decorating,' someone else advised. 'You can eat wallpaper paste. And the leather of your shoes of course. Although your shoes are your most precious possession, do not discard them lightly.'

'The winter nights in Siberia are very long. It is helpful if you can spare some of your bread ration because chewed bread can be used to make chess pieces to while away the night.'

'And do not forget also,' added Morgan the Enemy of the People, 'that when someone dies you must be quick – sneak out in the middle of the night and dig them up for their underwear: for this can be exchanged for a ration of cabbage which will keep your thyroid healthy.'

We were about to thank them for their kind advice when all conversation was silenced by a banging on the door and the words, shouted out, 'Open up, State Security.'

Chapter 21

ROOM IN a basement, off a long corridor with lots of doors. A corridor lit by single naked sixty-watt bulbs hanging from a dim cobwebby ceiling. The far-off sound of typewriters, gurgling radiators. No cries of pain. Yet. A ride through the streets of night-time Hughesovka in the back of a van marked 'Jones's Meat Pies'. I don't know why. I'll ask the interrogator. A room with the same single naked bulb. Walls painted in dark, sea-green gloss paint to halfway and a lighter paint of indeterminable shade above. The light switch next to the door jamb was a crude utilitarian metal box studded with bare rivets. You can tell a lot about your fate by the light switch. In the room, there was a table, two hard chairs, a lamp to point into my face, a manila folder and a pad of legal-size notepaper, for taking notes legal and otherwise. With my hands handcuffed behind my back I was made to sit in the chair. It wasn't comfortable; it wasn't meant to be. A man sat in the chair opposite me. Apart from the drab olive-green military tunic with the letters GKNB on the collar, he looked like one of the Cossack dancers performing in the bar of the Hotel Newport. He had a red, merry face with bushy white eyebrows and a big bulbous nose. He looked like a nice guy, I wanted to hug him. The soldier standing guard at the door might have been nice too but the emptiness in his face, the absence of solicitude suggested he could go either way: whichever way the wind was blowing. I yawned. The man sitting opposite me drummed his fingers on the desk and leafed through the folder. The first page had a photo of me. Somewhere in the night a church struck four. I yawned again and thought of Calamity. We had been separated shortly after arrest. Was she sitting now in a similar pea-green basement room opposite a granite-faced lady Russian hammer thrower who was leafing through a similar folder? I regretted bringing her along. I felt a keen homesickness for the comforting certainties of Aberystwyth, even the unpleasant ones like arrest. One good thing about Aberystwyth is, the cops like their sleep. The idea of interrogating someone in the middle of the night would be considered daft beyond words. The man leafing through the folder containing my life history sighed in a way that suggested it fell short of the mark. Finally he looked up, slowly and painfully as if he had a stiff neck.

'So you are a spinning-wheel salesman.'

I said nothing; it's the same deal in every country in the world: the point of an interrogation is for the cop to listen to the sound of his own voice; to marvel at how clever he is; if you butt in and interrupt the mellifluous flow of self-love you are likely to make your interrogator genuinely annoyed instead of pretend-annoyed. You have to let them gorge first on their own cleverness. It's the sort of cleverness that comes easily to someone who has another human being entirely in his power, but you can't say that for one very good reason: you are entirely in his power. Back in Aberystwyth, when Llunos pulls someone in off the street for questioning, he doesn't really expect to receive answers. You're there to listen to what he's decided you are guilty of. The main thing to remember is, you are of no importance.

'You don't look like a spinning-wheel salesman.'

'That's the secret of my success.'

He nodded thoughtfully and returned his attention to the dossier. He spoke to the pages. 'You are familiar with the story of Sleeping Beauty? Tell me, on what part of the spinning wheel did she prick her finger?'

I shifted in my seat and was overwhelmed by a flood of pins and needles from my wrists. 'Strictly speaking, there isn't anywhere on a Saxon wheel that could prick her finger, there are no needles, although there are cases where the distaff can get sharpened to a point after years of use if remedial action is not taken. It might be sharp enough to give you a jab, but not really break the skin.'

He made a steeple of his fingers and peered at me over them. 'It is interesting that you opt for a literal interpretation. You do not consider, for example, the possibility of a more . . . allegorical approach, looking for the meaning within the gestalt?'

'I must confess I had overlooked that particular avenue.'

My interrogator considered; a faraway look entered his eyes and, for a while, it seemed that I no longer existed for him. He thought for a long minute or two. I waited, fascinated by the sweep of the second hand on his wristwatch which was the only thing moving in the room. Eventually he spoke, but as much to himself as to me. 'A father forbids his daughter from visiting a big tower. You are a man and know what a tower symbolises, I do not need to be so indelicate as to spell it out. In the tower is a terrible secret locked away in a room. The father warns her that entering this room will be perilous. She agrees not to go there, but as she grows the secret room preys upon her mind. And then one day, many years later, perhaps at a time when she has almost forgotten this room, she becomes aware of changes in herself. Physical and emotional changes. It is the most natural thing in the world which all girls must pass through and yet to her, like all girls, it is deeply disconcerting. Perhaps she is distracted by these changes and follows a dark instinct inside her and, without ever consciously intending to, finds herself climbing the steps to the tower. She knows it is wrong, she knows that to disobey her father is the greatest sin a little girl can commit and yet somewhere buried deeply inside her is the knowledge that there comes a time when every young girl must commit this very sin. She reaches the top, her heart beating with fear and excitement and unfocussed expectation; and behold! The door is ajar. Almost as if this day had been preordained, which of course it had. She goes into the room at the top of the forbidden tower and finds a spinning wheel. She begins to spin . . .' He paused in contemplation. 'I must admit the verisimilitude breaks down a little here. This has always struck me as an unsatisfactory part of the story: would a teenage girl symbolically on the trail of her first sexual adventure sit down at mummy's spinning wheel? But no matter. She spins and the rest, as they say, is history. She pricks her finger, there is blood and the girl is ruined, save for the intervention of a good fairy.' He stopped and looked at me expectantly. 'You see?'

'Yes,' I said. 'I see.' I had no idea what he was talking about.

He grimaced. 'You do not see. You have no children and so for you the true significance will always remain purely in the realm of the abstract. But me, ah me! I have a daughter, a beautiful wonderful daughter who is more precious to me than the droplets of blood that visit the chambers of my heart. In this sad sordid world there is nothing as important to me as her happiness. To see her married to a respectable man who would look after her . . . I do not care whether he be rich, although being poor is not easy, just so long as he were a decent man who meant well by her . . . This is my only dream. And this humble goal is none the less a very difficult one to achieve because you and I as men of the world know well what dark qualities are to be found in the hearts of men. Yes, if you had a lovely daughter like mine, you would live this tale every day of your life.' He paused and said, almost sheepishly as if embarrassed to bring the matter up, 'You are not really a salesman, are you, Louie Eeyore-ovitch?'

'Truly, I am a humble salesman.'

'It will be much easier for you if you tell the truth. You might as well. Calamity has told us everything.'

'She wouldn't tell you the time of the next train to Devil's Bridge.'

'She wouldn't need to, we already have that information.'

'If you've harmed her, I will make you pay for it, somehow. One day.'

'Yes, I know, when you get back from the camps. They all say that. But twenty years carrying a pick in a subterranean labyrinth north of the Kolyma River is a long time to keep the flame of hatred alive. Those long dark arctic nights, when the sun shines for less than an hour or two, invariably give a man a different perspective on these things.'

'She's just a kid.'

'Then what are you doing embroiling her in a man's game? Tell me, why are you really here in Hughesovka?'

'I'm attending the Lower Don Collective Spinning Wheel conference.'

'They've never heard of you.'

I shrugged.

'Have you ever played the game known as tug-of-war?'

'Once or twice, at the donkey derby.'

'Do you know how they cut down trees along the Kolyma? We could give them chainsaws but that would be too easy. They might even enjoy it. No, we give them nothing and the clever ones, the survivors, tie rope around the bole of the tree and play tug-of-war to rock the tree out of the frozen tundra. Could you do that wearing nothing but kapok pyjamas in temperatures so cold your spit freezes in mid-air? You think, perhaps, you could handle it. I see you are a brave man, you think if needs must be you will die out there and it will not be so very bad. You think life is a treasure but we must all lose it one day, we must all open the chest to find it empty and acquire therewith the sickening knowledge that it will never again be filled. You think, faced with this, the most implacable fact of all facts, that it ill-behoves a man to quibble about the date of his exit; you think a man is nothing without dignity and to squeak and babble and moan about this is the mark of a man who has abandoned his dignity and is therefore not a man any more. You think all this, I see, because you are a brave and noble man. But you err, my friend, alas! How you err! Your God is not so merciful as to let you die out there in the frigid desert. He has a much worse fate for you in mind, a terrible fate reserved only for the strong ones, for the brave noble strong ones. You will survive! In temperatures so low it is impossible that a man could last a day you will survive twenty years. On a diet so poor and meagre, on a bowl of thin gruel once a day, you will chop down trees or break rocks and it will be impossible, and though it be impossible still you will do it. Every second will be a torment, and each of those seconds of torment will last the entire twenty years. It is impossible that a man so ill-fed, so badly clothed, so overworked could live to tell the tale, and yet you will. And then, when your twenty years are up, they will release you and two weeks after returning to civilisation you will catch cold and die. This is how it happens; no one knows why, but it does. I tell you this because I like you. Please, Louie Eeyoreovitch, I beg you, do not make me do this. Tell us what brought you to Hughesovka.'

'I've already told you.'

He opened a drawer and took out a photo. It was the picture of the levitated dog. 'Could you explain how a humble spinning-wheel salesman came to have this in his possession?'

'I found it on the beach.'

'That is not a good answer, Louie Eeyoreovitch. Mere possession of this item is a crime against our people punishable by a minimum of ten years' penal servitude.'

'I've done nothing wrong.'

'So you say, and yet I see you have cow-horn buttons on your jacket. It reeks of guilt. Who but a malefactor has such things? Did no one tell you we have canteens in our camps? And chess sets too, so there is no need to hoard your bread and chew rooks and knights in the middle of the night. In fact, all camps have libraries with modest audio-visual facilities. We are not so backward as you imagine. You insult us with your cow-horn buttons. Tell me about the photo.'

'I found it on the beach in Aberystwyth and put it in my pocket.'

'And travelled on the Orient Express with this photo which you intended delivering to a contact in exchange for a large sum of money.'

'No.'

'Do you know how much this photo is worth on the black market? Twenty thousand US dollars.'

'I didn't know.'

'Yes, because you found it on the beach. If you confess this, if you admit that you came to Hughesovka in order to sell this photo on the black market, I will help you.'

I said nothing.

'I will personally ensure that you are merely deported; and, what is more, I will tell you what you really want to know: I will tell you how it was that Vanya's daughter came to be possessed by the spirit of Gethsemane Walters.' He noted the surprise on my face and smiled. 'Oh yes, we know all about your errand. Jones the Denouncer has told us everything. We have been aware of the Gethsemane Walters case for many years now. The solution to the mystery can be found right here in Hughesovka. It could be yours, all you need to do is admit to something that we already know.'

He clicked his fingers to get the attention of the guard. 'Leave us now, Pascha. It is time you went home. The hour is late. Do not come back tonight, no matter how terrible the cries of pain you hear.'

The guard clicked his heels in acknowledgement and left. My interrogator watched the door and then gave me a sad, wistful look, the one headmasters wear when they insist the punishment they are about to inflict will, through some miraculous mechanism unknown to biological science, hurt them more than you. He sniffed and dabbed a tear from his eye.

'Louie Eeyoreovitch, you are a brave spy. Your country should be proud of you. As my parting words to you I will give you a piece of advice. In the camps you will hear many stories, most of them are not to be credited. Do not eat the wallpaper paste, it will make you ill. And as for selling the underlinen of dead comrades for a crust of bread . . . once many years ago it might have been possible but not now, you will merely be ridiculed, and quite possibly attract a further five years for desecration of the grave which belongs to the State.'

He paused and stared at me quizzically. I shrugged. He stood up and strode past me to the door. I twisted round in my chair to watch. He turned to me and put his index finger to his mouth, commanding silence. He seemed to be smiling like someone playing a practical joke. He opened the door with exaggerated care and peered outside, then withdrew his head and softly closed the door again. He returned with a broad smile upon his face. 'Louie Eeyoreovitch!' he shouted. 'My dear, dear friend Louie Eeyoreovitch!' He threw out his arms, grabbed me in a bear hug and dragged me to my feet. He unclasped me and then with renewed fervour threw his arms round me again and squeezed me. He kissed me on both cheeks. 'Louie Eeyoreovitch!' he exclaimed. 'How can I ever thank you? My daughter, my lovely daughter, my dear heart's blood, lost to me, alone in the world full of evil predatory men, and through the exquisite offices of our benevolent and ever-merciful Lord, she met you! My darling dear Natasha has come back and all because of you, the noble, thrice-blessed Louie Eeyoreovitch!'

Chapter 22

H IS NAME was Pyotr. He drove with one hand lazily
caressing the wheel and the other making gestures in
the air to amplify the effect of his words. We drove south
through town, down the broad tree-lined avenue of Praspyekt John
Hughes, into Petrovsky Pereulok and then Merthyr Tydfil Naber-
ezhnaya. He said we were heading for Sadovaya Ulitsa.

'You can imagine how I felt,' he said. 'I knew sooner or later the
moment would come. For years I worried about it, how I would
cope without her mother to guide her. At times like that, when a girl
starts to become a woman, she needs the company of other women. I
flatter myself I did all right, together we managed to get through the
trials of those years. Yes, there were boyfriends, some of which I
disapproved; others I tolerated. Then a few weeks ago she came
home and said in the sort of voice a girl uses to say she wants to be an
actress that she wanted to be a honey-trapper. Imagine it! I was
thunderstruck. Of course, I didn't want to stand in her way . . . She
thought it was glamorous, being a spy, a Mata Hari, but I knew
better, I knew how the world works, especially the grimy shabby
shadow-world of secret agents. I told her, it's not like in the James
Bond movies: you don't get many counts and countesses, handsome
spies and debonair millionaires travelling on the Orient Express
these days. It's just a train, like the one to Dnipropetrovsk, full of
bourgeois riff-raff. She wouldn't listen, of course.' He made an
especially dramatic wave of his hand. 'Who would be a father, eh?
Louie Eeyoreovitch, who would be a father!'

We turned into a street of solid nineteenth-century civic buildings,
and parked outside the Museum Of Our Forefathers' Suffering. The

chain was hanging loose, the jaw of the padlock open. The door was ajar. We climbed the steps and entered.

'And then, after everything I told her, what does she do? She meets a handsome James Bond on the train, the wonderful chivalrous knight Louie Eeyoreovitch who shows her the error of her ways and sends her back to her father.'

We walked into a lobby of scuffed linoleum and faded paint. Pyotr pressed the button on an old wire-cage elevator. There was a rumble from the basement and far above our heads wheels and pulleys creaked into motion. The cage arrived and Pyotr pulled back the concertina door and bid me enter. We travelled up to the second floor.

'We closed the museum about fifteen years ago.'

'Why did you close it?'

'Budget cuts, as usual. It was my initiative. I was in charge of the five-year plan for dream husbandry at the time.'

We emerged on to a landing. Next to the door leading to a gallery there was a table, chairs, vodka and Vimto. A girl sat at the table leafing through a dossier, pencil perched on her ear and an earnest expression on her face. It was Calamity. She looked up briefly from the dossier. 'Oh, hi Louie, good you could make it.' Her attempt at nonchalance was betrayed by the wide grin which flashed across her face. I rushed forward and, as she stood up, I hugged her. 'How was the interrogation?' she asked, struggling to breathe under the pressure of my arms.

'A lot nicer than the ones you get in Aberystwyth, but I was worried about you the whole time.'

'I was worried about you, too.'

Pyotr sat down and poured out the vodka and the Vimto. He drank to our health. Calamity pointed to the dossier on the table. 'It's Uncle Vanya's file.' On the cover there was a picture of a young man in Soviet labour-camp clothes staring blankly into the camera. Pyotr took the photo of the levitated dog out of an envelope and placed it on the table top.

'Natasha has asked me to apologise to you for stealing the photo.'

'It doesn't matter.'

'She is very upset. She has enrolled on a course to become a speech therapist for children with learning difficulties, and all because of you, Louie Eeyoreovitch. You restored my daughter to me and now you are my brother to whom I will be eternally in debt. However, duty dictates that, for reasons of State security, I must confiscate the photo. As recompense I make the exhibits of this the former museum available to you. It is my belief that you will find the answer to your quest here in the dust.'

I placed my fingers on the dossier and twisted it round to face me.

'Vanya's case is very sad,' said Pyotr. 'Twice he was denounced and sent to the camps. And the years in between were worse: he was captured by the Germans in Stalingrad and spent two years as a prisoner-of-war eating bread made of floor sweepings and leaves. When finally he returned to Hughesovka he did what he had to in order to survive and this meant taking employment in the criminal fraternity. His life was heading for the abyss, but then a remarkable transformation occurred. He was engaged to assassinate a woman for reasons that are now lost and, by all accounts, he fell in love with her face presented to him down the sniper scope of his rifle. He sought out the girl, paid off the people who wanted her dead, and proposed. How could she refuse the gallant man who had forborne to shoot her because he was so struck by her beauty?'

'This much I know. He married Lara and Ninotchka was born, and then he was sent to a labour camp.'

'Yes, of course, you are anxious to learn the truth behind this great mystery. You have come a long way and desire to know how it was that the spirit of Gethsemane Walters could inhabit the body of a little girl here in Hughesovka in the mid-fifties. Please, sit.'

I took my place at the table and chinked glasses with Pyotr and Calamity and tried to keep the impatience from my face.

'It is indeed a very strange story,' said Pyotr. 'You see, not long after Vanya was sent to the camps there was an outbreak of diphtheria in Hughesovka and Ninotchka fell ill and died. And for reasons known only to her, Lara kept this terrible news secret from her husband. It is not hard to imagine her motives. She intended no doubt to spare Vanya the extra suffering. The camps along the River Kolyma were infamous, everyone knew that a spell in the gulag was the worst fate that could befall a man òr woman and of this the worst of the worst was to be found in Kolyma. Lara must have thought that the extra burden of this evil news would have been too much for her husband's poor heart to bear. She didn't tell him, and thereby though acting from the most honourable of motives she constructed a trap that ensnared her. Because what was to happen when Vanya came home? It must have preyed on her mind a lot during those years. She found work as a cleaner in this museum. Then one day a strange event happened. They had just taken delivery from Mooncalf & Sons of some traditional Welsh furniture which would form part of a reconstruction of a typical nineteenth-century peasant's cottage. And in a Welsh dresser they found some curious items: a bottle of dandelion and burdock, a tin of corned beef, and a child's colouring book. One evening, a few days later, as Lara was mopping the floor she found a little girl hiding in the basement. This girl was Gethsemane, who it seemed had been hiding in the Welsh dresser and inadvertently shipped from Wales to Hughesovka. The streets of Hughesovka in those dark lean days shortly after the war were full of waifs and strays – so many mothers and fathers who went to war and never returned. It was a common thing to find a poor shivering half-starved child hiding in the warm museum at night. The girl was about the same age as Ninotchka would have been had she lived, and looked similar. Vanya had not seen his daughter since shortly after her birth; suddenly Lara saw a way out of the trap she had built for herself in the lie she told Vanya. She decided to adopt Gethsemane, to pass her off as Ninotchka and deceive her husband.' Pyotr paused and refilled our glasses for the fourth time. He raised the glass and held it to his lips without drinking, lost for a moment in contemplation. 'But of course there was a problem. The child stubbornly refused to accept the name of Ninotchka and not unreasonably insisted that she was called Gethsemane and was from Wales. And so, Lara invented this astonishing story about the imaginary friend in order to dupe her husband when he returned from the camps. "My darling, something very strange has taken place. Last week I gave our little daughter a Welsh doll from the museum and now she has acquired an imaginary friend from Wales called Gethsemane. I thought it was charming at first but recently the imaginary friend seems to have taken her over. Our daughter no longer answers to the name Ninotchka and insists that I call her Gethsemane. Yesterday she told me I was not her real mummy and asked for a strange dish of lamb and cheese called *caawl*. I am at my wit's end, whatever shall we do?" What a completely brilliant and totally crazy idea! Who knows whether such a subterfuge could ever have hoped to work? But Fate was not kind to the ingenious Lara. Shortly after Vanya returned home Dame Fortune inserted another player into the scene: Laika, the first dog in space. Gethsemane was fascinated by Laika and spent entire days glued to the collective TV set. Laika, the sweet yapping mongrel, staring out at us from her goldfish-bowl helmet, her eyes bright pools of trust for the masters who had put her in this strange contraption, and who had only ever shown her kindness . . . Laika sitting wearing a soiled nappy stencilled with the motif of the glorious Soviet Space Command. But as you know, Laika died up there above the clouds. Of heat exhaustion, they said. When news of her death broke, Gethsemane was inconsolable, and Vanya, unable to take the tantrums of his daughter, hit the bottle. He took to beating his wife, perhaps in some deep dark recess of his heart he blamed her or suspected that she had – in some way he was unable to divine – been responsible for the terrible turn of events that had so ruined his happiness. One night, he hit his wife a little too hard and that was that. He found himself behind bars for murder and the girl was taken into care. There the truth slowly emerged. It would have been a trivial story but for a twist to the tale that assumed dimensions of State security. Laika, you see, had been recruited for her heroic role during the visit to our town of Premier Nikita Khrushchev. A stray was presented to Khrushchev during a visit to Hughesovka and he in turn presented it to the Space Programme. But it turned out that the puppy belonged to Gethsemane and had followed her from Wales by the same route; no doubt by following the scent. Imagine it! Laika, the national hero, the pride and joy of our nation and proof to the world of our technological and moral ascendancy over the United States, was not a Russian dog as we assumed, but was Welsh. The puppy of Clip the sheepdog, now housed in your museum on Terrace Road. For the sake of our national honour all traces of this fact were duly expunged from the historical record.'

'What became of Gethsemane?'

'I do not know. In the fifties, after they started emptying the camps, there were many people moving to and fro across our vast land; so many fates and tragedies. Who knows where she ended up? She may be dead but there is no reason to suppose it. I like to think she is still alive, that she journeyed along the same railway line to Vladivostok that her father took before her and that somewhere along the way, perhaps some insignificant wayside halt, she got off the train. Perhaps there she found a man and a home and had children of her own; perhaps there she found that most ardently coveted of treasures, human felicity.'

'How did Natasha know I was travelling on the Orient Express with the photo?'

'Mooncalf told us, of course. There is a substantial reward available for information leading to the acquisition of these photos. We do a lot of business with Mr Mooncalf. He is a great man.'

'So people keep telling me. Why didn't he try and steal it from me in Aberystwyth?'

'Mr Mooncalf is an honest man, not a common thief!'

'Why not simply wait until I arrived in Hughesovka and arrest me?'

Pyotr looked apologetic. 'Call it bureaucratic inertia, if you like. These things have always been arranged this way. Reform is long overdue but who wants to throw thousands of honey-trappers out of work?'

Calamity took me into the gallery and showed me the exhibits. The room occupied the height of three ordinary floors and was open to the skylights high in the ceiling. It was like the nave of a vast cathedral, one in which the false god of Aberystwyth had been worshipped for a while before the people forsook the old ways. Most of the hall was in darkness, but occasional shafts of dawn light illuminated areas like sunlit clearings in a dark wood. Calamity led me to a tableau representing, according to the dusty sign, a typical Welsh serf's dwelling from the 1950s. There was a hearthside and a false roof of low timbers. Two rocking chairs were drawn up before the fireside. There were brass fire-irons, a soot-blackened kettle and teapot complete with tea cosy. Next to the fireside was a pen for the livestock which, it was said, wintered in the same quarters. Another tableau entitled 'Mysticism and Superstition' detailed, through life-size waxwork figures, the three-way tug of love for the serf's soul between the Church, the spiritualist and the dispenser of opiate for the masses in cornets, the ice-cream vendor. Next to this was a stack of framed photos recording the historic bank holiday food riots. Starving peasants dressed as Teddy boys fought with members of the local constabulary, using deckchairs as weapons. Calamity led me to a traditional Welsh dresser with a large cupboard.

'This is the dresser that Gethsemane stowed away in.'

'How do you know?'

'They found out when she went to the remote-viewing school.'

'Do we know who it belonged to?'

She looked at me with excitement gleaming in her eyes. 'Yes.' She opened a drawer and took out a photo. 'Mrs Mochdre,' said Calamity. 'It was her Welsh dresser.' I turned my gaze from the picture and looked at Calamity and we stood in silence, both host to a slight tingling sensation that signalled the end of a long treasure hunt. 'Her own sister,' she added.

I made a clicking sound in my throat that signified bafflement at the cabbalistic ways of fate. I put the photo under my arm. 'I guess we are allowed to keep it.'

Calamity carried on walking down the aisle with me following. The golden light grew stronger, mysterious objects glittered, it was as if we were walking into the belly of a mountain towards a dragon's treasure. We reached the end of the aisle and entered a golden cavern containing a reconstruction of the Pier amusement arcade from the late 1950s. A shaft of light from a skylight above us danced on the polished chrome and shiny glass of the machines. There was a laughing policeman, a mechanical gypsy fortune-teller and a machine for recording your own voice and cutting a vinyl disc. Next to that was a bingo console. Ghostly voices echoed down the years. I recited, 'Eyes down, look in . . . first on the red, it's key of the door two and one, twenty-one. Next up it's on the blue, droopy drawers or all the fours, forty-four! Remember, ladies and gentlemen, any row along the top or down the sides, or from corner to corner. Next up it's on the white, ooh! Never been kissed, it's sweet sixteen, one and six, sixteen. Following that, Kelly's eye all on its own, number one!'

'Bingo!' shouted Calamity.

I smiled. 'Sorry, chum, the authorities don't seem to have acquired the prizes. No Roy Rogers hat for you.'

'No, I mean bingo! As in, bingo!'

'I know, but . . .'

'No, not bingo I've won a prize, but bingo! As in eureka!'

'I don't follow.'

Calamity put her hands on my forearm as if to make sure I was listening and then said slowly, 'I've worked out the aural signature on the séance tape.'

'You have?'

She twisted and pointed at the machine for cutting your own vinyl record. 'Mrs Mochdre made a recording on that. Remember the maniacal laughter we heard in the background? It's the laughing policeman. The ghoulish squeals are the seagulls. And the bit we thought was French, *quelle ee* something? It's Kelly's eye, the bingo call. On the morning before Gethsemane disappeared Mrs Mochdre took her to Aberystwyth to buy a birthday present for her mum. They could have gone to the Pier and made a recording. Then Mrs Mochdre kept it and played it secretly the following year at a séance.'

'Or maybe she didn't really play it at the séance, maybe there wasn't a séance, she just made it up.'

'That's right. And remember Eeyore saying that he arrested Mrs Mochdre once for smashing up the new gypsy fortune-teller? Look! This one has been repaired.' I looked and beheld. Calamity was right: the gypsy's face had dents in it. Up in the sky above the museum a cloud moved, the shaft of light, refracted by the cloud, grew suddenly stronger. It illuminated Calamity's face and made her glow like the icon of a saint. 'It's all here!' she said with breathless excitement. 'It all fits. Mrs Mochdre was jealous of her sister marrying the balloon-folder. Maybe she made the recording and then when Gethsemane disappeared kept hold of it. The following year she sends it to spite her.'

'I can't believe she would put Gethsemane in the cupboard and send her off to Hughesovka.'

'It's her cupboard.'

'That doesn't prove it was her who did it.'

'No.'

'Anyone could have done it.'

'Yes, or she could just have been hiding in the dresser. All the same, it all points to Mrs Mochdre.'

'It's intriguing. But even if it is true, even if she made the séance recording, I don't see how we could prove any of it.'

'She'll confess,' said Calamity with quiet confidence.

'You think so? Mrs Mochdre doesn't strike me as the sort of shrinking violet who breaks easily, even if Llunos is doing the interview.'

'I know a way to make her confess. We'll make her confront her accuser.'

'Who's her accuser?'

Calamity pointed at the mechanical gypsy fortune-teller. 'Remember that technique I told you about, the one the Feds use, called reverse horoscopy?' She looked at my face and mistook slight bafflement for a rebuke and hurried through her sentence as if expecting me to cut her off before the end. 'I've been thinking about superseding the paradigm and all that . . .' She let the words trail off. 'I guess you think we've heard quite enough about all that, right?'

'No, go on and tell me what you have in mind.'

Still looking unsure, she carried on. 'Why would Mrs Mochdre attack the mechanical fortune-teller with a hammer?'

'Because she objected to its tone of voice, or thought Satan was speaking to her or something.'

'What if the fortune-teller told her she would one day go to prison for what she did to Gethsemane?'

'But how could a mechanical fortune-teller do that?'

'It couldn't, but Mrs Mochdre could have imagined it. We know she complained about Satan talking to her all the time. That means she was hearing voices, so just think if Gethsemane really was on her conscience and she felt guilty and then . . . what's it called when . . . when . . .'

'Projection, it's called projection or transference or something. She was racked with guilt and paranoia and heard the fortune-teller accusing her of a terrible crime and predicting a lifetime behind bars for it. So Mrs Mochdre shuts Gypsy Rosie Lee up with a hammer.'

Calamity looked at me with uncertainty in her eyes. Her face fell. 'It's a bit silly, really, isn't it?' she said.

'Yes,' I said. 'But don't let that stop you. Don't forget we are superseding the paradigm.'

'We need to get her in an interview room with the mechanical gypsy and decorate the place to pretend the year is 1955. Then we'll tell her it is the day before Gethsemane went missing and we are going to ask the gypsy fortune-teller for Mrs Mochdre's fortune for the next day. Llunos can arrange it.' Her brow darkened as a thought occurred to her. 'Llunos will never buy it, will he?'

I grinned with sheer joy at Calamity's crazy scheme. 'That has to be the nuttiest crime-fighting idea anyone has ever had in the history of detectives. That doesn't just supersede the paradigm it melts it down and turns it into a brass chamber pot. Llunos will love it. Llunos will absolutely love it.'

On the way out I returned to the dresser in which Gethsemane had stowed away and began to close the drawer that had been left open. I slid it shut, stopped and pulled it open again. The drawer was lined with a copy of the *Cambrian News*. I took it out. The front page was carrying a story about a bank holiday riot, a fight between Teddy boys and local police. The main photo was a dramatic close-up of a young hoodlum punching a policeman on the jaw. It was the same edition Calamity had retrieved from the archive in Aberystwyth, the one that had been censored by having the photo removed. Suddenly I knew who had been responsible for the act of censorship. I recognised the young man punching the cop. It was a long time ago, and he had changed a lot with the long passage of time; he had grown from an angry young man into a gentle and mellow old man who shuffled slowly along the Prom. It was my dad, Eeyore.

Chapter 23

LLUNOS WAS wearing 'drapes', velvet collar and drainpipe trousers, and strutted up and down the interview room; his hair was carefully sculpted into a quiff at the front and combed into a duck's arse at the back. From the expression on his face it was evidently the most fun he had ever had in an interrogation. I didn't know, but suspected he had missed the Teddy boy phenomenon first time round, not because he was too old or too young, but simply because it was inconceivable that his father would have allowed him so much as a feather of a duck's arse and almost certainly regarded rock'n'roll as moral poison. I read the copy of the *Cambrian News* from 1955 carrying the story of a girl from Rhyl who had been hanged at Holloway prison. Just another girl from Rhyl who had a bagful of troubles and ended up on the end of a rope. It could happen to anyone.

In a corner of the room a Wurlitzer played 'Rock around the Clock' and you could tell this was the type of music that Llunos liked. Mooncalf had done us proud. I attributed his willingness to help to the expression on his face when I walked in with Calamity; it was the expression of a man who had not been expecting to see her back. We made a deal: I would undertake the difficult task of not throwing him out of the third floor window if he would get hold of the ingredients of a 1950s party for us; nothing too fancy, just enough to fool a mechanical gypsy fortune-teller. In the space of a few days he managed to dig up the *On the Waterfront* cinema poster; the jukebox and its precious cargo of vintage vinyl; he found the drapes and blue suede shoes that Llunos and I were wearing, and all in the right sizes. He gave us the steam radio and rigged it up with a tape recorder to relay the sad news of Einstein's death and the stirring story of Rosa Parks in Montgomery refusing to give up her seat on the bus to a white man. This was Montgomery, Alabama, not the one between Welshpool and Shrewsbury. There were seven or eight months separating those two events in 1955 but something told me Mrs Mochdre was no history teacher. The mechanical Gypsy Rosie Lee had been given to us by Pyotr along with the complimentary tickets on Air Hughesovka Flight 003 that had landed at Aberporth military base a couple of days before.

Calamity was outside watching through the two-way mirror as we reversed the horoscope and superseded the paradigm in ways the writers for *Gumshoe* magazine could never have imagined. She had spent the past two days making a concerted attempt to keep the smug expression off her face. It was a very mature performance and did her credit, but she was fighting a losing battle. It was good to see. I no longer had any worries about Calamity's crisis of confidence.

Llunos put another penny into the jukebox and selected 'Folsom Prison Blues' by Johnny Cash. Oh yes, he was enjoying himself.

> I'm stuck in Folsom prison, and time keeps draggin' on
> But that train keeps a rollin' on down to San Anton . . .

He paced around the room for a while to let the irony of his music choice sink in and then, as if inspired by a sudden decision, he walked up to the high-backed chair in which Mrs Mochdre sat, placed his palms on the table next to her and leaned round to speak into her face. It was the 'invading the personal space' routine that you saw in all the cop shows. He even had the authentic sweat stains under the arms. 'It's up to you, Mrs Mochdre,' he said. 'We already know the facts, about the terrible thing you did to your sister's little girl, but we need to hear it from you. You recognise Gypsy Rosie Lee here, don't you? You thought you'd seen the last of her, didn't you? Thought you'd done her in good and proper that time when you took a hammer and smashed her face in.'

I re-read the report in the *Cambrian News*, strangely moved, and threw it down on the desk taking care that the story fell under the nose of Mrs Mochdre. Maybe it would help concentrate her mind. A smarter woman might have noticed the yellowing and fading of the aged paper, or wondered why the masthead had changed, but a smarter woman wouldn't even be here. Mrs Mochdre held herself erect, too proud or stubborn to look at the newspaper. She held her handbag pressed against her chest and trembled. No one, not even a tough guy, knows how to play it cool in a police interview room. The ones who tell you they can are just bluffing.

Llunos grabbed a desk calendar which was opened to the date 30 August 1955 and slid it across the desk towards Mrs Mochdre. 'Tomorrow's the day, Mrs Mochdre. Tomorrow's the day you take little Gethsemane to Aberystwyth and tomorrow's the day she disappears never to be seen again. Tomorrow is when it all happens. We're a bit cloudy about the details, we don't know exactly what happens tomorrow, but we've got a good idea. And Gypsy Rosie Lee here knows everything. All I have to do is put the coin in and she starts singing. You remember the gypsy, don't you? You are probably surprised to see her back, in view of the beating you gave her. But mechanical fortune-tellers are not like little girls,' said Llunos, 'they can be repaired. We hunted her down and brought her back. She recognises you. She picked you out of the line-up. She remembers the beating you gave her. You see the calendar. As soon as we turned her on she took one look and presto! She thinks it's August 1955. It doesn't have to be that way, Mrs Mochdre. You could tell us in your own words instead. I don't say it would keep you out of gaol, but it might knock a few years off the time you have to serve. For someone of your age those few years could make all the difference. So you sit here facing a choice. Either you tell us in your own words, freely and uncoerced, how it was, or we ask the fortune-teller.'

'No court would take the word of a common gyppo.'

Llunos paused. He exhaled deliberately and wearily. He said nothing. All cops know the right words to use, but the real smart ones like Llunos know how to use silence; at the right moment it can be crushing. He put his forearms on the desk next to her and buried his head in his hands. Still he said nothing and Mrs Mochdre began to tremble. Llunos straightened up and began pacing up and down.

'Underneath it all, Mrs Mochdre,' he said finally, 'I'm a human being and I believe in human beings. It's the only reason I can still bear to put on this uniform every morning. And I believe in you too. I don't believe any of this was how you intended. It couldn't be, it's not possible. Not to your own sister. I don't believe you are insane, probably not even wicked. I think you are weak, and stupid and mean and not very smart. But you're no fiend. There has to be an explanation for what happened. I can only think it was an accident, it got out of hand. As a cop, I've seen this sort of thing a thousand times before, you'd be surprised how common it is. People who do a small crime and would never be capable of doing a big one end up doing the big one to cover up the small one. In fact, I'd say that's how most criminals are except the real psychos. You never meant it to happen like this, did you? It just somehow started and once it had started, it was like a snowball rolling down the hill, you couldn't find a way to stop it. Even now, thirty years later, you still can't believe what has happened. Isn't that right, Mrs Mochdre? Isn't that how it was?'

'Yes, yes, something like that.'

'Tell us what happens tomorrow.' He pointed at the calendar, and then at the mechanical gypsy. 'Or we ask her.'

Mrs Mochdre loosened her grip on her handbag, as if coming to a decision, and put it slowly down on the desk in front of her. 'I never meant . . . she was such a naughty girl, she knocked my cruet set over and scratched it. Well, it was the last straw . . .'

'Let's start with the first straw, start at the beginning of the day, start with the séance tape. Tell us about that.'

'It was her mum's birthday the following week, you see. I took her into town to buy a present and we went to the amusement arcade on the Pier as a treat. They had one of those machines where you can record your own voice and make a disc, like that one.' She pointed to the machine against the wall. 'So I paid for her to have a little go. The disc was going to be the present. I kept hold of it. After that we had a milkshake in the milk bar and went back to Abercuawg. Then, once we got back . . . she was always such a naughty girl . . .'

'Just tell it.'

'She threw her lunch on the floor so I . . . put her in the pig pen. I told her, little girls with no manners can eat with the pigs.'

Llunos didn't bat an eye but this was news. We assumed she had packed her in the cupboard.

'Then what happened?'

'I went out for a little while and when I came back . . .' Sobs overcame her and Llunos waited patiently. 'When I came back, she was gone. The pigs had eaten her. There was nothing left except a single shoe. They'd eaten her, just like people said they did to Goldilocks's mother.'

Llunos sighed and sat down opposite her. We had departed from the script. 'OK, so the pigs ate the girl.' He shot me a glance and I did my best to communicate that this was a surprise to me too. 'Then what?'

'I told the Witchfinder. He promised to help, if in return . . . if in return I agreed to marry him.' She collapsed into sobs, and held her face in her hands. 'Thirty years I've been paying for it, every night. He's . . . he's . . . oh, I can't bring myself to say!'

'Then what happened?'

'He took the shoe and buried it in Goldilocks's garden. He told me not to breathe a word to anyone and they would all think Goldilocks had done something with the girl.'

'So where does the séance tape come in?'

Mrs Mochdre paused, thinking perhaps about how far she had to go.

'Don't contemplate, just tell us, Mrs Mochdre. The time for contemplation is past. Today we need the truth.'

'I thought . . . I hoped . . . Alfred the balloon-folder would still want me, even though I was married to that beast. I thought he could rescue me. But he was too broken-hearted over the loss of Gethsemane. I thought if he knows she has died he will stop grieving and come to me. So I sent the tape. But he just took to his bed. He said, "She's in heaven now and there's nothing left for me on earth. I'm taking to my bed." And he did, too. Died of a broken heart. It all turned out wrong.' She made token dabs at the tears with a screwed-up handkerchief.

'And that's it?'

'Yes,' she said quietly. 'That's all.'

'You're a liar, Mrs Mochdre.'

'No!'

'That's not what happened at all. This stuff about the pigs is a fairy tale. You locked her in the cupboard, didn't you?'

'No, I didn't.'

Llunos slammed his hand down on the desk. 'Yes! I say, yes! Tell us everything, Mrs Mochdre, or you'll die in prison, would you like that?'

'Why should I care? What have I got left to live for?'

Llunos let that one rest and played another card. Silence. No one said anything and for a while the only sound was breathing. Eventually, Mrs Mochdre began again. 'It was me he loved. He said so, he was going to break off with her. Then she fell pregnant, the scheming little hussy. I saw straight away what her game was. She knew, you see; she knew he loved me, not her. He was too decent for his own good. He went along with it, even though he knew that he had been tricked. Have to make an honest woman of her, he said. I said why? And he told me he couldn't bear the thought of a child of his entering the world as a bastard.'

'So then you packed Gethsemane off in the cupboard—'

'I didn't! It wasn't like that . . .'

'Yes, and then you went out for a walk and when you came back the cupboard was gone. It had been collected by Mooncalf. You realised what had happened, but you didn't say anything. That was the time to say something, wasn't it? But you chose not to, you chose not to because a little thought had wormed its way into your head: without her around, maybe, just maybe . . .'

'No, no . . .'

'Of course you did, anyone would. It would be the first thing you thought of. It's only human, Mrs Mochdre. We like to pretend that we don't have thoughts like that, but we do, we all do. They are the first ones, what's in it for me? That's how it was, I know that's how it was, it had to be. You thought, if I say nothing and she goes away maybe Alfred would come back to me. But he died of a broken heart instead and you ended up handcuffed to that old creaking wooden bed for the next thirty years shuddering beneath a man wearing a goat outfit. Tough break.'

Llunos stormed out of the interview room and left the two of us. After a pause I followed him. Outside, the three of us stood watching her through the window. She picked up the paper and glanced at it, then put it down and waited. Llunos put his arm on Calamity's shoulder. 'I have to hand it to you, kid,' he said. 'This is genius.'

'Not really,' said Calamity.

'Forty years in the force and never seen anything like it. I wasn't sure if she would fall for it, but she did. What's it called again?'

'Superseding the paradigm,' she answered with pride.

'Amazing!' Llunos took me by the arm and pulled me to one side. He beckoned me to follow him. We walked up the corridor out of earshot of Calamity.

'It will never work,' he said simply.

'No?'

'She won't sign. What do you make of the pig-pen story?'

'It must be true. I can't believe she would invent it. Gethsemane must have escaped from the pig pen and left a shoe behind in the mud. We need to find out who put her in the dresser.'

'Maybe Gethsemane just hid,' said Llunos.

'With a tin of corned beef? Only an adult would put something like that in. If a kid was packing stuff to take with her she wouldn't think of that.' I smiled. 'Don't they teach you anything on your psychology course?'

Llunos looked puzzled for a second until he realised what I was talking about. 'I stopped all that.'

'You did?'

'It wasn't me. It was the detective version of mutton dressed up as lamb. I prefer the old ways, the ones I feel comfortable with.'

'Abercuawg isn't the repressed unconscious of Aberystwyth then?'

'It's just a lake filled with old prams. Come, I want to show you something.' He beckoned again and I followed.

'Where are we going?'

'Someone's confessed to killing Arianwen Eglwys Fach – in the interview room at the end.'

My skin prickled. 'The Witchfinder?'

'Why him?'

'I don't know. I don't like him.'

'You would make a good cop.'

It was difficult to know whether he was being ironic or sincere. Most of the cops round here worked on a similar principle to the one I had outlined.

'It wasn't him,' said Llunos. 'Look.'

I peered through another two-way mirror into the interview goldfish bowl. Meici Jones was sitting at the table across from two cops.

'He says it was his mum,' said Llunos. 'Smashed the girl's head in with a rounders bat.' He paused for a second and said, 'Your name was mentioned. Again.'

A grisly image of Arianwen lying bloodied and face-down in the gutter flashed through my mind. My voice was thick with passion: 'The guy is in his thirties and wears short trousers; he lives with his mum and she hates him because he smothered his little brother to death when he was three. He's never had a girl in his life or even a friend and because he took a shine to Arianwen and saw me talking to her this is what happened. He saw me talking to her. Imagine how it makes me feel. She was a lovely kid.'

Llunos put his hand on my shoulder. 'Sorry, Louie. If you want to go in there and sort him out I'll turn off the sound.'

'Back to the old-fashioned ways, huh?'

'Murder is a pretty old-fashioned sort of crime, isn't it?'

I went back to Mrs Mochdre and chose another song for the jukebox.

> When the moon hits your eye like a big pizza pie
> That's amore . . .

I sang along softly, Mrs Mochdre stared disconsolately at the table, occasionally looking up at me with the hostility of a cornered beast. I stopped singing and spoke. 'Who killed the students?'

She said nothing.

'I think it was the Witchfinder, but what I want to know is why.'

'If you're such a clever dick I'm sure you'll think of something.'

> When the stars make you drool just like a pasta fazool
> That's amore . . .

'I can help you, Mrs Mochdre, but you have to help me.'

She gave me a look that symbolised a silent snort.

'What would you say if I told you Gethsemane didn't get eaten by the pigs? If I told you she climbed out of that pig pen and walked away alive?'

Mrs Mochdre forced herself to stare down at the table but it cost her a lot of effort.

'What would you say if I told you I have proof, that I am the only one who knows? If I say nothing, Llunos throws the book at you. But if you help me, I produce my evidence. You're a free woman.'

'You must think I was born yesterday falling for a trick like that. I know how it works, good cop, bad cop; my husband does it too when he's interviewing witches. Llunos will be out there watching through the mirror.'

'You watch too many cop shows.'

'Just don't try and take me for a fool.'

'OK, I'll level with you. This is the truth. I don't know whether Gethsemane is alive now, but she was back then. She didn't die. The pigs didn't eat her and your husband the Witchfinder knew it all along. I'm not saying the pigs wouldn't eat a human given half the chance but it would take a damn sight longer than—'

She looked up slowly and I sensed in that motion the dropping of a penny. Thirty years of conjugal beastliness and pent-up hatred gleamed as sharp twin points of fire in her eyes.

'That's right, Mrs Mochdre, he knew. Of course he knew.'

'H . . . h . . . how do you know?'

'Anybody would have known. You were terrified of what they would say if they found out you locked her in with the pigs. My guess is, it wasn't the first time you had mistreated her. You were worried about what would happen if they found out, so you panicked. You didn't think clearly. If you had, you would have worked it out too. There wasn't enough time for them to eat her. Gethsemane just climbed out and the mud caught her shoes. That's all. The second shoe is probably still there. The Witchfinder just—'

'He knew? He knew!' Her jaw gaped and her eyes became wide as saucers as the full implications of his trickery settled in. 'The bastard!'

'He just played along to entrap you into marrying him.'

She bit her knuckle.

'I'm not here to make you suffer. I don't approve of what you did to your sister, but I can see you've paid a price in your own way. I just want to know who killed the students. You tell me that and I promise to tell Llunos what I know.'

'The Witchfinder killed the students of course. To stop nosey parkers. When they paid that actress to impersonate Gethsemane it got him worried. He thought if he killed them and made it look like what happened to Gomer Barnaby people would think Goldilocks had come back and would be too frightened to start digging up the past.' When she stopped speaking she collapsed in on herself slightly, as if she had been punctured.

'Thank you,' I said.

She looked up at me. 'He really knew?'

'I'm sorry.'

She nodded as if only now fully understanding. She spoke in a dream, 'All those years . . . that bed . . . You know, sometimes he liked to dress up as a wolf; Heaven knows what for. And all along he knew.'

'If I go and get Llunos you can sign the statement and then go. I don't think he'll keep you here.'

Mrs Mochdre pulled herself up and sat erect once more, the flame inside her visibly rekindling. 'I'm afraid I won't be signing anything today, Mr Knight. I don't have time. There is an urgent matter I need to attend to.' She pushed back her chair and stood up. 'It concerns my husband.' For a second, before turning away, her eyes bored into me and I saw a repressed fury so intense it made me wince. For most of his adult life the Witchfinder had been exorcising and casting out demons; he had summoned and beaten, so they said, the finest champions of hell. His c.v. listed victories over Belial and Leviathan and Belphegor and Beelzebub and Asmodeus and probably Lucifer too. But that look in his wife's eye told me nothing in his professional life would have prepared him for what was coming when he got home for tea that evening.

Chapter 24

THE REAL question was, who put her in the cupboard? Who put the corned beef, the dandelion and burdock and the colouring book there? Why go to such trouble? Vanya had worked it out. He had guessed it all because he was smarter than me, worked it all out that day I saw him sitting on the beach with Clip the sheepdog. That's when he decided there was no purpose carrying on. He found out that there never was a spirit possessing his daughter, no imaginary friend, he found out it was a real girl who had replaced the one he had loved. He worked it out on the same afternoon that he saved Gomer Barnaby's life. Who did he see? Who told him? Sometimes it takes us a long time to see the obvious. Who would you go and see after saving the young Barnaby's life? Who would give you a phial of Ampersandium in recognition of your brave deed? Who else but Old Barnaby?

The old lag at the rock foundry told me Ephraim Barnaby was expecting me. He showed me up the stone stairs to the first landing and then to a door in the corner. It led into a tower inside which was a spiral staircase. I climbed; the inside of the tower was dark and cold, almost damp. I wondered if it was like this for Sleeping Beauty. There was a door slightly ajar at the top. I hesitated on the threshold and a voice from inside bade me enter.

He sat in an armchair next to an electric bar fire, toasting muffins on a long brass fork. An arched window behind him looked out over the rooftops of the town and beyond to the deep blue sea. I sat in the other chair, next to the fire, flesh prickling with sweat.

'Vanya told me everything,' I said.

Barnaby skewered another muffin on the end of the fork. 'You wouldn't be here if he had.' He held the muffin out to toast. I undid the button of my collar. 'Sometimes at night I wander the streets dressed as a tramp, asking people for the price of a cup of tea,' said Old Barnaby. 'You gave me a fiver once outside the Spar.'

'I don't remember.'

'I admire you.'

'You know who put Gethsemane in the cupboard that ended up in Hughesovka, don't you?'

'I didn't know where it had ended up until Vanya came to see me.'

'How did he guess?'

'He didn't. He saved my boy from drowning, and so naturally I invited him up here for a drink. He told me his life story and what had been so baffling to him – the peculiar story of the imaginary friend, the diphtheria outbreak while he was in prison – it all seemed so obvious to me. So I told him. Your child died of diphtheria, and your wife, anxious not to break your heart while in that prison camp, adopted Gethsemane and made up the story of the imaginary friend.'

'Who put her in the cupboard?'

'Goldilocks's sister. She came to see me after she had been to visit her brother in prison. While on death row Goldilocks had asked to see a priest; they sent the Witchfinder. Goldilocks told him the truth about what had happened; about how Gethsemane had stumbled on the Slaughterhouse Mob torturing my son, how he had never harmed so much as a hair of her head but had been reluctant to speak out for fear of getting his comrades in the gang into trouble. The Witchfinder promised he would do everything in his power to get the conviction quashed. But he did nothing, he was happy to let Goldilocks hang. That's when the sister came to see me. She offered me a deal. If I agreed to help her brother escape she would tell me what happened to my son. So I agreed. I arranged the escape and helped them leave town, Goldilocks and the girl; they are still alive.'

'What did the Slaughterhouse Mob do to your son?'

Barnaby stood up and walked over to a cupboard. He opened it and took out something that looked like a hedge clipper. He brought it over and placed it in my hands. The handles were insulated with thick rubber tubes, and at the ends instead of blades there were spikes with electrical contacts.

'It's an electric cattle-stunner,' he explained.

'From the slaughterhouse?'

'Yes. The two prongs are applied to the temples and render the beast unconscious before it has its throat cut.'

'It breaks your teeth?'

'Convulsions. In the early days, when they gave patients electro-shock therapy in psychiatric hospitals they often made the voltage too high, it used to give the patients convulsions so strong they would break their own teeth. Goldilocks was familiar with electro-convulsive therapy because they administered it to his brother at the asylum. He must have told the mob about it and given them the idea. It's called a slaughterman's lobotomy.'

'They did it to your son? Applied this to his head?'

'Yes. All afternoon. He wouldn't tell them what they wanted to know, and so they just carried on. Lost his teeth and his wits, made his hair stand on end.'

'Is this how the Witchfinder killed the students?'

'I have no information about that, but my guess is, yes. He probably wanted to make people think Goldilocks had come back, frighten them a bit.'

'They tortured him for the secret formula of your rock?'

'Yes.'

'Why didn't he just tell them?'

'He did tell them, but they wouldn't believe him. He told them and told them, he screamed and shouted, but they refused to believe him.' He picked up an envelope and handed it to me. 'This is the secret formula. If you take a look you will understand.'

I reached inside and pulled out a piece of paper. There was nothing written on it. 'Nothing?'

'Nothing. My great-grandfather discovered one of the most fundamental and strange proclivities of the human mind, and inadvertently stumbled upon the essence of branding. It was like the ampersand in the company name and the bogus partner name, Merlin. What do these things add? Nothing, except in the psyche, to which they bring an indefinable magic. The people heard about the secret formula and the ritual on top of Constitution Hill and convinced themselves they could taste the difference. For over a century we have made exactly the same rock as everyone else and the whole world has been willing to swear that ours tasted superior.'

'Where does Gethsemane fit in?'

'She stumbled on them in the barn when they were torturing my son. She escaped from the sty and wandered into the barn. She saw them at work, saw too much. While they were deliberating what to do with her, Goldilocks's sister stole her away and hid her in the cupboard. She gave her some food and drink. She had no idea the cupboard was due to be collected by Mooncalf. She told me all this, sitting in that chair many years ago.'

I stood up and thanked him for his time. I had one final question. 'What did you do with the bodies?'

He hesitated, his smile shrank a fraction. 'What bodies?'

'The bodies of Goldilocks and his sister. You wouldn't have done all this and let them get away.'

'Oh, but I did! We had a deal. I told you: they started a new life somewhere safe and far away.'

'Maybe. Over the years every member of the Slaughterhouse Mob, except the typographer downstairs, has been murdered or died violently in obscure circumstances. Most people reckon you had a hand in their deaths and I tend to agree. My guess is, if your intention was to hunt them all down, there was no way you would have allowed Goldilocks and his sister to live. Maybe they are safe, but probably not far away. Maybe they're asleep in the dam.'

'Well if they are you will have a devil of a job finding them, won't you?' He reached out a hand to shake. I ignored it and turned to leave. As I reached the door he stopped me in my tracks. 'Of course, you know what Vanya's real purpose was in coming to Aberystwyth, don't you?'

I paused in the doorway, teetering on the threshold of leaving.

'Murder,' said Ephraim Barnaby.

I half turned, unable to restrain myself.

'He came to find Gethsemane's murderer and kill him. During those long years in the gulag after he killed his wife he reflected deeply on the litany of pain that had comprised his life. And, as any man would, he brooded intensely on the short period of happiness he had once enjoyed with his wife and little daughter. A happiness that was destroyed when, he supposed, the wandering spirit of a murdered girl took up residence in the soul of his own little Ninotchka. In those dark bitter winters he came to the conclusion that the man who had murdered Gethsemane was the cause, albeit indirectly, of all his woe. The murderer had shattered the only episode of bliss Vanya had known in this world and for that had to be punished. This thought alone, this burning desire for revenge, was what sustained him during those prison years. But, as we know, there was no murder, no wandering spirit. No one was responsible for the tragedy, apart from Vanya's wife. When he learned this bitter truth sitting here in that chair there was nothing left to sustain him. His spirit was extinguished like a snuffed candle. The rest you know.'

I nodded slowly, stared bleakly at Ephraim Barnaby for a second or two and walked out.

Eeyore was sitting on a deckchair overlooking the harbour. There was a spare folding chair and a cool-box full of beer. He looked up and smiled. 'Good to see you back, son.' He reached down and drew out a beer and pulled back the ring. I took the can and we knocked them together and drank. We stayed that way for a long while, watching the golden light fill the sky in the west. I took out the copy of the *Cambrian News* from Hughesovka and unfolded it.

I handed it to Eeyore. He chuckled. 'I thought I'd cut out all these pictures.'

'If it's none of my business, just say so.'

He chuckled again. 'Of course it's your business, son. It must come as a shock after all these years to discover your father was once a member of the Slaughterhouse Mob.' He paused and looked at me with a mischievous glint in his eye. There was a playfulness in his manner at odds with the unsettling revelation. He continued to stare at me, grinning, making me feel uncomfortable. I shifted position. Finally he chuckled and spoke. 'I was undercover. Got a job in the abattoir and joined the Slaughterhouse Mob. Used to hang around the Pier tea shop with them. We were trying to find out what they did to Gethsemane and Gomer Barnaby.'

'Bit old to join a bunch of teenage hoodlums, weren't you?'

'I was a tough guy, they looked up to me.'

'Why punch the cop?'

'To establish my credentials in the gang. The cop was expecting it.'

'Did it work?'

'Not really. It backfired.'

'The gang didn't buy it?'

'Oh they were impressed. It was your mum that objected. She was always asking me why I hung round with that crowd, kept saying I was better than they were and I was wasting my life. Once she told me how I reminded her of her father who had been a policeman before the war. She said, if only you were a policeman, Eeyore! Then I would love you even more. Of course, I was a policeman, but I could hardly tell her. My! How I ached to tell her, how I ached! When the newspaper ran that picture she was waiting for me in the café after her shift. As soon as I saw her face I knew I was in trouble. She wasn't angry, just . . . unbelievably distraught, no, worse than that, disappointed, that was it, her face disfigured by a terrible bitter disappointment. It might not have been so bad if I could have explained things, but halfway through our conversation the mob turned up and so I had to act in character. So I said, "What's the big deal about chinning a lousy pig?" She walked out of the café. Next day handed in her notice and left town. No forwarding address. After that, I was pulled off the case, they sent me up to Llandudno for a while. Then about Christmas time she turned up. Someone had tipped her the wink, so to speak, about me being an undercover cop. And would you believe it, she was with child, seven months gone. That was you, Louie. We got married the following day.'

Eeyore looked at me shyly, in fear and also joy as if telling me of his role in the Slaughterhouse Mob he had shed a great burden. 'We were only together three months but there was more happiness in those months than a lot of folk see in a lifetime. I always try to be grateful for that.' He took out a large white handkerchief and blew his nose. 'It's a shame you were too young to remember her, Louie.'

I smiled. 'In a strange way, I think I do. This picture of you punching the cop, it's quite a good likeness, why cut it out?'

'I was ashamed.'

I took out my wallet and removed the scrap of paper I had torn off the envelope that had contained the séance tape. I waved it under Eeyore's nose. A look of surprise and delight flashed across his face. 'My, oh, my! That takes me back,' he said. 'Haven't smelled that in years. You know what that is, don't you?'

'I've got an idea, but I'd prefer to hear it from you.'

'We used to smell that a lot in the old days, very distinctive it is.'

'Yes?' I looked at him the way a dog watches his master reach for the tin opener.

He said simply, 'Tram. That's the smell of a tram.'

Sospan's box was open again. When he saw me, he looked bashful and busied himself with unnecessary chores. 'I went on a journey, you see,' he explained. 'On the train – I got a good deal off Mr Mooncalf. I was going to seek my fortune, but to tell you the truth, the further I travelled the less I found I really wanted to seek my fortune. I missed Aberystwyth terribly and it occurred to me that I already had a fortune, here on this beloved Promenade. I began to ask myself, why am I doing this? Why am I running away from a paternity suit? And then an incident occurred that changed my life.' He paused and the skin of his neck became suffused with a pink tinge. 'It's a bit embarrassing, to be honest, but while on the train I met a lady in a stovepipe hat. A Russian girl. A thoroughly nice girl she was, and . . . well, I don't want to delve into the intricate details of the business that we transacted, Mr Knight, but this lady was kind enough to initiate me into certain practices . . . ones that, it may be, I have wrongly neglected; timeless rites, I suppose you would call them, that pertain to the sacred communion between a man and a woman . . . ones that the Lord back in that first garden . . .'

'It's OK, Sospan, you don't have to explain. I understand.'

He smiled with bashful relief. 'In the early morning, as I lay in my berth watching the condensation running down the chill train compartment window, I reviewed my situation and experienced a passing and unfamiliar melancholy . . .'

'Oh yes?'

'It was a peculiar mood that I understand has been known since ancient times as post-coital tristesse.'

'I've heard of it.'

'In the cold light of that dawn it became clear to me that I had been the victim of a cruel hoax. I realised that the charge of siring a fish through the vehicle of ice cream, as laid at my door, didn't hold water – if you will forgive the pun. I decided to return to the town I love.'

'Perhaps it's still not too late to have a son by the conventional method,' I said.

For answer he gave a thin smile that said more clearly than words that, in this respect, the die had been cast long ago and he had become reconciled to it. 'What can I get you?' he asked.

'Any of the autumn specials left?'

His face brightened. 'I might just have one or two tubs still.'

'What was the tree that survived the atom bomb blast in Hiroshima?'

'Ginkgo.'

'I'll have one of those.'

I took the cornet and wandered the Prom. It was late afternoon and September had arrived. That soft month poised between the edge of summer and the rim of autumn, when quite often we are given a taste of summer that frequently eluded us earlier in the season. There were fewer people on the Prom. The beginning of the school term had drained the town of visitors; the paddling pool was an empty rink, but all this afforded the necessary quiet for contemplation. The sun was still warm, though the slight wan tinge to its shining made clear that it had passed its acme, not just in the technical sense, for this, so the druids tell us, took place in June, but in a spiritual sense. I had an appointment with Calamity at the railway station. She had spent the past few days out at Abercuawg. The water there was so low now, they said, you could walk down the main street. For some reason that I could not name I had a disinclination to go myself so I had sent her on a special errand with a pair of wellington boots in search of something that would bring a degree of closure to this strange and unsettling case.

Llunos had let Mrs Mochdre walk. She wouldn't sign the confession and the word of a mechanical gypsy wasn't enough to take before a judge. But that didn't mean Llunos had given up. He was a patient man and happy to bide his time. He just needed to build a case. Obligingly, the Witchfinder saved him the trouble by dying of a heart attack while leaving town suddenly. For a man in his seventies that's a tough decision to come to: leaving everything behind, everyone you know, everything you've worked for. But he had compelling reasons. It must have been something to do with that look in his wife's eye, a look he had never seen before, when he came home one day and found the cattle stunner missing from the secret hiding place. And then when for the first time in thirty years of wedded misery she volunteered to tie him to the bed with his own handcuffs . . . In that moment, he must have heard the soft insistent whirring that signifies the final curtain being wound down. They call it the slaughterman's lobotomy but there are other options besides lobotomies. Yes, it's tough leaving town at any age and his heart registered a violent and final protest in the back of the bus to Aberaeron. The following week, when news leaked out about her role in the disappearance of Gethsemane Walters, Mrs Mochdre put her head in the gas oven and left it there. Llunos was angry about the leak and worked hard to find out who was responsible. His anger puzzled me for a while until I remembered our conversation outside the interview room when he said he was going back to the old ways. That's when I knew: it was Llunos who leaked the information.

I turned into Terrace Road at the point where Eeyore said the trams once turned. At the far end of the street the railway station sat blocky and angular, as if built from giant sugar lumps. It had a lemon tinge in the afternoon sun. Everyone travelled by tram in those days and there is no great mystery about how an envelope could acquire that distinctive scent. And yet, my inexplicable contention that it reminded me of the mother I never met is not undermined by this.

There were still a few children playing in the paddling pool. They ran back and forth in the limited confines of the blue-tiled rink, like dogs in a wood, insane with a joy invisible to the rest of us; an ecstasy that seemed to express nothing more than the uncontemplated joy of existing.

Light, scent and music are the keys to the hidden chambers of our hearts. A musical phrase, a few bars of a song that played every day on the radio unnoticed during a forgotten period of our lives. The scent of ointment from the back of a drawer, or sunlight on the afternoon sea, late in the season as today. Sometimes the water scintillates like a shattered mirror; sometimes the light dances like moonlight on a pelt; at other times, when there is no breeze, the surface of the sea appears vitrified, a syrupy sea of molten glass with that same pale green translucence to be found in bottles of Victorian lemonade.

He said it was His human condition that let Him down, but where would I be without it? Sitting in an empty office staring at a client chair that was covered in cobwebs. It's the engine that drives everything. Though every case is different, really every one is a symptom for the same underlying malaise. In a world where the churches are locked people go to the doctor but all she does is give them bottles of pills and after a while, when the joy begins to pall, they can't help noticing the void in their heart has not been filled. At such times, they go to the witch doctor; his name is Louie Knight. It can be a risky policy sometimes. He's careless with his clients – the Chief of Police called him the undertaker's friend – but he knows a secret that is not vouchsafed to a great many people; it's a secret revealed to him in a story he once heard about the convicts from a penal colony in Siberia surviving twenty years' hard labour and dying of a cold two weeks after their release. The secret is this: don't look down. It's like those animals in cartoons that run off the edge of a cliff and carry on running. They are fine until the moment they look down. Vanya had always known the quest was futile but he also kept that knowledge secret from himself. That is a marvellous trick. Maybe, too, this was what God was trying to tell me about Sadako and her origami cranes; it wasn't about whether it worked or not, the mere act transcended such considerations. This is the medicine they buy from Witch Doctor Louie. It's called Ampersandium. It's not perfect, but it works as well as anything can. The alternative is to be like Mrs Mochdre and spend the rest of your life pickled in sourness and your own bile.

I missed Vanya. Of all the clients who had sat across the desk from me, he was one of the very few I actually liked. I grieved for him, but I didn't kid myself I could have saved him and because of that I know the pain will fade. I grieved for Arianwen too and with her I am not so sure. Despite all the comforting words people give me I know in my heart her death was my fault. I should have foreseen it. That's what I get paid for.

I don't know whether Old Barnaby killed Goldilocks and his sister, and really I don't care. As a witch doctor it's not my job to tie up all loose ends, that's what cops are for, and even they understand that sometimes ends are best left untied. If Goldilocks and his sister really are in the foundation of the dam they are probably better off. Life didn't deal them much of a hand; sometimes life doesn't and there is nothing in all the world you can do about it except play with what you've got or quit the game. Now they are at peace. And they have a concrete headstone provided by the Corporation, which is more than most people get; the biggest ever, too; not even Barnaby will get a bigger one than that.

Calamity was waiting on the platform holding a small package wrapped in newspaper. She grinned at me and I did not need to ask how she had got on with her errand, the glee burning fiercely in her eyes already told me. I reached out and tousled her hair, aware of an upsurge of love in my heart. I made a mental note that if she ever wanted to start out on her own again I would definitely stand in her way. Calamity's place was in my office, because sometimes even witch doctors get sick.

We walked down the platform to where an old lady stood waiting with a small suitcase at her feet. It was Ffanci Llangollen, the singer who once made a trademark of singing about how it would be a lovely day tomorrow. When a great tragedy struck she went on the road and continued to sing, travelling on nothing but the fuel of hope. We greeted each other. Clasped under her arm was a folder from Mooncalf Travel, covered in the stickers of the grand hotels and the railway companies and shipping lines. We told Ffanci we were sorry about the loss of her sister and she thanked us graciously.

'No shopping trolley,' I said with the deliberate banality that sometimes helps us through the difficult moments.

'They don't allow them on the Orient Express, so Mr Mooncalf was kind enough to give me this nice suitcase. I feel just the part now, like a dowager. He's been ever so helpful, gave me the tickets gratis on account of my recent . . . misfortune. He wished me luck on my quest. He mentioned you: said you seemed to have got a wild fancy into your head about the tickets he gave you last time. He seemed quite put out about it. A simple oversight, he said, which you have misinterpreted out of all proportion. You will go and make your peace with him, won't you?'

'We'll go directly after seeing you off.'

She smiled and waved something which she was clutching in her hand. It was a talisman.

'A ticket to Hughesovka,' I said.

'Not just there but all the way to Vladivostok if need be.'

'It's a big continent.'

'I know. I once met a man who surveyed it and told me it was as wide as the human heart. I have never given up hope. And I never will as long as my heart beats. This isn't just a ticket to Hughesovka, Mr Knight, it's a return – for two.'

Calamity unwrapped the newspaper package and revealed a little girl's sandal. It had once been bright red but time and mud had now reduced it to the colour of burned umber. The guard blew his whistle. Calamity gave her the shoe.

Acknowledgements

I would like to thank my former editor Mike and my current editor Helen, and my agent Rachel. In addition, a substantial part of this manuscript was written while struggling with illness. I would therefore like to express my sincere thanks to all those whose help and support helped me get through this difficult period, particularly my family in Aberystwyth, David and Anwen, Andy and Lynda, Mitchy, Martin, Richard and Betsy, Nick Topley, Karen Penry, Boot and Rachey.

A NOTE ON THE TYPE

The text of this book is set in Fournier. Fournier is derived from the *romain du roi*, which was created towards the end of the seventeenth century for the exclusive use of the Imprimerie Royale from designs made by a committee of the Académie des Sciences. The original Fournier types were cut by the famous Paris founder Pierre Simon Fournier in about 1742. These types were some of the most influential designs of the eighteenth century and are counted among the earliest examples of the 'transitional' style of typeface. This Monotype version dates from 1924. Fournier is a light, clear face whose distinctive features are capital letters that are quite tall and bold in relation to the lower-case letters, and decorative italics, which show the influence of the calligraphy of Fournier's time.

ALSO AVAILABLE BY MALCOLM PRYCE

ABERYSTWYTH MON AMOUR

'Spot on. This rollicking black comedy should be ludicrous but isn't. Huge fun'
ARENA

Schoolboys are disappearing all over Aberystwyth and nobody knows why. Louie Knight, the town's private investigator, soon realises that it is going to take more than a double ripple from Sospan, the philosopher cum ice-cream seller, to help find out what is happening to these boys and whether or not Lovespoon, the Welsh teacher, Grand Wizard of the Druids and controller of the town, is more than just a sinister bully. And just who was Gwenno Guevara?

*

ISBN 9781408800676 · PAPERBACK · £7.99

BLOOMSBURY

LAST TANGO IN ABERYSTWYTH

'A sustained masterpiece of dark imagination … I am already looking forward
to future volumes in this marvellously surreal Welsh noir series'
DAILY TELEGRAPH

To the girls who came to make it big in the town's 'What the Butler Saw' movie
industry, Aberystwyth was the town of broken dreams. To Dean Morgan
who taught at the Faculty of Undertaking, it was just a place to get course
materials. But both worlds collide when the Dean checks into the notorious bed
and breakfast ghetto and mistakenly receives a suitcase intended for a ruthless
druid assassin. Soon he is running for his life, lost in a dark labyrinth of druid
speakeasies and toffee apple dens, where every spinning wheel tells the story of
a broken heart, and where the Dean's own heart is hopelessly in thrall to a porn
star known as Judy Juice.

*

'Pryce is in a league of his own … effortless and hilarious … Pryce's novels show
disturbing signs of becoming a cult. If only Aberystwyth was really like this'
TIME OUT

*

ISBN 9781408800669 · PAPERBACK · £7.99

BLOOMSBURY

THE UNBEARABLE LIGHTNESS
OF BEING IN ABERYSTWYTH

'Malcolm Pryce is the king of Welsh noir ... he dishes up a dastardly mix of gothic comedy where Edgar Allen Poe meets *Phoenix Nights* in a flurry of blood-stained absurdity'
SUNDAY TELEGRAPH

There is nothing unusual about the barrel-organ man who walks into private detective Louie Knight's office. Apart from the fact that he has lost his memory. And his monkey is a former astronaut. And he is carrying a suitcase that he is too terrified to open. And he wants a murder investigated. The only thing unusual about the murder is that it took place a hundred years ago. And needs solving by the following week. Louie is too smart to take on such a case but also too broke to turn it down. Soon he is lost in a labyrinth of intrigue and terror, tormented at every turn by a gallery of mad nuns, gangsters and waifs, and haunted by the loss of his girlfriend, Myfanwy, who has disappeared after being fed drugged raspberry ripple...

*

'Marvellously imaginative ... You'll weep and laugh, on the same page. Wonderful'
GUARDIAN

*

ISBN 9781408800690 · PAPERBACK · £7.99

BLOOMSBURY

DON'T CRY FOR ME ABERYSTWYTH

'Hilarious'
DAILY TELEGRAPH

It's Christmas in Aberystwyth and a man wearing a red-and-white robe is found brutally murdered in a Chinatown alley. A single word is scrawled in his blood on the pavement: 'Hoffmann'. But who is Hoffmann? This time, Aberystwyth's celebrated crime-fighter, Louie Knight, finds himself caught up in a brilliant pastiche of a cold-war spy thriller. From Patagonia to Aberystwyth, Louie trails a legendary stolen document said to contain an astonishing revelation about the ultimate fate of Butch Cassidy and the Sundance Kid, but he's not the only one who wants it. A bewildering array of silver-haired spies has descended on Aberystwyth, all lured out of retirement by one tantalising rumour: Hoffmann has come in from the Cold. Louie Knight, who still hasn't wrapped up his presents, just wishes he could have waited until after the holiday.

*

'Inventive, funny and dark, Pryce packs more style into a sentence than most authors could hope for in volumes'
BIG ISSUE

*

ISBN 9781408800683 · PAPERBACK · £7.99

B L O O M S B U R Y